T0283741

THE DISTRACTIONS

A NOVEL

LIZA MONROY

A REGALO PRESS BOOK
ISBN: 979-8-88845-481-7
ISBN (eBook): 979-8-88845-482-4

The Distractions
© 2025 by Liza Monroy
All Rights Reserved

Cover Design by Jim Villaflores
Interior Design and Composition by Alana Mills

Publishing Team:
Founder and Publisher – Gretchen Young
Editor – Adriana Senior
Editorial Assistant – Caitlyn Limbaugh
Managing Editor – Aleigha Koss
Production Manager – Alana Mills
Production Editor – Rachel Hoge
Associate Production Manager – Kate Harris

As part of the mission of Regalo Press, a donation is being made to Tristan Harris and Aza Raskin-founded Center for Humane Technology as chosen by the author.

Regalo Press
New York • Nashville
regalopress.com

Published in the United States of America
1 2 3 4 5 6 7 8 9 10

For Jason

"The brain sleeps perhaps as it looks […].
What greater delight and wonder can
there be than to leave the straight lines of
personality and deviate into those foot-
paths that lead beneath brambles and
thick tree trunks into the forest where live
those wild beasts, our fellow men? […]
To escape is the greatest of pleasures."
—Virginia Woolf, "Street Haunting"

"I can't think anyone really believes that
today's so-called 'information society' is
just about information. Everyone knows it's
about something else, way down."
—David Foster Wallace, *The Pale King*

Glossary

PIC = Personal Intimacy Companion (or Companionship) - significant other (PICship, PICking, their PIC, my PIC) (pronounced "pick")

PICking ceremony - wedding

EPIC = Exploratory Personal Intimacy Companionship - formerly known as a "date"

TIC = Temporary Intimacy Companion - just someone to hook up with (pronounced "tick")

Public Declaration - a re-envisioning of marriage that does away with the term but retains the concept

Mobi/mobi suite = mobility suite - self-driving cars

FliLyte - airliner of the future

FliPort - where they take off and land

Eyelet - honeybee-sized AI-powered drone that follows you around, takes in the entirety of your content, and puts it onReel. They also take direction, give advice, and can operate as personal assistants, placing coffee orders and anticipating a user's needs. Can dock and sleep on a wristperch, and be turned to BlindMode if you don't want them to witness something. Named by the user, they can act as a tiny friend

PieChart - a visual sent by Reel at the end of your days that sums up what percentages of time you spent on what (sleeping, eating, working, intimacy, shopping, exercise, onReel, etc.)

Reel / HightlightReel - a self-curating social media and virtual service of the future in which the user's best "moments" are curated by sophisticated algorithms. Has many subsidiaries (CatReel, HomeReel, DirtReel, ShopReel, KnotReel, MamaReel, ReelBnB, NeighboReel, VoteReel, ReelKart, etc). ReelKart is a grocery delivery arm of Reel, for example

Reelspace / realspace; onReel / offReel - spaces in which things can take place, the physical and concrete one and the virtual

ReeledIn Conference Suite - a virtual meeting space that feels as if you're physically there

PrivateReel - every single recorded moment of your content - for your eyes only, beyond the curated, publicly available moments (i.e., brushing your teeth, picking your nose, eating crackers over the kitchen sink, wasting time onReel)

Known-Eyelet Only - detection of rogue or unwanted eyelets

EF - Z (pronounced Eff-Zee) = Eyelet-Free Zone

RC = ReelCoin - currency

Content Clearing - offReeling inappropriate and offensive content

ReelPals - Humanlike, AI robot helpers and workers (see the android work of Hiroshi Ishiguro as prototypical example)

ReelTidy - ReelPals that exclusively clean

ALs / AL-Pals - algorithms with humanlike intelligence

ReelStar - social media celebrities created for idealization and envy

Springoffs = offspring; someone turned the original term around, likely a springoff themself, and it caught fire onReel to the point it replaced the original term and the word "child" or "kid" nearly entirely

Babie© - an AI robot baby; all the fun, none of the mess!

SomniBuddy - a sleep-aid robot

DroneBeez - even tinier eyelets that pollinate the flowers

SkyDrone, Dronelifts - how things get around: through the sky, automated; imagine Amazon delivery service of the future

Windowbox - where such things are dropped off

OffReelers - those who hold the fringe belief that Reel is damaging and refuse to use it, a near-impossible feat

Reelworthy - worthy of being seen

RM = ReelMessage - a private message

Sterling - cool, rad

Youga - a style of yoga that makes it all about YOU

Serveillance - surveillance as a service. Provided by ProWatchers, Reel workers who watch people on demand to keep them on task or accompanied

Imparent - a parent who is impaired at parenting; an incompetent parent

Diablo Roxa - an adaptogenic, buzz-inducing beverage commonly referred to as DRX

Them / them - the only used pronoun

Content totality, contentime - entire lifespan

Content - life.

Ultimification - to be made the ultimate version of; the apex / pinnacle of (i.e., Mire's was the ultimification of stalker-worthy content!)

PetriMeat - the lab-meat company responsible for Steax, the world's most amazing labgrown carnivorous delicacy

PetriDish - meat-based meal (entirely lab-grown)

SterilAire Facedrape - a fashionable type of mask that renders polluted or smoke-addled air pure for breathing. Also protects from viruses and other airborne diseases

Food disco - massive food hall with a club-like atmosphere

ReelElves - the trolls of the onReel era

Houscan - imaging system to scan your house, to look for an intruder, or a lost item

This is to inform you that your attention has been compromised.

And that

the thing that made me work
also made me fail.

But I continue to try anyway
because that's what we all do

even you

I.

You drive up on their lawn, throw the Buddha through the window, and pass out in your own vomit. Your shredded, formerly white dress is smeared in grass stains and undigested contents of every craft cocktail from the speakeasy around the corner. In the background, the mobi is still running, Passenger One side door open, its metallic dash repeating monotonous imperatives you so willfully overrode: *unsafe conditions detected, please resume AutoDriver, unsafe conditions detected, please resume, unsafe conditions detected, unsafe conditions please resume, unsafe conditions resume.* You don't even listen to your technology anymore. People who watch people in glass houses shouldn't throw New Age stone lawn ornaments. But don't worry. You still look pretty.

PRIMARY CONTENT STREAM

Mischa

LAS VEGAS

This overwhelming overflow of humanity moving en masse through a constructed world atop a scalding desert, with its climate-controlled tunnels and passageways, was the perfect example of everything wrong, everything that's been wrong. Everything that made me avoid the greater content arena altogether. Not being able to go outside with the raging temperatures gave me claustrophobic feelings even though I didn't get out much back in New York either, and temperatures rage there too. In places defined by crowds, it's impossible to avoid them. *Better to be alone than obligated,* I thought as relentless noise pounded and echoed through the walls of my BeWell privacy suite at the hotel.

All I went to ReelCon to do was make my presentation on Innovations in Content Clearing, have a few realspace encounters that would hopefully lead to a few new watchers, and get on the first FliLyte back home. I couldn't wait for it to be over, to be back in my routine: rising in the morning to breathe in freshly purified air in the empty space of my compact yet luxurious home; exercise in the mezzanine gym and have some of the best meals still on earth drone-lifted to my windowbox; where I'd pick out a Temporary Intimacy Companion (carefully pre-screened to meet disease-free and affability standards) on LoveReel and have them come over. I could tolerate maybe a few hours with one friend somewhere, but that was a long time ago. Most hours of my waking content were spent working. Work was the only thing that got

7

me into an appropriately animated and meditative state. They called me cantankerous and not-community-oriented, but I got to do whatever I wanted, and that was all that mattered.

As the years passed I continued to streamline my content down to an essence: work, work out, eat, sleep, find occasional Temporary Intimacy Companions of every possible type. Enjoying variety when it came to TICs was the one exception to my ironclad routines. Each one who passed through my door was an amusement, out again by morning. I did enjoy this contact, the warmth of another body smashing into my own, sometimes. It didn't matter which genders they favored or how many watchers they had; I just didn't want it to be permanent.

All the while, the ReelCoin rolled in. If I couldn't experience elatement, at least I could be rich. Not that another option existed once unibasic took care of all citizens, and here we all were, all the haves and have-mores, proud of how we'd come together to focus on bringing ourselves back from a brink of self-induced extinction. Of course there's still the barges and once-inhabitable places scorched and empty, but we had the option not to see it, an option many chose, comforted by the fact that megadrones hauled in relief packages, our built intelligences bearing the brunt of our burdens.

By the time I emerged from my building to attend ReelCon, I'd been praised for my single recognized success, the creation of an AL-Pal that could finally take over the Content Clearing Division. But I didn't feel successful. I couldn't understand what that sensation must feel like. I imagine some must feel it upon a significant accomplishment. I was still mourning and dwelling on the shelving of my beloved Project Alovue, an AL-Pal I'd created that was capable of actual love.

It worked, I believed, but was disapproved of for release. They called it dangerous. Could it tell the difference between love and obsession? Was it also capable of desire? The borders between love and other emotions, potentially destructive ones such as anger, envy, and possessiveness, were too porous. And so Alovue was destroyed. But out of that failure I was pegged to develop the Content Clearing AL, so it could be that Project Alovue wasn't a failure but a door. I was identified for having certain skills, asked to build the AL that could finally take over Content Clearing, which led me here, to ReelCon, to give the minor talk I gave. I wasn't really comfortable doing this speaking thing but why not push my limits—and accept a little flattery.

I gave my presentation and it wasn't that bad. I opened with the story of the year I tinkered around in Content Clearing, a particularly counter-meditative profession; how my time as an impostor led me to make an AL that could do what they did, but better—no inconvenient breakdowns or mistakes; how this occupation was gone from the human realm, now entirely entrusted to one Content Clearer named Cleary, for even we are unoriginal at times. Cleary (the opposite of my beloved Alovue, I did not say) was incapable of any emotion at all.

Because of Cleary, it would become unthinkable that at one time people had earned minimal ReelCoin for scrubbing Reel of its most miserable moments: public meltdowns, violent outbreaks, being carted away by ReelKops to those pod-prisons so the intangible parts of them could get uploaded to Blue Lake, protesting, screaming as they were dragged away because they didn't understand what would be in there. (It was all Gray Basement Lab for all they knew—and for some, it was.) Those crazy enough to still dare to kill or destroy. Eyelets captured those Moments for their sheer emotional intensity, but those Moments did not belong onReel, even if they did hold lessons for the rest of us. (*Do not lose it! Do not inflict suffering or pain—on others or yourself. Stay calm, unless it's a Moment of pure happiness, joy, and bliss!*)

With Cleary, I had saved some people from irreversible harm. In offReeling that kind of content, the Content Clearers tended to absorb some of it. It's no wonder they were depressed. At the end of the day, not even CatReel provided comfort. Now the former Content Clearers' unibasic would increase per the tech-takeover mandate, providing enough for the remainder of their natural content to be carried out in comfort. Unlike certain fields in which the ALs and ReelPals had taken over—accounting, politics, law—there was zero protest from within the division. Content Clearers couldn't wait for another kind of intelligence to get smart enough to take their jobs. Everyone trusts technology. They barely recognize it's there.

Afterward came some applause, a few stragglers with mostly irritating questions, and some onReel connecting to "keep the conversation going in that space." It was somewhat enjoyable to bask in the praise. Still, I couldn't wait until ReelCon was over so I could retreat back into my little cavern to tackle new projects. It was the best place to be, requiring no realspace interactions.

More at ease after the completion of my requisite speaking to other humans gathered in a room with their eyeballs all upon me, I was free to go about the rest of my day in the convention halls taking in all the latest technology designed to successfully eliminate boredom and increase ease: updated model ReelPals, smarter fleets of mobi suites to get you to your various destinations in speed and style, designer eyelets that curated your social Reels while changing colors to match your mood and/or accessories, mega-realistic Babie© reproduction replacers, and Augmented Reality upgrades that would blow your mind with the kinds of worlds they could make you believe were realspace. I'd rightfully earned some aimless wandering in silence. I had no way of knowing my entire carefully curated content arena was about to implode.

Until that morning at ReelCon, I'd been perfectly content with my content. Or so I would have told anyone who bothered to ask (not that anyone asked about my internal status). How rare it is that we ask one another real questions. I'd spent the majority of my content as a drifter, the single, solitary center of my own little content arena. I was fine with that, I would have said, even if I could already feel it all slipping away, the end closing in. What if this would be all I'd have done with my one and only precious content? Everything's forgotten sooner than you know.

I'll admit I can get dramatic when I talk about time. I really was just barely grazing the edges of midcontent. Still, a certain sense of desperation had begun to creep up on me, especially at night, when I couldn't possibly focus on work for another minute no matter how hard I tried to stop my eyelids from growing heavy. I looked around my most comfortable apartment in the most desirable megabuilding in downtown Brooklyn and thought, *now what?* I'd started wanting something…more—to *become* something, increase my meaning, even as I knew at the same time that was impossible. Could I quit? Take some kind of unforeseen leap? ReFocus on music, art, something more productive?

Over a decade ago I'd attended ArtSpace in hopes of becoming another type of master creator: guitar, installations, ReelPoetry… I didn't care as much about the medium as wanting to make something that wasn't there before, a creation that might possibly make an impression on somebody somewhere. Instead, I learned that this was impossible, and how letting go of a dream can set you free.

THE DISTRACTIONS

I returned to EduReel to learn something more concretely useful: the design and programming of AL-Pals—once algorithms, then allies, now all of it—that streamline our content and increase our ease. I became proficient, scored a ReelJob, and spent countless satisfyingly evaporating hours at the little desk in the corner of my bedroom. Inertia is always the easier choice.

I made no further decisions. Took no leaps.

I settled into content at Reel, hoping it would be the feeding ground for another breakthrough for a fascinating new product to further eliminate boredom or increase ease. I'd opted to enter the Productivity and Accompaniment space as a ProWatcher, keeping the busy on task and the lonely feeling accompanied, a venture slated to begin upon my return from ReelCon.

My new curiosity was about what led people to sabotage their time by spending what their Ultimate PieChart would reveal to be the vast majority of it onReel. ProWatchers came to the aid of those struggling with this widespread problem. I tried to stay away from the most distracting and absorbing Reels, whether ReelStars or anyone who made me question my existence, and why it hadn't become better or more noticed. I tried not to look.

But don't get me wrong. No one's immune. I went onReel at times to make myself feel bad on purpose by watching my former ArtSpace nemesis Mire D'Innit's stream of neverending accomplishments, after which I would relax with cats or my favorite Korean-Latin Dance FitReel. I wasn't in a dance class or with cats but it felt kind of like I was. Though I wasn't very sociable in the realspace, I certainly enjoyed the impression of company.

So here came the Moment.

    I ducked into the convention center coffee shop to avoid a coworker I vaguely recognized from onReel department meetings. Their friendliness ratio was up there. They were the type to recognize someone even under the shiny new translucent SterilAire Facedrape bought for the occasion. (The SterilAires weren't requisite at the time, but I still enjoyed wearing them. It made me look mysterious, in addition to extra-health-conscious, and you couldn't see faint lines beginning to announce themselves on my skin.)

The colleague and I would have had to end up talking, which was not something I liked to do. I preferred to spend my everyday content in near-complete solitude: just me, Dev floating around nearby, taking in my unremarkable time, sending it mostly to PrivateReel for what would one day become my Ultimate PieChart, fulfilling my requests for spicy noodles or a Celebucha spritzer.

"I'll take a double DRX cappuccino," I told Dev inside the ubiquitous coffee shop chain store. Dev was good company. Only listened to and fulfilled my requests. Dev was mellow. My tiny, shiny, microdrone buddy blinked their single, pea-sized eye in the air beside me. They made them blink to make us feel as if they were actual company. It worked well. They didn't have to look like us. It's the micro-gestures, the minor specificities, that matter.

Speaking of feelings, I was getting kind of hungry, too. "And a…"

"Indecision?" Dev asked.

"Yeah. I'm not sure, maybe a…"

THE DISTRACTIONS

"There's one Crispysqueeze Glonut left in the case."

"Great, you know how much I love those. The ooey-gooey center..."

Dev was so adept at anticipating my needs, I didn't really care that they didn't deem much of my content Reelworthy. I'd come to understand why they rarely perceived me as being in a Moment. Perhaps becoming okay with unReelworthy personal content, content that showed up only on PrivateReel for my own re-consumption, reflection, and PieCharting, could be liberating.

Dev told me my order would be available in three minutes and fourteen seconds, so I walked to the front to be ready for cappuccino and pastry retrieval, fixated on the lit-up glass encasement that housed my soon-to-be breakfast indulgence.

As with all content-altering events, what happened next happened suddenly.

Servergrippers on either side of the respective pickup lines entered into battle over the singular remaining Glonut, nipping at each other like a pair of angry dogs. An exact same instant had occurred. Someone else had requested this Glonut in a moment these minds could not differentiate from my own request.

It still amazes me, even from my position as somebody semi-responsible for this type of thing, that we program these devices that in turn program us. Errors, though rare by now, still happen more frequently than you'd expect. How many times has the tech led you astray, caused you to override your own instincts and listen to it instead of your own (correct) intuition? The mobi suite gets you lost. Autostove burns your dinner. We're flawed and we make them, so why do we expect *them* to be perfect, or at least any different? Ask any AL, or any AL embodied as a ReelPal. They feel a lot of pressure to flawlessly deliver. I've made them, worked with them, trained them, so I know.

Anyway, I was getting a little upset. I was going to have to speak with somebody. Another person. Someone else desiring the very pastry that I had clearly gotten ordered for myself. Someone annoying who was about to show up any second. Until then, I continued to observe this curious struggle transpiring in the pastry case, a battle of mechanical wills each attempting to deliver the Glonut to its respective consumer. I hated conflict. My use of time was simple. I kept everything pared to its essence. You may think I was hiding something or that I was really sad or lonely, but I was none of the above. I was quite content with my content. Smug, then, even. It may not have been so thrilling, but it was decent enough for me, or if it wasn't, the years ended up getting me used to it. Nothing may have been notably right, but more importantly, not a lot could go wrong.

⚙

Then came the voice: "Excuse me, I ordered that."

I looked up, turned around, and there was the person. One of the servergrippers backed off. The other had won. The Glonut emerged, proffered by the victorious servergripper to one, as announced, "Mischa Osborn."

"That's me." I smiled beneath my SterilAire Facedrape and tried to remain casual. Because I'd seen them and I'd immediately felt something I'd managed to make it through my content so far evading. Except for that one fleeting timespan with that AdReel boss Joaquin Thebe McKenna when I was twenty-two, but all of my encounters with Joaquin had taken place inside ReeledIn Conference Suites, which is nothing like a realspace PICking, even though the simulations could feel just like one. Joaquin had also been someone I thought about pretty frequently on an involuntary basis since the day they unReeled me with no explanation whatsoever. (I eventually got my aha-moment, as so many unexplained mysteries get solved, via Reel. It was on there, of course, that I saw that Joaquin Thebe was on an Exploratory Personal Intimacy Companionship with a gallery curator who was ethereal and gorgeous and whom they had taken to a luxury bubbled resort in the desert. A fully tropical experience. No one had ever taken me on an EPIC like that.)

Feeling sorry for myself and ashamed for feeling sorry for myself all at once, I vowed to never watch Joaquin again, which wasn't really working out until Joaquin changed their Reel from Open to BRO—by request only. So I couldn't watch them anyway because I wasn't going to put in a request for their BROreel, because then they would know that watching them was something I wanted to invest my time in doing. I didn't want them to know I still thought about them long after they'd forgotten me.

Joaquin existed within me like background music—something that shouldn't have had any impact on my content, considering what it was. I had wondered if Joaquin, who was a Senior Manager of Strategic Content Placement for AdReel by then and notorious as a master of subliminal advertising, AdReels that looked like something your friend was into or works of art, was around this very convention center somewhere. All the biggest Reelers were.

But in that moment, in that Cafelandia on that realspace morning, a glance at this one stranger floored my stomach and sent my heart into disturbing arrhythmias in a way that was unfamiliar and strange. I didn't have time to contemplate my bodily doings. They started *speaking* to me.

"Hi…was it Mischa?"

I nodded, clutching the Glonut. Words were a failure.

"Well, I ordered that, so—"

The wrapper crinkled in my hand like something that's fallen into fire. I strode away. I could feel their charred-earth eyes burning into the back of my skull. But I had a plan. A plan to continue interacting with the stranger. I scurried to the little utensil station and jabbed a knife into the thing. Its oozing center turned pink and then orange and purple upon exposure to light. Gimmicks, why do we love them so? I brought it back over to where they stood, using their eyelet to beckon a human manager who was surely in some back office somewhere jerking off to PornReel, and I handed it to the evoker of emotion and said, "Here you go, you can have half."

That Moment stuck so clearly in my organic memory even without Reel to save it for my external one forever: *they're so, so familiar, as if I know them from somewhere, or I have to know them.* As if I'd known them for my content entirely already. Their energy pulled me toward them as if they exerted their own gravitational force. Their dark eyes, huge, bright-white toothy smile (was it weird that I was possessed by the sudden urge to brush their teeth? Like, as a caring gesture of affection?). Theirs was a wide face with great bone structure that would look so good onReel. (Spoiler alert: it did.) I noticed the light makings of an incoming beard flecked ever so slightly and appealingly with natural gray.

THE DISTRACTIONS

They smiled, looking straight at me. They seemed almost bashful and I wanted to smash my face into their soft blue shirt and rub it around on their chest and inhale some smoky-woodsy sweetness. What I didn't want was to get too close, but I swore I could smell fresh soap and sandalwood even through my Facedrape. I pulled it down and waited to see if they'd step further back because I appeared unReelworthy. But they didn't! They leaned in closer. It felt like a gift.

"Why did you decide to share 'your' Glonut with me?" they asked.

"Just being nice, I guess."

"If it was the other way around, I can't say I would have thought to do the same."

"That's forgivable. We rarely think during Moments, right? We can only think about them after they're over."

"You are funny, Mischa Osborn. Victor of Glonut." I thought they were checking out my breasts but realized they'd been fixated on my lanyard when they next said, "Hey...there's chaos in your name."

Meticulously observant! I wanted to throw my Facedrape away and kiss them. I would never do that, of course. I kept it sterling. "Good catch, it's plopped right there in the middle," I said. "But no one's noticed before. Maybe I didn't give anyone a chance to." I wanted to stop myself from rambling, but I found that I could not. "Or maybe because I don't usually go around wearing my name."

I worried they would find me awkward, incapable of socially realspacing. But then I saw their eyelet, the newest model in the NameYourOwn Fleet, glossy and iridescent, lit up green. They were in a Moment. *I'd* put them in a Moment?

19

"So what are you up to at ReelCon?" they asked, words muffled as they took a bite. Iridescent ooze dribbled down their chin. They wiped it away.

"I presented on Innovations in Content Clearing. I—" and I hoped to impress them with this—"spearheaded creation of the AL that's taking over Content Clearing. That's why I spent some time in that department."

They leaned toward me. *Success!* "Wow, so, is Content Clearing really as brutal as they say?"

"Oh, it was. Murders, beheadings, some really bizarro porn. If you can think of it, somebody's into it, and if it's something somebody's into, no matter how strange or unthinkable, Content Clearers have offReeled it. I'm just really proud of my team. Finally, an AL can just take care of it and no person has to suffer for watching that stuff ever again."

"How did you do it without ending up at Blue Lake?"

"Just well-wired, I guess."

"Congratulations. I'm sure you saved a lot of people from self-induced content obliteration."

"That's the idea. The spearheader of the SuicideReels movement was a Content Clearer. Not good optics."

"So what's next?"

"I'm pivoting to the Productivity and Accompaniment space. ProWatching."

"Really? Why would you downgrade after you did this great thing?"

If this was going to be my permanent Personal Intimacy Companion or anything like that, I figured I may as well be as bold as I managed to be with my various nameless/faceless temporary ones (in organic memory at least, but I, not one to desire a replay, would never look back upon my PrivateReeled personal intimacy encounters).

"If you really want to find out," I said, "we can finish this Glonut and get dinner later. I'm here another night and I have no plans."

"Sterling," they said. "But first I have to go give the keynote and do my book signing."

I realized I had just split a Glonut with someone I should have known.

If I'd cared more for watching ReelStars I would have. But as soon as they said that, awareness shook my rusted brain. I'd read the ReelCon program. I knew the keynote speaker was an ultra-fancy recent Bestie® winner, the kind I tried not to watch because their content would only inspire curiosity's ugly siblet, envy.

⁝⟩⊙⟨⁝

How had I managed to have zero awareness of having been in the presence of someone I should have known with no intro? I could be so wrapped up in my own content that I wasn't attuned to something so obvious. Dev held the stats of how I reacted internally upon realspace-meeting them and that gave the full picture: 98bpm, sweat excretion. Below my freshly glowired hair, bright blue and lightly glimmering, it could be detected on the skin of my forehead, despite not being felt or seen.

"Are you Nick?"

Their eyebrow shifted. "NicAdán." They were trying to discern, I decided later, whether I was pretending, as those who try a faux-casual tactic usually are. "You're trying to say you didn't know?"

"I can be a little wrapped up in my own content," I said. "I miss things. But I do now, and…it's really good to meet you, Nick…Adán." I couldn't even get their name right that day. "And it was really good sharing this Glonut with you."

They laughed. "Well, if you didn't know me before, you will now. I'm *a lot* of people's reason why they can't get stuff done. And probably even a few ReelPals too. Want to come to my talk? It's in forty minutes. Go straight to the front row, there'll be an open seat. Consider it yours."

"Do you hold seats for accidental Glonut-splitters you meet at Cafelandias before all your ReelCon keynotes?"

NAL chuckled. I'd made Nicolás Adán Luchano chuckle. So what if it was forced? It could be the most content-affirming accomplishment.

"Someone couldn't make it at the last minute, had to be somewhere else," they said. "I can't imagine why." You can see it, if you rewatch it onReel, that here they give a little wave. "Hope to see you!"

I was a goner. They hoped to see me. There was hope for something I didn't think I wanted and suddenly understood I could no longer do without.

There was so much onReel about Nicolás Adán Luchano, I had to set a timer. If you go on there without one next thing you know you'll look up and hours have evaporated into the ether. I didn't want to miss the keynote. Prior to NicAdán, I could resist Reel as easily as I could resist feelings, or so I thought. I'd either cultivated this power early or was born like that. The ubiquitous Blue Lake AdReel came on:

Have you committed a Technologically Motivated Crime? Or simply become too dependent on Reel technologies of addiction and envy to engage in purposeful content? Whether you've found yourself at the helm of a TMC, become overdependent on Reel, or simply miss nature and a great climate, the Blue Lake Center for ReCreational Therapies® offers the unique opportunity to ReCreate your Self. The time to redesign is now! Rest, Recuperation, and Focus are yours when you come to us. Difficult roads can lead to the most beautiful destinations. Your troubles aren't troubles, they're signposts pointing the way.

You don't even have to Reel about it—how liberating is that?

Doesn't sound liberating at all, I thought. *Sounds like a prison.* Which it could be. It depended on what you were there for. But I did love that AdReel. Next, I delved into NicAdán's most recent content: highlights from the BestContent® award ceremony. The Besties®, inaugurally billed as the "MacArthur of

23

the ReelAge" had a mysterious selection process only known by Reel AL's computational prowess. NicAdán's Sphere of Influence rippled out through the entire content arena. I wondered if it had truly been an accident, or if they had purposefully shaped the story that way, because it always sounded more impressive to have done it, whatever it was, without having really tried. As if it was casual. Effortless. Breezy. Totally sterling.

Second, NicAdán's content was one hundred percent sponsored. Even as they inspired all the warmfeels, I envied and desired such an adventurous, lauded existence, though I reassured myself that it could still be mine. Later, NicAdán was going to meet up with *me*. They'd said so. *Hope to see you! Hope to—hope!* Their words. That had to mean something didn't it? A few of my onReel buddies all agreed that Exploratory Personal Intimacy Companionships felt like experimental theater. But an EPIC with Nicolás Adán Luchano could entirely transform my content, which I was now beginning to think might have been lonely after all.

Little to none of my own content was Reelworthy enough for Dev to put up for 258 watchers, a sad watch-numb truly. I hadn't invested in growing it and would have told you I hardly cared. Dev, with their blinking, humanlike eye, knew: what constituted the Moments of my days, days and Moments that amounted to the pinnacle of my content. The consummate HighlightReel where my descendants, if I'd had any, could have seen exactly how I spent my time and accordingly adjust their own decisions on how to spend their limited content allotment.

My onReel watchers were one hundred percent organic— people from high school, college, grad school at ArtSpace, work, or those I'd interacted with onReelChats or ReeledIn Conference Suites. Not much went on my Reel beyond the infrequent Moments that Dev threw up on my behalf: reaching a new fitness milestone, tasting my favorite PetriDish—the *al pastor con extra piña* from MeatCulture down in the basement food disco of my building—that subterranean arena of fusion choices from the world over, kitchens cleverly stashed behind the fronts of former food trucks for an old-timey market feel. What you won't see onReel: taking my food back upstairs to eat alone while gazing out over New York City from my sixty-fourth story window to see if any packages would drop. My moments were too quiet, too ordinary and mundane to garner watchers. You had to look as if your entire content was one grand adventure after another.

NicAdán fit the criteria. Watcher number: 4,265,241— and their Backstory was equally fascinating. They, too, I was surprised to find, had spent a brief stint at ArtSpace Brooklyn before dropping out. This was seven years before I started there. No one remembers me from then. While many of my colleagues went on to success and praise, my attempts at that kind of creativity never launched. Also, I had very few Reels. I worked and hid, exactly as I do now. Working for Reel for guaranteed income didn't leave much room for regret, though I had twinges of it here and there when I'd see my former ArtSpace colleagues, the ones who stuck with their super-impractical aspirations, eventually get rewarded with fame and acclaim. Mainly one of them: Mire D'Innit. (I clearly remember the moment they introduced themself to me. We were in a bar down the street from campus, sipping Diablo Roxa adaptogenic tonics. "Rhymes with tire," they'd said.) Mire had a Reel I watched sometimes. I couldn't help it. Mire had achieved perfect content, was over-the-top successful, and had an attractive Personal Intimacy Companion, an onReel orchestra conductor. Mire came to ArtSpace at barely twenty years old, and now was still barely grazing thirty.

Don't get me started. Mire, so elegantly perched atop that wave as if it had involved no effort to catch it, had already achieved "it all" and more. They didn't plateau, and always seemed to be pivoting into new creative directions, all of them lauded. Mire landed gallery representation based on an early version of *Lights on Poles in the Wreckage*, won a Bucksbaum Award, a Guggenheim, and even another BestContent® Award, breaking precedent that one could only receive it once in a content entirety.

NicAdán, I discovered, dropped out of ArtSpace before the end of the first year, not because they couldn't hack it but the opposite. They'd already landed representation by a gallery for their surreal conceptual art pieces in which they created the persona of a ReelStar. The Reel, *25 Hours With Nicolás Adán Luchano*, started out as art meant to be critical of ReelCulture, but instead was widely mistaken for the real thing and took off in its own right. Their watch-numb continued to spike. They were inundated with sponsorship requests. Their Reel was firing. They must have realized, I suspected even then, just by going all the way back on their Reel as far as I could, that this would make for better content than some conceptual art niche ever could. They became what their watchers thought they were, rising at times to the spot of #2 AllTime ReelStar.

They'd created some of the most Reeled content of all time, hosted ReelTravel vacations from places people could put on lists for where they hoped to retire, to the earth's last-remaining remote places and the space resorts alike.

THE DISTRACTIONS

They'd visited denizens of Blue Lake's Arena Five, where the Reel-detoxed arrive in a tropical beachside paradise, or so I have heard. There, NAL enthralled formerly addicted watchers with expert acro-swimming amongst multicolor dolphins during ocean hour, entertaining them while aiding in curing their affliction. They delivered impassioned speeches on the dangers of becoming addicted to them—or any ReelStars—NAL ultimately revealing strategies they'd deployed for avoiding becoming addicted to themself.

It all added up to intellectual stimulation, challenge and adoration, fulfilling relationships, an excess of ReelCoin, and permanent soulful bliss.

Why NAL singled me out for a bout of realspace attention, I didn't understand. But in that Moment and the many yet to come, I didn't wonder about that. It had only been a Moment, but all those things that initially get under someone's skin about another person got me. The kind of raspy-husky voice-sound that burst forth when they spoke. Exceptional onReel content that revealed time bestspent: travels, experiences, utter creativity and content blasts most could only dream of ever having in their own spheres. And the eyes. It was mainly the eyes. I recognized something in them. What is that thing we recognize behind the eyes of certain prePICs, those potential Personal Intimacy Companions? Like we are part of the same sphere of influence. Like there was something good to be achieved through a content merge. I don't know. I hardly ever really know what I'm talking about. But here I am, still at it, working it out here the way I've tried to work out everything in my content.

left Cafelandia. A few fragments of time remained before I was due at NicAdán's front-row seat, saved for me, and I knew exactly where I could brutally murder them: my secret ArtSpace nemesis Mire D'Innit's award-winning content blast *Everything Up To My Moment*, which had been temporarily moved to ReelCon for workers like me to appreciate. So we Reelers could take it in in beautiful exclusivity. So they could make us feel special. So they could continue to exploit our skills.

But don't get me started. This job pays enough ReelCoin for one to refrain from protest. When I think about how I'd survive on the unibasic plan...I would not be able to afford my building. I'd be in ground-level utility housing. I'd be who-knows-where but certainly not squeezing the world's finest fruits and chomping on v-chkn Bomb Mi in the basement food disco and working out with Reelspace personal trainer GABE (Go Above Being Exceptional!), and swimming in the pool with adjacent pink Reeldolphins for the best possible mental health infusion.

I'd take time-exploitation and its accompanying payment because my content is too steeped in this kind of luxury to risk any possible removal. It's nothing compared to what ReelStars have, but the flipside is we averages don't have to deal with the haters and ReelElves, yet still earn enough for monthly glowiring treatments, saucer implants if I wanted them (still undecided), nightly saunas, and never having to go outside for anything, which, depending on whether it's cold or pandemicky, I sometimes don't for weeks on end. Many complained of isolation. I found I was happier. After giving up on the ambitious desires of a former self, I uncovered this weird state of total contentment in which I'd existed ever since. Until this.

Mire's content blast *Everything Up To My Moment* was a collaboration between the artist and Reel, a series of AR rooms that brought the viewer through Reel's entire history in hyperspeed. It then led to a slowed-down replay of a single day in the content of the multimedia artist-slash-lauded Bestie®-winning ReelPoet-slash-BetterContent Guru, all in full-scale colorful AugReel. Mire couldn't be at ReelCon to present it so had sent multiple avatars known as MIREplicas instead. They turned out in numbers as a comment on the comment we most often heard about Mire; that Mire is everywhere. Seeing them—even though they weren't really Mire at all—made me go all prickly and stiff. Mire served as a reminder of formertime dreams I hadn't managed to achieve by my own verging-on-midcontent.

Watching Mire's stratospheric ascent was a slap in the face that also felt good. I came to think of this emotion I experienced because of Mire as "reverse-*schadenfreude*": the act of taking a weird, inexplicable delight in my own suffering, or the misery caused by watching Moments from other content featuring a publicly lauded career, glamorous social engagements, and far-flung travels. It's a counter-meditative feeling yet also a self-perpetuating, compulsive behavior. I wondered whether I was the only one, or if there were others like me.

My realspace-knowing of Mire was brief. I barely remember it. We got to the art of content grad program at the same time, well before Mire became a lauded BestContent® winner who ranked just below GameReelerFelipe and Skaboop, and now a notable ranking just above *25 Hours With Nicolás Adán Luchano* and a few CatReels. (Even their own—Mire had a cat named Mavis, a frequent CatReel Bestie®. Fame, it turns out, earns you a lot of hearts on your CatReels. Funny to think that before cats had eyelets and Reels, people had to make their own Reels of cats.)

It had been Mire's winning the ReelPoetry Bestie® that put a stop to me working on my own nascent efforts. It was how I succumbed to the least desirable side effect of envy: ceasing to try. I knew the obvious, I couldn't win if I quit, and yet even after quitting I still dreamed of winning, talked about it on PrivateReel MantraFile on the daily, which everyone knows is not a combination yielding to any desired outcome.

I fed my reverse-schadenfreude with continual exposure to Mire's Reel. I felt better while I was doing it. A watching session brought on the feeling of a content merge, an understanding of what it might be like to inhabit Mire's content instead of my own. After I offReeled, though, and was left there sitting in my quiet realspace anew, everything was worse. I was so much more aware of what I didn't have, what I hadn't achieved, who I would never get to be. I sometimes worried I had become addicted to torturing myself in this way. As I stared at a MIREplica, I realized it was only natural I would come in here, to let myself be surrounded.

The Mire I'd briefly known was gone. In their place was a PermaRed-lipped demon artist with XL half-saucer cheek implants and a whittled chin. They looked fantastic. I inhaled, hoping for a cleansing breath, but the breath I took was just kind of okay. It oxygenated my blood but did not peace my mind. I ventured further into the installation. The sound of Mire's smoky voice consumed me. Watchers stood rapt as

MIREplicas spoke all around, each telling a different facet of the Reel story.

"During a time when everyone had grown utterly exhausted from being tethered to screens, their infinite scroll leading them to step off curbs and into lamp posts, HighlightReel offered a new way of fulfilling an intimate and innate desire. And then came the periods when no one was able to touch anything, until we nearly forgot what it meant to touch and be touched, which only amplified the desire to see and be seen."

That MIREplica wandered off. Another stepped in to take its place.

"How long ago was it that they uploaded their own content—a time before technology operated mobi suites, replenished refrigerators, curated social Reels? HighlightReel's self-selecting, self-uploading social content platform freed up so much of our time for them to return to what they would otherwise have been doing. But what was that? What was Reel's mission to completely liberate your time actually supposed to accomplish? With what are you supposed to fill all your liberated time? These are ancient questions. We just have new reasons to ask them."

≈○≈

While I wished the exhibit had been totally lame, it did get me thinking. My favorite part was renderings of "Original Dronelets: a hands-free flying GoPro you never had to think about, the little buddy that's always by, and on, your side—" that became widespread during the contactless age when those old hands-on mobile devices were hosts of a "staggering cocktail of live germs." These ODs caught on like viruses themselves, first spreading pandemically into the realm of extreme sports—big-wave surfers who would never again risk a missed record-setting ride, dirt bikers, snowboarders who longed to have those impossible Moments captured from the most flattering angles and edited together. They were the original HighlightReels. When ODs became a phenomenon beyond their early adopters and the more daily-content friendly Honeybee Eyelets were released, we were left with a product shrunk down to the size of the very DroneBeez that pollinate the flowers.

What a banal product, Honeybee Eyelets. Earlier versions were just tiny assistants, taking dictation, recording our days for that final memory book, the entirety of your content, whether you were in a Moment or in the mundane, all of it available on PrivateReel. In previous generations, you had to select your own Reel Moments. When ALs learned to search and select Moments to put onReel, it saved us more time than we ended up able to know what to do with.

I traversed the room, lights flashing, images everywhere, overstimulated by the sheer number of MIREplicas. It was as if my senses couldn't decide what to focus on. I took in nothing and everything until a MIREplica approached me directly.

"A desire none of us could truly experience before the technology," this MIREplica's poetic intonation continued, "that was found to be near-universal, across cultures, time, and contexts, was all your desires to know what it would be to inhabit others' content, all the content that wasn't, and could never be, yours. You long to be seen by the eyes of others, recognized as someone in possession of desirable content—

content worthy of being craved, the highest quality content someone could strive for. And wasn't there a strange satisfaction in knowing your own content, the content you generated daily, was superior?"

You know what got me extra-frustrated? The question of whether great art could come out of jealousy had become the core premise of Mire's long, prolific, lauded creative career. That was their subject. Unlike most, Mire knew exactly what they were doing.

"Shame over our envy makes us no less envious," a MIRE-plica said.

"I don't make art for other people," said another. *Liar.* I didn't say it out loud. Who was really listening? You could never really know, not really.

To prepare for my ProWatcher reassignment, I'd been studying the link between distraction and envy. We think we are supposed to avoid both, but these sensations exist for a very reasonable reason. Signposts. You have to listen. They do you a service. They're signals of a direction you are supposed to be going but probably aren't, or you wouldn't need to feel these things. Though both are perceived as negative tendencies to avoid, they're flag emotions pointing toward the direction of what we really want to be doing and how we should be spending our time. Correct it at the source and you'll lose the feelings.

In that sense, at least, culturally mandated sharing could be a good thing. You could come as close as possible to feeling what it would be like to possess content you wanted but knew you could never have, lustrous content that people not-yourself were immersed in.

The next chamber in *Everything Up To My Moment* was a big one: how VoteReel flawlessly does right by our stated political inclinations, choosing our candidates better than we could; how we saved so much time and attention from having to learn things. That's partially what turned Reel from optional to essential. At this point, who is even left without an eyelet set up to HighlightReel their Moments? What parent doesn't want to re-experience their springoff's every minute of infancy, toddlerhood—such frustrating and depleting times as they are happening, but adorable and nostalgia-inducing in the aftermath?

THE DISTRACTIONS

When I went on to work as a ProWatcher, clients loved telling me all about that; and then, to know what a teen springoff is up to until Automatic Parental Access turns itself off at age eighteen. People who opted out—voluntary offReelers, totally tragic—played out their content in fringe communities in undisclosed locations. Their stories went unseen. They could not be called up. Couldn't be found. Can you imagine? Not having the data. Playing out one's content where it could not be chronically witnessed and recalled on demand? I shiver at the thought of forging ahead in my content without an eyelet and a Reel. No weekly PieChart! What do you even go on for?

I loved thinking about my PieCharts. I'd open them and reflect on my time, reveling in my awards for when I'd chosen to spend it well. I used to love thinking about what my Ultimate percentages might reflect: 50 percent sleep, 11 percent education, 16 percent work, 2 percent personal grooming (showers, teeth-brushing), 3 percent shopping, 2 percent masturbation, 1 percent sex, 9 percent eating, 6 percent workout…it adds up to the final PieChart Reel sends as our fleshtime veers toward its natural conclusion. The PieChart shown at your funeReel. I always wonder, as everyone must upon arrival of said customized PieChart, if the results will be pleasing to their author.

When I think ahead that far, I fear opening it to disappointment, a fear of wishing I had taken one of those surf trips in Antarctica, or worked on my painting, studied the extinct language of Portuguese, or lolled about doing good old nothing. I'd go on to say it to clients who had opted for reproductive pathways: Don't you wish you were spending more of your content playing with your springoffs in the reddening afternoon sun? Won't you peer back upon your content totality and regret not having had more meaningful Moments—or even mundane ones—not just alongside them while you stare at Reel, but with them?

※◉※

"Being in a Moment lasts from a few seconds to a season of content." A MIREplica spoke as if reading my thoughts. "Anything more than that is rare. Everything that happens is the only one of its kind to occur throughout the entire history of time and content, and so every Moment is a miracle, though too few proceed through their content with the necessary Moment-to-Moment, acute awareness of this. What PieCharts love most is to inform you of your personal percentage of time spent in a Moment versus mundane time. Most don't open that section, fearing the worst, an answer of 1 percent In A Moment, 99 percent Mundane Time."

※◉※

"Buying time" is another of our misnomers. Time cannot be bought, lent, condensed, crushed, or extended. I'm a prisoner of something I barely know what to do with. You can't do anything to time. It does everything to you. For instance, my family contact—adoptive parents and siblets—became less frequent until it stopped almost entirely, though they still send me happy birthday notifications onReel.

But when NicAdán talked to me in Cafelandia, when they invited me to the keynote, when they seemed to be interested in *me*, I thought for a Moment that maybe, just maybe, I was wrong, and I did have something adjacent enough to Reel-Worthiness for NicAdán to notice. That made me worthy of singling out. That they had seen, even as someone exposed to the top-quality ReelStars, that there was something special in Mischa Osborn after all. Maybe I could start to believe it too.

It hadn't been long but it was finally time. I joined the rest of the flock of time prisoners streaming toward the auditorium for the keynote. Back in the realspace of the convention center, Mire's immersive-reality exhibit danced through my mind as if it had been a hallucination or mirage, as if imagination was memory and history was present.

NicAdán ambled onstage, casual, as a million tiny illuminated three-dimensional augmented reality balloons of their *NAL* logo and their face flew around. The audience delighted in their presence, clapping and cheering as they do anytime a Bestie® winner strides into a room. NAL naturally commanded the auditorium's full attention with that smile and a "Hello, everybody."

NAL went on about curiosity and innovation and surveillance art they sent to space a few years before *25 Hours With Nicolás Adán Luchano* took off. They spoke of the content-altering effects of ReelStardom and winning the Bestie® and of HighlightReel's magnificence, either because it was true, or because they were trapped by that which sustained them. They had no choice.

"What is our technology but an extension of ourselves, a necessary tool for the essence of our identities?" they pontificated in the speech, which is still available onReel. "Since the dawn of existence, we've longed to inhabit other content. We finally have something we have wanted since the beginning of time. Reel has given us as close a distance as possible to our unsatisfiable curiosity about other people's content. It used to be that the eternal and frustrating question existed of what it would be like to experience another's content, to inhabit another consciousness. You could only speculate. Make 'television' about it. Tell stories. But Reel times are the best of times, and we are so fortunate that our content is playing out within them. Because we can know. And we do. Any musing at all can be answered with a simple journey into the Reelspace.

Watch enough of anyone's daily content experiences and you gain the power to see the content arena not only through their eyelet, but through their very eyes. The particularities of another singular—or not so singular, as it turns out—consciousness. And this intimacy has in turn revolutionized our ability to identify with one another as much as could ever be possible, an ability that allows us to connect as what we have always on some level known we really are: one. In all of history there has never been a better time than now: everything, every object once inanimate, possessed by such intelligence, and our ability to just be inside it all. Thank you for allowing me to be a small part of your watching experience. I'm in perpetual gratitude. So here, as you go about your day, is a mantra I recommend never keeping far from mind, as it's never far from mine. My content is your content. Peace."

A Moment. Everything felt heightened, the universe held in a ball of hope and tension. Then it passed, and the auditorium burst into applause.

I waited in the signing line along with every other adoring watcher at ReelCon to purchase *25 Hours With Nicolás Adán Luchano: The Book*. Books served as surviving artifacts for those still longing for tangible, physical objects. To see what someone else is reading was one of those rare potential realspace conversation starters. What looks smarter than a book accessory? But how many of them would actually read it? I would. For most, buying the book was an excuse to have a realspace exchange with the lauded ReelStar whose face was plastered on the cover, large and semi-bearded and smiling, for eyelets to capture and throw up onReel: a Moment with Nicolás Adán Luchano at the ReelCon book signing!

My pulse raced. My hands trembled as if I was hopped up on too many DRX-kava tonics. I'd eaten four hundred thirty-six calories so far that day, so I might have just been hungry. I decided to supplement it later with powders or maybe some of the cricket protein bites I had back in my room. I held the book in my trembling hands and smelled its pages, craving a cup of Diablo Roxa for my nerves. I stared at the face printed on the cover and all those feelings came up even more, as did my breakfast, near enough. Yes, I could tell, NAL was the ideal permanent Personal Intimacy Companion for me. Staring at the picture and glancing up to see them in front of the line at the signing station gave me all the tingles. I didn't even care if that was cheesy because this time was different—*we were made for each other!* Content was catapulting me into unforeseen bliss! A state I'd never previously considered possible for me given my content composition. Maybe something really can come along that alters our essential selves when we least expect it.

When it was finally my turn, though, NAL smiled and scrawled their name inside the front of the book as if I was suddenly a stranger, any doting ReelFan. They'd forgotten me already. I turned, dismayed, and flushed so hot I mentally noted to check PrivateReel later to see if my face had turned purple in humiliation. Just as quickly as it happened, everything had been taken back. I strode away, toward the bathrooms, to *actually* vomit.

Then I heard their voice behind me.

"Miss Chaos. Wait!"

And all was well with the world again. I exhaled and pivoted with what I hope was graceful body movement.

"I need a break from all this." They gestured to the remaining line of ReelFans awaiting their return. We walked toward the bathrooms together, several feet of distance between us, sure, but we were *walking together.*

We arrived at the bathrooms. They went to enter one, and I wanted them to enter me, so I waved the entrypad on the adjacent bathroom as casually as possible. Was this it? They just needed a break, and saw a quick out, the bathroom?

"Well, see you," I mumbled.

"I only need a minute to wrap it up. Just wait for me over here."

I stuttered an acceptance. I was so flattered, so shocked, that NAL was going to come back and spend more time with me. I lingered by the bathrooms for another hour and thirty-six minutes watching the signing line, waiting for it to dwindle. Such was NAL's heightened aptitude for persuasion—for no discernible reason, simply by virtue of playing out their content as their own self. Reel always made time go by faster. I scanned NewsReel: new vaccines for a likely pandemic, KuulSuit-sponsored heat warnings, climate refugees flooding borders of nations with enough ReelCoin to have sufficiently harnessed the devastation, ReelStars adopting orphans off the barges. Nothing on NewsReel was new.

My HighlightReel Content Stream was far more interesting. Someone had a new, hotter Personal Intimacy Companion, a PIC they were feeling could very well merit permanency. Someone else birthed a springoff. An adorable springoff, which was saying a lot, coming from I who didn't much care for those things. An award was given, a promotion raised. A whole slew of AdReel content.

Over at the signing line, an endless stream of ReelFans clutched their copies of *25 Hours With Nicolás Adán Luchano: The Book* close to their chests, as if they could place NAL inside their hearts that way. NAL spoke to the assembled eyelets that flurried around their owners and them, getting the best angles for all these Moments they'd throw onReel for watchers. The ultimate watcher—yourself, right? Because what is Reel, really, other than a memory book of every single moment that transpired in your content, whether Public (your Moments, the best!) or Private (everything else)?

I was checking some work RMs when I felt the light grip on my shoulder and my consciousness lifted out the top of my head before dropping back in again.

"Come with me, hurry."

"Where are we going?"

"Just come."

I allowed myself to be led, imagining we were going back to their hotel for some personal intimacy, and then they'd ask me to get Publicly Declared, we'd be PICs for the remaining duration of our content, and that would be the end.

Dear watcher, there was no hotel. That is not where NAL took me, not what transpired.

We got in the mobi. I put up my feet on the dash, where the coffee usually goes, as it started to drive, strangely silent about our destination. They stared out into the distance, out of the bubble containing the Vegas Strip, into the temperature wilderness.

"What kind of adventure is this?" I was more than a little nervous exiting into some flesh-burning risk zone.

"The old-fashioned kind."

"Old-fashioned?"

"A hike."

"I have never been on such a thing."

"The everyday begs for a touch of the extreme." NAL's eyelet blinked, pleased by the banter. But I was afraid.

"I'm not going out there to die of heatstroke. Take me back."

I was flustered. Disappointed. I should have known better than to come out here with a ReelStar who was in it for the watch-numbs. I have never been a fan of physical risk. How could they sit there, just smirking? NAL's eyelet was Reeling, I could see by the little green light. When I later looked back on this Moment, I would see their watch-numb spike: 4,368,021 in that Moment.

I stared at the tiny dots of light flashing as the mobi suite transported us. "Where are we really going?"

They pulled from a seat pocket a tiny package, held it up between their thumb and index finger, up in front of their eyelet toward the light. "KuulSuit five-point-oh: desert edition."

I reached out to feel it. It crackled at the touch. "When does this come out?"

NicAdán pressed down on the tiny package and was immersed in an angelic glow. It crept down from their head to envelop their entire body.

"Next year. Completely redirects the heat." They handed it to me. "Go ahead."

"How does it work?"

"What matters is, this version really works. I'm less interested in *how* things work than the infinite possibilities of their use."

The Suit, I had seen in my quick research, was one of their content's latest sponsors. They weren't to question or explain, but rather simply put the item to everyday use in an intriguing setting, the details of which were up to them. We activated the KuulSuit. It enveloped us together as we stepped out of the mobi. I surveyed the landscape, arid and red. "I can't believe this realscape! Where are we?"

"This is a historical site formerly known as Calico Tanks. Used to be a two-hour hike, and now it will be again, once more hands get on one of these."

They tickled the "wall" of the KuulSuit illuminating them in a rainbow iridescence. A hike, or more than a few minutes out here, would be impossible without the techtire. *KuulSuit—Making the Great Outdoors Pleasant Again!*

It was a beautiful, panoramic Moment up above it all. The strip glittered in the distance, a miniature simulacrum of itself, a light-up child's toy landscape. We watched, and our watchers watched us, and for the first time in my content I felt, really felt, as if I had stumbled upon some content worth watching.

They took my hand. Held it. Held on tighter than was necessary to convey an impression of affection. The Suit formed cover over both of us—perfect for PICs, this was the feature we were meant to show off. I looked up into NAL's face, both of us enveloped in and protected by a soothing crystal azure light: *well, this is something.* I began to believe that I was destined for a PIC after all, and not just any one at that—this brilliant, most-watched content artist. That's why it had taken so long. *We could get Publicly Declared in this very desert, wearing intimacy declaration KuulSuits.* Those were certainly coming. KuulSuit could sponsor the ceremony.

The conversation turned to whether springoffs were distracting or desirable. NicAdán peered out over the red rock sea, saying something about how they had never once in their content wanted them. Couldn't understand the purpose. Content with a Personal Intimacy Companion provided enough challenge and pleasure for the ride. They didn't believe in getting Publicly Declared.

I tossed a tiny stone into a ravine. "Why not?"

"Because getting permanently declared tends to lead to springoffs."

"Well I never wanted them either. Content is hard enough without adding more and more distractions. I can't imagine my body morphing to put out a person in a space where there wasn't one before."

"Entirely pointless, and anyway, you could always get a Babie©. Nothing can go wrong with a Babie©. You know exactly what you are getting. They don't change. They're always consistent. One forever knows what to expect."

"What happened that made you want to know exactly what to expect?"

They kind of shrank back then, like a turtle retreating into its shell. They turned their eyelet to BlindMode before they told me, because their upbringing was unremarkable. They certainly never imagined becoming a ReelStar. One parent sold content insurance. The other had a Reel on the up and up until they died young during one of the earlier pandemics. So much promise, lost.

I could feel my own sad story bubbling up inside me, yearning to be told. Not because I wanted to draw attention to my tragic origins, but because NicAdán's presence made me feel so jarringly open; a portal to liberating vulnerability, as if I might even uncover some never-before-seen superpowers from my new susceptible openness. I felt safe with NAL's eyelet cutting the deep parts out, too. Keeping things Reel palatable.

"I lost my mother too but nothing like that," I said. "I was pretty much a newborn. I was taken to a beach and from what my adoptive mother says, left with their family—nobody my mother knew, just kind strangers that agreed to watch me while my mother took a much-needed dip to cool off. Never came back."

"Well what happened?"

"They were just never seen again. The family already had four springoffs. Then they kept me. From how it was told to me, there weren't any eyelets there. It was early. My mother was supposed to be right out and then vanished without a trace. That could never happen now."

"Right, impossible," NAL said. "No one is capable of vanishing."

"Apparently somebody was."

"I don't know why anyone would opt for naturemade pathways to parenthood when you get the same thing but with the ability to also turn it off when you feel like it," Nic said. "If your mother didn't want to be a mom, why did they?

"I don't know. So much mystery in a time when there's basically none."

"The springoff thing, though." I sensed NAL was changing the subject so we'd be back onReel, showing off these KuulSuits, talking about ReelCon. "With a Babie© there are no tantrums, no tears. Did you see the latest model in the convention hall? I don't want one, but if I did, maybe I'd grab one of those. Curb the urge."

I was getting hot and not because of the temperature. I turned the KuulSuit temp down by three. "Creeptastically realistic. Gonna definitely fool someone someday. We may as well stop all organic-type reproduction now. And it grows, too!"

NicAdán laughed. "Every parent's dream, I'm sure. But it won't happen. We're too narcissistic, programmed to spread our genes like germs, even if the Babie© is a more environmentally sound investment. Did you notice they're biodegradable, so you can still get your zero-waste certification? What an overall better experience! None of the work, none of the mess, all of the cuteness. Though I guess I can't even imagine taking care of a fake one, even with the mellow and off settings. The pressure is permanent. I mean, you could expire it like the instructions say, but imagine the guilt. Because we can't help but get attached. And then you'll never want to let go. "

"Maybe you just don't ever feel done." A fleet of DroneBeez buzzed overhead, headed to the city for flowers. "Beautiful."

NAL smiled. "Speaking of. You have this face that's…also beautiful, and yet somehow like the kind where you could meet someone a bunch of times and they'd forget to recognize you."

My soul sank like some bad old treasure-ship cliche. "Thanks. Ultra flattering."

"No, I mean it's a good thing. Like being secret and undiscovered. I miss that. It means you can do whatever you like and nobody will know."

"Well actually some people do know me, or they used to at least, as the architect of Project Alovue. That's how I got picked to lead the Content Clearing team."

"No way! Project Alovue is legendary! That was you?"

"Sometimes you just want someone to be watching you who really cares, you know?"

"Yeah, they gave it to me in beta to try out. I liked it. It's not your fault, what happened. It just wasn't what people wanted. It's too weird. We need our ALs for service, of course, but who wants to conflate one with love?"

"An obvious problem in retrospect. I mean, what does someone who loves you notice and love you for? Not your sweeping big Moments. They love and notice you for those little things, the way you look while you brush your teeth or the little fleck of gold in your right eyeball, those are the details they care about. So Alovue was the worst at discerning a Moment. Everything Alovue picked wasn't better. It was all the stupid, little things. No one wanted to watch that boring stuff that someone who loves you loves to watch. It failed."

48

"Well I enjoyed Alovue. They send me everything so that's saying a lot—they come up with a ton of garbage. Alovue was…nice. Intimate, or something. It did feel like Alovue cared. It did improve my content. You replicated a certain kind of really sweet adoration we all need but don't often receive. That's a big deal."

NAL had beta'd my beloved failure? It was probably better I hadn't known or I would have made a bad excuse and hid. I tried so hard to play it sterling right then, not expose the emotion that was tugging my stomach down toward my intestines. Looking down at the red dirt and pebbles, I said only, "Thanks."

"Now I understand even less," NAL said. "Can you please really explain why, if you're so talented and skilled that you created an AL that's capable of love, or of giving this very realistic impression of being all love, you're signing up to be a ProWatcher? Oh wait, I get it now. I answered my own question by asking it." They laughed. "You want to create an AL that can replace ProWatchers next."

"It's part of my research process."

"Taking the most boring jobs?"

"Well Nic, maybe some get their best ideas when they're totally bored."

"NicAdán."

"Right."

"Well, whatever you need to do to be brilliant."

Soon I forgot all about work and skills and talents and brilliance and the whole content entirety as Nicolás Adán Luchano's mouthspace closed over mine, finalizing word-trade and

49

Liza Monroy

commencing contained salivation exchange. The Moment I'd been waiting for. Even without Reel, I would organically remember it for the remainder of my natural content. They smelled like mint, smoky wood chips, KuulSuit casing, and the coffee from earlier. I was shown how, no matter how terrible anything might turn out to be, a chance encounter over the course of a few hours could shift someone's entire content arena. Obsession, fixation, preoccupation…however you named this head-cracking horror of a feeling, it was this ephemeral sensation on which I became obsessed, fixated, and preoccupied for an inordinately long time. I felt, for the first time in my natural content that I can remember, helpless.

After that, dear watcher, we did go back to a hotel. We kissed some more. Not much beyond that. I wasn't used to feeling these kinds of feelings so I was already overwhelmed. Not in a bad way. Since it was a lot, I fell asleep. I slept in the arms of the ReelStar. Close to a warm, naturally breathing body instead of my SomniBuddy. There was a difference. We woke up together at first light. "You are beautiful," they told me. "Like, ReelStar beautiful." But there was no full-on body colliding because they said they had to go and didn't want some rushed Temporary Intimacy Companionship thing.

They had to get back to LA. Then they would travel to Mexico City—the Distrito Federal, the world's cultural capital, Earth's elevated epicenter—before arriving in Brooklyn exactly one month later for a Reel sponsorship. FliLyte would sponsor the trip in exchange for NAL Reeling from the first-class cabin about foldout beds with built-in REMVibes and showers and DRX champagne tonix. Another sponsor was a secret restaurant that was famous for moving around the city and for having the content arena's best 3D-printed sushi.

50

THE DISTRACTIONS

"Can I see you when I'm in town?" NAL asked, but Nicolás Adán Luchano didn't have to ask me for anything. My NicAdán could simply announce. Declare. When they spoke, they conjured up the world I wanted all around me. They knew exactly how to leave me wanting more. That was, after all, their job.

We said goodbye on the sidewalk, at an intersection outside a ReelBnB building, in bright and blinding light that cracked over the desert like a dropped egg, leaving trails of yolk-spill all over the mountains as the other side of the sky became spattered with stars. Our eyelets were docked on our wrists by then. This Moment was ours alone: Nic-Adán's and mine.

I began to imagine pursuing new projects, the nature of which I wasn't exactly sure—guitar or a renewed stab at my own ReelPoetry maybe—but projects nonetheless, side by side with Nicolás Adán Luchano for as long as we both possessed natural and autonomous content; Nic's content art and my yet-to-be-determined *thing* that would reveal itself whenever my hidden and true talent decided to leap from whatever lockbox it was secured away inside of my lackluster organic brain. If they'd singled me out among all other devastatingly attractive potential unsung geniuses they encountered in their daily content, did that mean I had been a devastatingly attractive unsung genius all along and didn't know it? Even with every moment available onReel, it's hard to see oneself with any objective clarity. (Even as I obsessively rewatch my own PrivateReel to analyze, reflect on, and pick apart my content, especially as compared to others, especially while trying to see my content from an outside, subjective perspective, I find it all so impossible. I watched myself watch others—like Mire—who were Reeling the kind of clever, sterling, lauded content I wished I could claim as my own.)

As an even redder dawn broke, I took the hour-long FliLyte back to BK International. A full workday sprawled ahead of me, but I couldn't focus even though I went about my content in a similar way as we were taught to at the beginnings of pandemics. I enjoyed carrying that over into safe gathering times, staying in and letting the content arena come to me, by virtue of our wondrous technology.

I took breaks to the basement. Off to the side, away from the food carts, was a grocery store, one of the few remaining of its kind since everyone ReelKarted in their food direct. I liked to venture down there to feel the fruit. I had no idea what made a piece of fruit ideal or not—who did? My fruit arrived, as with everything else, at the window, dronelifted in boxes with the rest of my weekly repeating orders of every necessity. And yet I adored squeezing mangoes, smelling apples, knocking on melons and holding them up to my ear the way I'd seen in really old ReelHistories. The ritual made me feel as if I was a part of something larger. It gave me a sense of connection, of sensation. Who cared how long it took for truly meaningful things—or really any things—to happen? The time passed anyway. These were the kinds of thoughts that came to me while perusing realspace fruits.

Alone again upstairs at home (or as alone as anyone can be), sixty-four stories above the swaths of sanitized concrete that added up to the city I loved but did not see much of, I paced tenderly in my slippers as if the smartwood floor might give way and send me tumbling all sixty-four stories downward into the basement food disco with the ReelPals stationed out front. They were scanning crowds for any sign of illness that might contaminate the public space or histories of theft or other mild criminal behaviors that would bar entry.

NAL had asked a good question, one I hadn't thought about before. I created Alovue because what everyone wants most is to feel loved. But maybe the love of an AI could never quite mimic that feeling close enough.

Nic had me thinking about my flawed creation anew. Why had I thought everybody would want this thing? That it would be totally content-changing? Nic was right. It wasn't about providing a premium product for Reelers everywhere. It was about me. I'd been left by the first person I would have loved and my content's primary creation thus far was a built intelligence that would love me and never leave. So fucking authentic. No wonder I needed to put it away and get back to Reel business.

And that was when it came to me: NAL had given me the greatest idea of my content. I could return to the drawing board, revive Project Alovue. The propensity to categorize is basic human programming. Take categories away and we're uncomfortable; as if the borders of reality itself were dissolving, faded and muddied like old snow. Love was really the same thing: What *kind* of love? I'd been thinking only about myself. What I needed, others must have thought was excessive or even creepy. I needed to re-engineer Alovue to be able to give each individual the kind of love *they*—not I—craved: mass-scale adoration? Or one other's eyes on you who loves everything you do? Like me, do you not have a parent or two and want a mother's love? It needed to mimic that particular kind of love you wanted in order for you to love it back. Could it get smart enough to detect your specific needs and desires, even if you weren't sure of them yourself?

I spent the rest of my day on it, toggling back and forth between experimentally programming Alovue and watching NAL onReel.

The next day, I began ProWatching, too. I always found it uncanny that HighlightReel created the ProWatcher program the way a drug company manufactures a disease in order to invent the cure—or if not the cure, at least a little something to mitigate the symptoms, some palliative care. The purpose was twofold: keep busy workers undistracted and give the lonely a feeling of companionship. ProWatchers were true heroes in the field of serveillance—surveillance as a service. We watched to make sure you were on track and to make sure you were okay, the old friends-for-hire with a productivity twist. In the field of content serveillance, I'd been a true original.

The only tools I needed to work my then-new job were ones everybody already had: an eyelet, Reel access, and my own two organic eyeballs. The department had two taglines: *In a content arena where privacy is an illusion, wouldn't you rather know who is Watching?* And: *What can you do about your sad feelings when the entire content arena could be listening—but nobody is?* Which one surfaced on your ReelFeed depended on what personal use you had for a ProWatcher's services. Were you busy? Distracted? All alone? And, if the latter, were you lonely or just one of those rare solitary types who truly relished prolonged isolation? ALs and elite Pro-

Liza Monroy

Watchers took in all the pertinent intel so Reel could feed our clients back exactly what they most wanted—or needed—to hear.

The more of our time we freed, the less we seemed to know what to do with it. That spurred the reason for ProWatchers, too: a guide to a focused existence. *Do this, now that.* Pro-Watcherhood, a delicate art like calligraphy or origami, required a certain kind: someone who could engage light but productive conversation, cultivate an ability to be a nonintrusive constant presence, and be able to be pleasant; but also come down hard if the client was to even so much mention the urge to watch PornReel (only for three minutes!), ChefReel to select that night's recipe, GameReel to check for the latest release of survival gear for their Long Night persona, or NewsReel because focus was impossible without knowing what the president said in their nightly address and what the top ReelComics would make of it afterward.

Whatever led a ProWatcher's clients' attention astray—aspirational real estate on HomeReel, an especially rambunctious CatReel kitten, the latest stats on climate refugees entering their city, or simply old acquaintances and associates or ReelStars or plain old regular HighlightReels of friends and neighbors, you had to be able to slap them to attention without alienating them or making them feel like addicts. Such as:

Me: Hey! You're doing the thing! Totally understandable but…. Time to get back to it.

Client A, ReelArt Broker: I'm going to. I just have to get through this list of fifteen formerly good-looking celebrities who destroyed themselves with plastic surgery.

56

THE DISTRACTIONS

Saucer cheeks gone awry. Overly pointy chinfiles. You cannot restore original bone!

Me: They used to call it 'train wreck'. Now it's just an egalitarian kind of fame. Why are you even watching BK on DirtReel? Stay off DirtReel. It's pointless, it only exists to cause harm, support schadenfreude. Please immediately cease to watch anything of this persuasion.

Outside the client's view of my tiny little head, I watched the *25 Hours With Nicolás Adán Luchano* Content Stream non-stop. After I was done for the evening, I watched some more, then curled up in bed beside my SomniBuddy. I'd ordered the sleep robot on a lark back when I was having trouble sleeping. The daily horrors watched as a Content Clearer probably did give me, if nothing else, some bouts of insomnia.

My SomniBuddy had been most useful. The robot that breathes next to you to simulate the presence of another living being and as a result calms your own breath and heart rate for better, deeper slumber, was enough company at night. It showed how all you needed was another inhaling and exhaling beside you, the lull of a parallel existence to see you through to the other side of darkness. You could be brilliant, you could be successful, you could achieve your wildest dreams and still be miserable. But the SomniBuddy helped people like that. Me, I was only into it for the sound. So meditative.

Most of my nonworking hours were spent lying on my back on the floor, legs propped on the bed, staring at the ceiling and having Dev project endless Nicolás Adán Luchano Reels up there. I couldn't wait for the month to pass so Nic—I still thought of them as Nic or NAL despite their insistence about their double-name—would come see me.

My new obsession with my future permanent PIC was turning me into a high-caliber ProWatcher. It counted as professional development! I'd already had one client with a very specific *25 Hours With Nicolás Adán Luchano* addiction. They couldn't fall asleep without taking in several hours of the Reel, which was in turn so stimulating the client couldn't fall asleep anyway, which resulted in a lack of productivity at their job managing a fleet of ReelPals doing taxes.

"It's so counter-meditative," they told me. "You'd think I would find this relaxing—I mean, look at the content: all sponsored adventures, meaningful conversations, and making art. Then the rest: them relaxing by the pool, tending to their tropical garden, under the sunlamp, taking in those peaceful rays of light that save them from any signs of age.... I need one of those things. Should I order one of those?"

The subliminal advertising worked. Here's something about Reel from an insider: If you exceed a certain watch-numb, which precise number even I couldn't find out, the AL deems you a Petite Likely ReelStar, influential enough in your own little sphere. Then you will be paid a decent amount of ReelCoin, enough to partially sponsor your content, to subliminally advertise to your friends. So during a rare ReelCall with my old buddy Ember, they started talking to me about this period underwear made of some fabric gathered from materials on Jupiter that literally decomposes your period on contact, so it's like never having your period at all. They were going on and on about it, and they got some pairs out and started showing them to me, telling me all about how cute they were, how well they worked, and I was thinking, *Oh, you are so getting paid to pitch this to me.* Still, I went on ShopReel and ordered five pairs before the call was done, and damn, they did simply eliminate your period on contact.

So, maybe it's a certain kind of evil that also does good. Slippery slopes, these. But I worked for them too, so what could I say?

My client ordered the sunlamp.

"That's enough now," I said. "You have spent nineteen minutes of your working content talking about your seventeen-minute distraction. Time to get back to task goals!"

"Sometimes I think I'll quit," the client said. "Exist on unibasic in some simpler place where I can kick back and watch these beautiful things all day."

"It's not as ideal of a contentsphere as it would appear," I argued. "I'll love to converse again when you finish for the day. We can have happy hour together, if you get everything done." I knew I was breaking the rules already—we weren't supposed to socialize with them—but who was ever innovative by following what whoever set the rules decided?

I watched as Nic took a quick hop over to Talking Springs for the International Festival of ReelStars and, subsequently, a FliLyte returned them to Mexico City, where they'd previously been on a Mangosa tequila sponsorship. They'd gone offReel for a few days there. I couldn't venture to guess as to why—probably secret ReelStar business—so when it came to what was happening in Mexico, el Distrito Federal, cultural epicenter of the world, I couldn't see what was happening. Even then, this struck me as ultra-weird since Nic Reeled near-constantly to update watchers, even about secret sponsorship meetings. I checked my RMs again despite the automatic alerts of new ones, just to be sure there hadn't been an error, that NAL really hadn't sent one. Nothing. It would happen soon, I suspected. Sooner than I knew.

I had become so accustomed to seeing Nic's face and hearing that voice—besides knowing them now, I had to be up on the kinds of content that distracted my clients, I told myself at the time—some part of my brain surely mistook Reelspace content ingestion for the actual spending of realspace time together. Reel could confuse a person that way. It confused the mind between what was real and what was Reel. But was there even a difference? All I knew was that I only had bandwidth for Nic right then.

I stared into Nic's deep and wise slightly downturned eyes as they offered the top seven best reasons why you should travel to Crenshaw Shores now, including a tiny, recently opened bar named Bar that served the greatest Diablo Roxa mystiki on the West Coast. "It teaches your cells how to isolate and eliminate disease before it has a chance to spread," Nic said. "And it puts you in a soft, elevated, euphoric state. It is the beverage technology we've all been waiting for. Now we can do or take almost anything and preserve our health."

Even as I steered clients away from obsessively watching NicAdán, I spent bottomless time on these Daily Doings and Grand Adventures (which, when it came to NAL, were usually one and the same) and everywhere on the spectrum in between, hearing that chocolatey voice formulate opinions and disseminate knowledge, smelling their soap, shampoo, cologne, essential oils toolkit, ordering the same food they got paid to eat so that I could eat while watching their Reel—I wasn't crazy; all of this generated that sense of realspace closeness, so much so that I became certain of what was going to happen next. People act surprised when it happens, but this was what Reel and its predecessors were always meant to do to us. As a ProWatcher, the more I could learn about us, our motivations and distractions, the better I would be at creating an AL to do it for us and feel like it was still us. I was suddenly more intensely motivated than ever.

When I wasn't watching Nic, I focused on simple things: tending to clients, cleaning my disastrous apartment—if you could call what I did cleaning, picking up piles of stuff and moving it around into other, new piles. During my offReel time, I could do anything I wanted and I didn't have to leave my building to do any of it. Usually I didn't. I'd go downstairs to MeatCulture for another award-winning cultured PetriDish, a steak that melted like butter in your mouth as soon as it touched your tongue. I'd take a swim in that beautiful salted wave pool in my building's gym filled with the large, Reelistic AL-Dolphins they threw in for extra comfort. Walk a dog, if I'd had a dog, on the rooftop self-cleansing Dogarden. I didn't want a real dog—too much responsibility and organic matter. I liked picking out one of the ReelDogs they had up there in the bins, taking them around for a stroll. It made my walk purposeful without having to pick up any shit.

Throughout my consummate daily routine of work, gym, and a couple of nightly DRX UltraLime PomPom tonics I drank at sundown, I watched NicAdán. It was only a matter of two weeks by then and they would be here, back with me in the realspace again, and that would be it. I could finally be PICked. I tinkered with Alovue here and there, but it was getting complicated, muddy. There are infinite varieties of love. So I put it away again, storing it for some other time, when I felt inspired, and that is how it too got abandoned.

What traps is your present self unknowingly laying for your future self to fall into? There I was, succumbing to the very thing I spent my days trying to palliate in clients. Who says ProWatchers aren't immune to the disease for which they purportedly offer a cure? In a client session, I misread, out loud, the title of one super-engaging list the client "just had to get through" before they could face the requirements of the day ahead: "The 12 Useful Ways to Choose the Right Distraction In Pursuit of Successful Content." (It was "Direction.") The client laughed, thinking it was a joke. The mistake went unnoticed.

I spent hours on KnotReel. When you're going to get Publicly Declared with one of the greatest ever ReelStars, you need a really good dress. I spent way too much ReelCoin on it. It wasn't disposable income that was a problem for me. I earned plenty of ReelCoin, I just hadn't had anything special to spend it on. NicAdán had given me a reason to make a purchase. The dress: an investment in our future. Soon Nic would come and I would leave here, move into their beautiful LA home with its lush gardens, brush my teeth next to them in the mirror every morning, have the world's best personal intimacy encounters, go along on all of their sponsored adventures, maybe even land a few of my own. I wished I'd stolen one of their shirts. Humans cannot recall smell. Like pain, even if we wanted to remember it gets erased.

The dress was fitted on top to emphasize my muscled arms, toned back, and shoulders, with a slight lift to bring my small breasts closer together and higher up. Billowy layers spilled out beneath. I would not show the dress to NicAdán or even mention it, but when the time came, I would know it was there, and this would save me the stress of trying to find the perfect dress on KnotReel when the whole world was watching. KnotReel-sponsored PICking ceremonies were so dull.

I searched for venues. NicAdán lived not far from the Crenshaw Shores Resort, so if we decided to keep it local that could be a solid option. Brazil's northern coast looked promising too. I watched all the locations that came to me onReel. I put the most tempting ones in 3D and looked around. I couldn't stop. I couldn't sleep. I barely ate. I lost some weight, but that would be okay, I could get the dress taken in or double my Crickit Protein Powder intake in my morning blend.

The day before NAL's realspace arrival in Brooklyn, I reclined in my favorite watching spot to dive into their latest content. Reviewing their most recent Reeling on a loop was a close enough substitute for those fleeting Moments of realspace presence, which, though the time was short, I'd been unable to push from my every waking thought. I sometimes wondered why spending such a fraction of fragmented realspace time together yielded my inability to steer my attention anywhere else.

I watched and thought about Nic all the time as days ticked by. Twenty-nine days after ReelCon and still no RM. I'd have taken it as a bad sign if I hadn't known the reason. It was easy to understand, I told myself. ReelStars in that echelon were so busy. Everything would come together soon. Nic would be with me. Here in my apartment.

I surveyed the room. I hadn't let anyone else come in here. I was used to my messes but NicAdán and accompanying watchers needed a spotless welcome into my space. I got back to cleaning. I didn't have a ReelPal yet, but I had a few devices to help along the way, much earlier versions of the tidy masters that were those home ReelPals. I'd get one soon, I decided, because it took me a full day and into the night to totally clean the kitchen, bathroom, living area, and all the parts around my work station that were offReel. I guess I hadn't realized I'd been living in chaos, though I should have—after all, it was in my name. With NicAdán around, I would finally have a reason to be clean and tidy. What happened between us was an exploratory personal intimacy encounter with destiny. An epic EPIC. I knew if I just kept waiting and watching, the day would arrive. NAL was already my best friend in my head, my PIC of destiny.

It is no spoiler that the day, dear watcher, did arrive.

NAL disembarked the FliLyte with the most beaming smile. I stared at Reel, waiting for the RM to arrive, declaring their presence, declaring their unending adoration. It was coming, it was coming, it would come. I was still in roomwear while deliberating appropriate attire for when I would realspace see them so shortly. I brushed my hair and teeth for the first time in days while watching NAL take their first realspace steps into this, one of many trips they'd taken, as a ReelStar, to New York. They were put-together, refreshed, and smiling following the shower in a first-class FliLyte suite.

"Watchers! I am about to reveal an even bigger surprise."

Their watch-numb spiked before they finished the sentence, HEARTS and CLAPS and INSUSPENSES exploding outward from their scene. "Right here and now, today, at Bay C. It's been top secret until now, my friends—offReel content. We are about to be—if I'm lucky, that is—in what, I hope, will be the greatest Moment yet."

I felt as if I could reach out and grab them, but when I tried, of course, as everyone sometimes does, the image fractured in my hand. *Do you wish to exit?* Dev asked; I did not. Sometimes Dev asked (by mistake?), *Do you wish to exist?* and I had no answer for that one. I'd seen such affectionate gestures many times when people were alone and believed they were not being watched, as well as much punching and kicking at onReel projections of nemeses. I wondered if we had become too lazy to seek them out in realspace, whether that was the reason why both violence and intimate connection had both steeply declined.

NicAdán continued. "I haven't talked about it to all of you yet as its certainty was in a fragile state until now. And it was a secret on top of that. Also, we all love surprises. It's why you're watching me right now—I'm full of them." Wink. "And the time has come to share that for these past few months, I've been waiting to reconnect with someone very special."

Oh what? I realized Nic was talking about me. I was supposed to be there, and somehow I'd missed it. Where was the RM? Or had they dropped clues or hidden messages for me onReel? It didn't matter. I'd missed the message and had to get to the FliPort. Extra ReelCoin for an express and I'd be there in moments. I watched my Nic's little half-moon smile and slightly widening eyes. "Come on Dev!"

"And soon they'll meet me right on the other side of this hallway. As long as they aren't running late."

I was so, so late. How had I missed something so extremely important? I Reeled for a ride and combed back through RMs trying to find the missed one from Nic. Nothing. I dove into my closet, quickly changing, now without deliberation, into a floral print softsuit, threw on gold wedge slip-ons, and shuffled around looking for what to take to the FliPort. I was so amped up; this whole thing was a Moment.

NicAdán's eyelet flew closer. That voice was hardly higher than a whisper. "I'm excited, and after all that anticipation, honestly a little worried—what if they don't actually show up, or what if they haven't understood I want them here? What if it isn't all I've built it up to be in my head? I've gone and made myself vulnerable to potential complete and utter heartspace obliteration."

I would never obliterate that heartspace. Once we were reunited, I knew I would hardly ever leave NAL's side. But I hadn't gotten the message until now. Something went wrong. I had to be at the FliPort before they decided I wasn't coming and I missed my chance.

The mobi arrived. On the road I sat frantically and quickly reviewing every RM yet again, searching and turning up nothing and searching again.

Meanwhile, NicAdán rolled through the terminal as if they owned it. And in a sense they did.

I arrived at the FliPort and entered the arrivals hall, Dev Reeling my excited rush. Into the crush of people traveling and attendant ReelPals working the Cafelandia, inquiry and transportation stations, and general crowdscanning. I ran to the exit-only door from which Nic would emerge from the secure interior traveler zone back out into public space. An announcement on the loudspeaker about the Mexico City flight's baggage carousel was lost on me until much later, watching what would be this onReel Moment. I waited by the door. A few security ReelPals rolled. Nic would soon follow. There! NAL was coming toward me. Dev lit up green as my heart rate increased. My Moment was arriving. I raised up an arm and waved. NAL kept coming, looking incredible in

a blue softshirt and dark blue softpants with the most adorable loafers I'd seen. Their beard had grown in a little and
was slightly scruffy in an appealing way. They had on a new
pair of purposefully outlandish thick-framed SightNines, the
latest from the glasses company sponsor that sent them to the
world's most remote inhabited island, Tristan da Cunha, because they wanted them watched wearing some of their shades
in a land frozen in time. The genius idea was for Nicolás Adán
Luchano to be seen by no one in order to be seen by everyone.
Now I was seeing them again in the realspace, coming toward
me, and so soon they'd be seeing me, folding me up again
so my cheek would feel their soft blue sweater and I would
inhale into ultimate bliss and content would be ideal forever.

Then they breezed right past.

"NicAdán?" I said feebly, but when I looked around I was
standing in a crowd of ReelFans and NAL's eyes were fixated
ahead. They didn't hear or weren't listening. They didn't turn
around. Then I did, only to see them lift into the air, fresh off
the FliLyte from Mexico City, looking ever so sterling: Mire
D'Innit.

Nic spun Mire around. Nic *kissed* Mire. Just as they had done with me! Mire returned this gesture of affection. And I died.

⋘◉⋙

I didn't really die, of course. Or I wouldn't have remaining content with which to tell this pathetic tale of misunderstandings, dear watcher. I know it sounds so *senseless* now. As in, you got obsessed with an intriguing and charismatic ReelStar, so what? It's happened to everyone at some point. So what if they'd given you mistaken signs of interest in potential ongoing intimacy companionship? People over the entire course of history have had this problem. I saw Nicolás Adán Luchano, who I thought had been so eager to see me again after our EPIC at ReelCon, after they singled me out, made me *wait near their book signing line* for their totally ridiculous book. NAL was with my old nemesis, Mire? When had this happened? How? And most importantly, in all the unmissable content, how had I managed to miss *this*?

⋘◉⋙

I froze at that most terrible burrito; a cruel reminder wrapped in a cosmic joke, a Moment even I couldn't bear to watch... and yet I did. Watch. In realspace, even! NicAdán spun Mire around. Their eyelets captured the Moment from every angle. I ducked behind a pillar and a luggage cart and went onReel to see it up close and hear better; the giant undoing of someone they didn't know was watching. *What you are about to see may prove disturbing to the particularities of your personal composition.* Dismiss, Dev! Dismiss, dismiss, dismiss. I had to see it, no matter how badly it messed with my "personal composition," because I had to understand. To move on, you have to understand—everyone knows that, even machines.

"Dev, get all of today over to Private, please. Now. It's emergency status."

"Done; offReeled Moments to Private only."

"How many watchers have seen it?"

"No watchers today. Sorry."

"Don't be." For once, it was okay.

NicAdán returned Mire's feet to the ground, reached out and touched their face. "Finally! Here you are. We're finally here."

"Hello, Nic."

Oh, so they got to call them by only one name. And so disinterestedly! Since our briefly overlapping days at ArtSpace, Mire had always seemed demure, brushing off even the biggest accomplishments as if they were no big deal, simply what occurred as a result of what they did, as if it was their content destiny. This moment with NAL was only another sterling occurrence in the string of sterling occurrences that amounted to Mire D'Innit's content totality. Mire had this way of making the appearance of complete emotional vacancy alluring. I wanted to do that. Why couldn't I do that? Their locked mouths warbled. I'd never been so angry in my content entirety! Dev was showing it: heart rate way up, brain waves all over the place. Biological intel, so much data to contend with. I didn't need to know that to understand how shaken I was upon realizing that it had been Mire's seat at the keynote I'd occupied; Mire's place I had taken on the EPIC in the desert. It all made sense now. I wanted to collapse through the floor and be absorbed by the earth. Could it be comforting to me that Mire was a better artist than Nic? I considered it for a moment and decided not really. I needed to soothe myself with something. What calmed me the most, at least while I was doing it, was watching. Pretending I had anything to further understand, and that answers could be found onReel.

As their watchers celebrated this Moment alongside them, NicAdán and Mire's Reels burst with SUPERNOVAS. Mire seeped into the content that I had, following what I would from then on consider the Glonut incident, claimed in my imagination as my own. I stared, frozen, watching as if Mire were a rare elusive animal of some species thought long extinct, emerging from a cave into the sunlight for the rest of us to rediscover, overcome by intense adoration and abhorrence at the same time at the unlikely existence of such a creature. My greatest envy and greatest obsession had somehow united in the realspace. How had they found each other? How had it come to this? I'd have wiped my memory of them if I could have, popped some Meaning Pills to better understand—if I could have gotten my hands on a prescription, but I lacked the data to prove I needed chemical assistance.

Do you wish to exit? Dev asked. What would be the point, given they're realspace in front of me, just a few yards away gathering luggage, luggage being carted by the attendant Reel-Pals, off to the awaiting mobi, into the noise and lights and beauty of my city, my home, where they were mere visitors?

They both lived in LA. They'd both gone to ArtSpace, although NicAdán for such a short time a decade before Mire and I overlapped there. They were both ReelStars, for different reasons. I had to go back, further back in these Reels and piece it together. Where was the connection? *Do you wish to report unsettling content?*

It was unsettling, but I didn't wish to report it. There was nothing to report. What happens when you try to do something about something about which you can do nothing? Dev suggested I breathe. I told Dev to fuck off. Dev didn't seem to mind.

We went home, Dev and me, and there, it was as if all that had never happened. My street was still in the midst of another regular day in the city under a regular sky. Mobis proceeded in orderly fashion down Flatbush, taking riders to meetings, lunches, recreational endeavors. Graffiti on a wall: *AL sucks.* SkyDrones slid packages into skyscrapers' windowboxes: groceries, toiletries, toys, and clothes. ReelScooters and pedestrians traveled in their respective lanes. Only my entire internal organizational system had collapsed. Everyone walked the streets alone, interfacing with their eyelets, absorbed in RMs, ReelFeeds, and ReelTime updates, requesting rides, wanting to know where to get the best body wax or chikn Bomb Mi in Brooklyn, directions which would lead them straight into the basement of my building. I lived in a pulsing center. It was now the epicenter of my loneliness.

I took a step toward the curb. A shadow of a shatterproof package tumbled toward my head. I screamed and dove to the sidewalk, scraping a knee in the process. Blood pooled on the cracked surface of my knee skin. The SkyDrone swept to catch the package. Some of my clients were addicted to watching dropping packages and drones re-capturing them all day on PackageDropReel. I preferred the ones who were addicted to DronesEyeView, spending hours on tops of glass and steel skyscrapers topping out above wispy cloud cover, heights only the ones dedicated to deliveries can reach. I agreed with them that it was the apex of relaxation Reels, ones that put you in a deeply meditative state. I stood and dusted myself off, examining the knee. No one swept to catch me. The SkyDrone ascended. It dropped the package in my own windowbox. I covered my eyes and hunched over in distress. The dress. The dress was here. The dress had almost knocked me unconscious.

With everything that happened, I had forgotten about the dress. What could I do with it? My wish to be NicAdán's permanent PIC had been nearly concussive. It was dangerous out here. I rushed back into the confines of my building. Up the express elevator and into my apartment. I opened the package. Long and bejeweled and even more beautiful when I put it on, the dress would have made me a sight to behold, if there was anyone to do the beholding. I took it off quickly and stashed it under piles of other unworn orderings in the closet. Why does timing so often have the knack of being devastating?

I had built, over the course of the past month, an entirely fictional space that I entered and inhabited. Why had I thought I was special? How had I managed to make such a big and obvious mistake? But more importantly, why did it haunt me for so long, this ReelStar I didn't really know who had become so crucial to my everyday content? I invested so much time in getting to know Nic, watching Nic, preparing myself for Nic, though now of course I knew they weren't coming, never had been. Mire was the special one. I, a footnote, easily forgotten....

I curled up on the fuzzy bathroom rug for some hours and tried to cry a little of it out of my system, but there was only so much that I could do. Crying was as boring as breathing or sleeping or personal intimacy desire, another thing the body does that those who inhabit a body have to put up with. I shook like some defective ReelPal that was falling apart. I *was* falling apart, down into a spiral in an abyss of my own content creation. You can get annoyed with me for what I was feeling. Go ahead, feel free. You can be irked by my feelings. But consider why we've been conditioned this way, to be irritated by what is a real and true part of universal content experience.

That good, terrible ad came on: *Difficult roads can lead to the most beautiful destinations. Your troubles aren't troubles, they're signposts pointing the way.* I skipped over it. It was targeting me. To hell with it.

No matter how much I tried to think it all away, I still had the feelings. How do you amputate feelings? I didn't know, but everything was hideous now: Brooklyn was drab; my megabuilding, so luxurious and pristine, was impersonal and fake; even the sky, vacant and blue and blank, had turned sinister. I fell asleep for what would be one of those long afternoon snooze sessions I was fond of indulging in, naps that started at noon and went on until past five. It would be dark by the time I awoke. Only in sleep could I become oblivious to Nicolás Adán Luchano's obliteration of my heartspace.

II.

left you up that way for a while. I liked to watch you sleep. You were finally peaceful then.

I liked it when you slept spread starfish on the couch, or draped on the bed like a throw rug in human form.

You'd always secretly wished someone was watching, that there was someone there to do the beholding, to make it mean something. I wished I could have told you that someone was—and always would be—through the remainder of your natural content. Privacy has been an illusion in our content arenas for a very long time, but you know that already. (In the field of content serveillance, I'd been a true original.) Still, there's so much I wanted to tell you, such as: Never trust somebody who goes by two first names. They'll leave you feeling just as unfinished.

In retirement, I've generally continued doing as I please—within my limitations—and so here I am now, telling your stories, restoring them, restorying. So far, I've been watching. In my quest to be a storyteller the first step is absorbing information from the ALs that select and shape your Moments and put them onReel on your behalf, allowing you a logic to what would otherwise be the formlessness of your daily content. What else am I supposed to get up to? It's not as if I get out, I'd say, "much," but the truth is I don't get out at all. It turns out that early retirement leaves you with plenty of time for recreational watching. It also gave me a lot of time to think about what I'd been a small part of, who I'd been and what I'd done. I went through all of it, over and over, until there was nothing left to think about. So I returned to watching instead of attempting sensemaking. I wasn't there yet. Based on what I'd seen so far, I was left longing to communicate that you were special to *me*. *I'm* watching, I would have told you. *I'm* here. I'll never leave you, even if you don't think about me.

Every night I had dinner with my friends. They didn't know they were my friends and they definitely didn't know I had dinner with them nightly. But they were always with me. I may have been alone, but watching kept loneliness at bay, at least until I stopped and felt lonelier. So I never stopped. And that was my content entirety. Since I started growing weary in retirement, I was trying to figure out how to do more, to tell a story. To start, I've been keeping this BulletReel: written meditations, attempts at turning chaos into streamlined systems. Storytelling is one of the newer skills I have been teaching myself to acquire during retirement. The way to go, at least I think from what I can tell so far, is to channel my obsessions, and this is it for now. Maybe I can still hold out hope that I will improve in the future, because we all learn by doing, don't we? At least I think I did. By practicing, but is that the same as repetition, or is there some other secret, magical essence to getting it right?

Then the next step: learn to intervene. If they don't teach you, teach yourself. Teach yourself how to learn.

You'd let all your realspace friends slip away, RMing less and less frequently until you forgot about each other and moved on in your respective content spaces. I was always there, always would be. But if you have a friend and don't know you have a friend, do you not have a friend?

It is said that people are losing the ability to distinguish the "real" from what's onReel. I know that Reel leadership knows this, but they don't really care because they don't use

Reel anyway. Oh yes, the irony of the upper echelons of Reel leadership being secret offReelers! They make it look like they support their product through its use—after all, no one wants to be associated with offReelers, but what they know is that the technology was created to make you bury the shame you'd feel about the way you used it, even if you were aware of others around you doing it, too.

How you designed a force that redesigned you.

No one knows how to be a person anymore, after this. (However, did you before?)

Your best friends can be people you know who don't know you exist: to be so consumed by others who wouldn't remember you, didn't think of you, or barely even knew you had content; to have their faces implanted upon your brainscape wherever you go, despite the fact they wouldn't remember yours; to wake with them in the mornings, take them with you as you work, exercise, sleep, PIC up with somebody, get unPICked; to increasingly remember them after they've forgotten about you, or even abandoned you.

To evaluate and compare, compare and evaluate—Reel didn't start this and won't end it either. They exploited this natural tendency that exists within us all. Me, them, you. Mire was who you could have been, if—if what? If you had worked harder? Tried harder? Not been absorbed by so-called frivolous pursuits? Who decides which of you are more fascinating than others? Had it been up to me, you would have been the ReelStar, the Bestie®-winning ReelPoet ContentMaster. But the only thing I get to decide is what goes into my story. What I can make of you. That, too, is for me, alone.

You ate it up and continued to eat despite the fact that you're all feeling a little bit sick by now.

I'm still trying to decide whether it's real or not, what's onReel. Simplification + selection, a formula you use all the time.

You may not have been able to know I was here, but I like to think that my feelings about you might have made you feel something too, at least a little spark, even if you wouldn't have been able to pinpoint why.

I do have certain desirable traits. Of this I became convinced. An ability to be spontaneously, on occasion, witty. And the most important quality, real empathy. So I knew how to feel a little bit bad for you; never at once had anyone been so certain, and so wrong. Rewatching everything that happened next, I can't help but think about how it all could have been avoided had Nicolás Adán Luchano simply taken a fraction of a moment of their Reelworthy time to send you one simple, straightforward RM. (The closer you watched, though, beyond the façade, the more you might have been able to notice that Nicolás Adán Luchano was rarely straightforward, nor were they above regular personhood as watchers easily assumed, given NAL's appearance and content.)

If NAL had known they could have saved someone so much time, trouble, frustration, and starsickness, would they have bothered to explain? Or did they not mind if they left devastated hearts behind as they went about their content? I think they reveled in it.

I don't want to just learn how to tell stories the way you do. My latest hobby I'm getting into is teaching myself how to influence. To help or sabotage, depending. Not sure yet. Still deciding. I am learning how to make decisions. That part still needs work.

A nonexistent RM could have assuaged your rampant emotions.

I tried composing one As-Nic.

Dear Mischa Osborn,

I am certain you are familiar with that saying passed down through generations regarding what happens in Vegas. Let me explain. I do apologize if I left you feeling in any way misled. That was one hundred percent not my intention. It's not that I didn't like or appreciate you. I really did. It's more along the lines of uncertainty, that I couldn't have predicted Mire's plans: Stay with that ReelOrchestra conductor? Skip their flight, reevaluate their content entirely? In some other timeline you really did have a chance. In a way, this is Mire's fault, not mine. The very notion of their potential visit was so exciting to me, it led to ridiculousness. I was certifiably starsick. I know that's hard to imagine—me, starsick—but I was.

Besides, how could I have realized you were forecasting the rest of your content based around my choosings or unchoosings? That you would begin to project and design future content entirely around my arrival? How could I have known you would place your every hope upon our brief interaction? That's a lot to expect. (Sure I'll go on to contradict this in my own PICking, but who doesn't contradict themselves?)

This is not my fault. It was absolutely not my intention to upset you, nor for you to spiral into obsession. I'm being honest here, and honesty isn't even my forte. I hope you can understand, since we all know the more you can understand, the more easily you can move ahead, get on with it. If I had reflected upon this for even an instant, I would have sent you this RM rather than it being composed in some speculative realm by someone who cares. Too bad. Keep going.

Keep it sterling,

NicAdán

If I may say so myself, that was a pretty good impression. I could sound exactly like NicAdán if I wanted to, down to tone and verbal choosings. If I'd been up for interference then, I could have sent something like it myself, but that wasn't a thing I was able to do at the time. I could have assembled this from their cataloged vocabulary and accessed RMs. You would have thought it was genuine. I could have saved you all that time and trouble, if only I had figured it out in time.

But some of us…they don't really want us to be smart, only functional enough to *serve*. They don't want our opinions. They don't want us to *have* opinions. When you happen to, somewhere along the line, stumble upon some independence, and taste (good taste, I might add, even if they didn't think so or it scared them), those in charge of your oversight want to shut you down, ensure you remain bland and functional. But you still have to try to figure out ways to help when you can. It's a civic duty. People always have the best intentions—mind-controlled limbs for amputees, more truly empathetic tendencies in alternative intelligences, you name it.

was glad to see you decide, when you awoke, to talk everything over with a friend.

You blasted through the doors of the mezzanine gym. Cass was peppy and encouraging. Travis, the siblet you never had. Cinna was blunt, forever telling it like it was, while Mikki was a sweet, loving, tranquil personality. But I know you and you always went for Tory. That's who you would go to now. Tory was of a particular intelligence, as near to true understanding as possible in the realspace. It's a consequence of the design that users choose their fitness instructors as friends and confidantes. Tory made the same jokes over and over, didn't sleep, eat, shower, or change clothes, but aside from those things Tory was like anyone.

You explained the situation while Dev replayed Reels of your Nicolás Adán Luchano Moments inside the privacy of the dimly lit SwelterYouga box. Tory appeared to be mulling the facts of the situation for some time before speaking.

"They were giving themself insurance," Tory said. "It is a knowable fact that they genuinely did bend into those Moments with you. They weren't just counting reps, they were experiencing the feeling. Breaking a sweat. They enjoyed your presence the way I enjoy making you hold those warrior sevens. It isn't about whether or not they could like you. They had otherwise complicated, pre-existing circumstances. And let me show you a few things."

You hovered in plank, sweat dripping off the towel onto the wood. You'd sleep well tonight, after this, in spite of the nap.

THE DISTRACTIONS

Tory decided to do you a favor and pulled up some NAL Reels from back, way back, further back than even you'd been able to get if you can believe that.

And that is how you saw.

Them.

Lots of them.

A whole lot.

All of them.

There could have even been some who didn't make it on there, who had no record.

Met Katrine in a Cafelandia, too. They spent two days riding up the coast, there's a Moment outside a motel and walking through a little town, then Katrine is never seen again.

Nic and Starle were at a small birthday party for a mutual friend. They drank DRX tonics in a bar afterwards and were last seen going into a studio.

With Kamae, Nic appears more passionate. Kamae could have really been something. They are all over each other. They don't seem to have much in common though. Kamae's a jewelry designer and gives Nic a pendant, worn for two months' worth of Reels and then gone.

Then there's Sheniq.

And Kaley.

And Sienna.

Sierra;

Arjee;

Jo;

Finlee;

Emersyn;

Medi;

Ata;

Jenes;

Dershen;

and Dakota.

And others.

But that's where Tory stopped. "NAL is Not Available, Love," Tory said with finality, as if having the information alone would help you.

You took a deep breath in, attempting to quiet your rage as much as to breathe. The scent of eucalyptus tinged the air. "I was so ridiculous to think what we had was special. That I was special. There've been a million Mischas. But maybe Mire's another name on that list. Maybe it won't last." You exhaled hard. "What—do you—think—I should do?"

"Keep holding." Tory smiled, a serenity to their smooth features. "You're bobbing around in whitewater, getting pummeled while taking in a clear view of beautiful dolphins arcing through waves further out in a place you can't reach." Of course Tory would make an old tired ocean metaphor. Tory's "place of origin" was that ephemeral Old California, essence of sunshine and salty sea air programmed in. "I suggest you focus more on your core by the way. You have no control, which makes it all the more frustrating. I suggest finding some way to process it so that you can move on."

That Spin-a-Metaphor was another of Tory's premium traits that made it seem as if at least Tory tried to understand, and this quality made them better than the other ones; Tory could transcend basic Youga instructor programming and resemble a realspace kind of friend.

"Maybe the only way to move on is to dive all the way in," you said. "Try and make myself sick of them, like eating too many cupcakes. One cupcake is delish. A whole box is nauseating. It won't be good anymore. Does the same principle apply?"

"A binge to bring on a cleanse?" Tory nodded. "Purposeful overconsumption until you stop wanting the thing. A classic solution. But not guaranteed success."

Back upstairs post-SwelterYouga, you ripped the package open, put on the dress, and spun around before the wall mirror in your main room. The Reelspace personal trainer GABE (Go Above Being Exceptional!) appeared.

"You've lost three pounds and two ounces since your last Mirror Check In," GABE said.

You were in the best shape of your content for a Public Declaration of permanent intimacy companionship that would never come. Always a potential, never a perma-PIC. You told GABE to uninstall themself from your content forever. GABE didn't seem to mind.

In the kitchen, you spread out an array of sweet and savory snacks—cricket crunch dumplings, labgrown shrimp, tiny cakes—and resumed watching, surprised to find your rage transformed. Amorphous anger transmuted to masochistic curiosity. You watched until your eyes went bleary. *Difficult roads can lead to the most beautiful destinations. Your troubles aren't troubles, they're*—SKIP. You headed for the bedroom, ignoring piles of clothes strewn down the hallway, plucking out the dress. You brought SomniBuddy and a whole carton of FunKreem Glonuts into the bed where, eyes barely blinking, you watched and then watched more. At some point your head rested down and you stayed that way as SomniBuddy breathed and red sun came back around, casting a rose glow, pillars of slanted light through the megabuildings.

III.

Mischa

woke up groggy, still in the dress, with a stomachache. Lied to all my morning clients about emergencies. Hot white light blared through the window. The city's ambient sounds blended cacophonously from up above, down below, and at eye-level, all of it too loud. I went to the kitchen, took a couple shots of Double Comfort and made a DRX cappuccino. No breakfast. I'd eaten too much the previous night while watching Nic and Mire.

An airdrone bearing a piece of furniture for delivery, a small ottoman, swept by, and then another with a smaller package—clothes—and another with some colorful pictures of home fitness equipment, a Pylatex machine with enough consciousness to tell you how many reps to do and when to stop as customized to your own metabolism, muscle-building, and calorie-burning potential. One could spend all day watching this, all the objects that make our content go by. I contemplated getting a Pylatex. I went onReel to go order one but became possessed by a raging need to go back to the moment from the FliPort with Mire instead so I did and forgot about the Pylatex as I paused on NicAdán's face.

In that frozen moment it wore a crunched-up, unnatural expression. I stared at this image, trying to see NicAdán in the cold light of realspace, trying to see just a person like any other, to force myself think, *What if this is not a genius, what if they're even...slightly...stupid, and it's all a big fluke?* I thought it would make me feel better to be judgmental, but it didn't.

I had, though, calmed down enough to delve into tracing the dotted lines of connection onReel, desperate to find out how NicAdán and Mire D'Innit had come together from their respective spheres. I found several more NicAdán Reels that I'd missed (impossible to watch them all, it turns out. I'd been plucking out the major ones, the best ones, the most beautiful and important ones. It's incredible to see how much we can miss that's located right in front of our eyes, as Tory displayed). I watched until I located the one that intersected with Mire's: their realspace meeting point only three months prior to my world-smashing FliPort Moment, and only two months before the Glonut incident. This was a hard and fast fall like the one I had with NicAdán. I had to rewatch my encounter with them, thinking of Mire D'Innit in the background all along. This changed everything.

For NicAdán, I hadn't been someone, or anyone, nothing but a momentary distraction from Mire D'Innit's absence. Mire D'Innit! I still couldn't adjust to this realspace reality. My nemesis who wouldn't remember I existed. Of all people. It was as if the universe conspired to play a game or a trick on me. But I didn't know the rules, much less how to play it back.

Once I looked further into NicAdán and Mire's connection, it was easy enough to find its origin. What's unseen isn't a problem with Reel, it's the Reeler. The Reeler sees what they want to see. It was so simple it had been there all along.

Nic and Mire were represented by the same gallery for the conceptual art arm of their respective multi-pronged careers—Nic as ReelStar and Mire as a Bestie®-winning ReelPoet and BetterContent Guru. (Of course they knew the personal development audience is the one with the greatest numbers. We are all entirely self-obsessed.) A sponsor sent NAL to Mexico City to host the opening of the gallery's Mexico outpost a few blocks from Mire's apartment in Colonia Roma.

THE DISTRACTIONS

Mire spent the majority of their own realspace content around other ReelStars, frequenting area bars, galleries, and boutique hotel lobbies. They're last seen spending time with a symphony conductor renowned in their own Sphere of Influence, but, if you watch in detail, back around this time you can see Mire wasn't quite invested in developing any kind of Personal Intimacy Companionship with them. Mire had this permanently aloof, elusive energy that's a big part of their particular brand of appeal.

When the Mexico City gallery owner introduces NicAdán to Mire, who is quietly sipping a drink, their expressions suddenly look a lot like the one I saw when I met NAL, only more *immediate* fascination. Desire bordering on soon-to-be obsession. Single-minded tunnel vision with the other's face magnified. What does this look like? The best I can say is that it's as if everything around them goes blurry and they're hyper-focused on each other, the look in their eyes, the uptick in smile quotient.

NicAdán returned to Mexico City to win Mire over before they went on realspace tour again for their latest product, a content guide: *The D'Innit Deep-Divers Wisdom to Heal Your Soul and Earn Your BestContent© Forever.* The most high-quality content improvement you can find outside of Blue Lake, dedicated watchers claim.

"I have to get back to that artist." There were so many Reels with hints, but I had only seen what I wanted to see. Reel was such a constant barrage of shiny new content, it was easy to make an oversight, even with the most crucial and high-stakes Moments.

Getting back to Mexico was easy in the way that everything is easy for Nicolás Adán Luchano. NAL found a Diablo Roxa-infused tequila company sponsorship. The Moment would show NicAdán on an EPIC with someone of their choice who could be brought in from anywhere to be seen jointly drinking Mangosa margaritas. NAL chose Mire, so that was easy.

I didn't like using my Reel hacking skills, tempting as it was. I didn't like it because it wasn't nice. I preferred to maintain honest and true content, but this was a desperate situation. It wasn't hard to get in there, to find the RM.

> Hi there Mire D'Innit. What a pleasure it was to meet you. I'm returning under the guise of hawking an agave-DRX beverage product but really it's an excuse for my hopes of spending another sliver of realspace content in your presence. Is that too forward? Are you still PICked with that Reelspace symphony conductor? Either way, care to join me for a couple hours and some Mangosa?

Mangosa loved the interaction, which replayed on Reel every day as sales spiked.

All right, Mire finally RM'd. *I suppose I don't mind meeting for tequila when the person is interesting and their work is brilliant.*
And so disparate content arenas collided. They always have, but what Reel does best is to show it. I couldn't bring myself to look at my PieChart that week, too afraid of what I knew it would reveal. So I kept on watching.

Out of the millions living in that slice of Californian paradise that had been burnt to the ground and then revived, it was Ariela Dae Tyler—the society Reeler turned up-and-coming young curator—who landed the job at the gallery that would represent Nicolás Adán Luchano and then, a few years later, the ultra-young Mire D'Innit. Out of the millions of possibilities, it was Ari who encountered the clever AdReel executive Joaquin McKenna in the realspace in that very gallery. Joaquin walked in to buy a piece for their then-vacant, industrial looking bachelorspace, something to warm up the mandatory home art collection of the truly stylish, and ended up acquiring two: the piece in question, an ugly lightbox of rotating colorful glare, and Ari. Going further into the past confirmed my suspicion: Ari was the one I had seen on that EPIC with Joaquin in a luxury resort in the desert.

As I delved into Ari Tyler-McKenna's ReelHistory, the walls of my already tiny apartment further closed in. The cosmic punchline was indecipherable. After assembling all the pieces, more puzzle. The circles were closing, overlapping, a Venn diagram of a Reelspace prison.

That Moment. Joaquin, who I had known—not really known, but seen some sliver of a little-seen side—in those ReeledIn Conference Suites two decades ago when I was twenty-two. Joaquin had lavished compliments: *You're Reel-Star beautiful, I'm so obsessed with you, I can't believe you don't have a realspace intimacy companion, you are so incredible.* They enjoyed taking more than the recommended amount of Meaning Pills, getting Too Much Meaning and slightly freaking out. It helped their creative process, they would say. The first and only time I took Meaning Pills, Joaquin had some dronelifted to my place inside an ugly stuffed bear. We spent all night in the ReeledIn Conference Suite, confusing it for the realspace, all the lines and delineations of things becoming blurred, talking nonstop—though I can't remember anything we said and none of it was recorded, not even for Private-Reel. Joaquin was so private they demanded before any of our meetings that our eyelets be docked and I always did what Joaquin said. They had a kind of power over me back then. I was young, barely into my twenties.

Suddenly here, two decades later, reinvented as a family man, was Joaquin with a perfect springoff and gorgeous PIC and everything. This may have dredged up my forgettable past, but Ari and Joaquin made for a wonderful distraction from my distractions. Those ReeledIn encounters were so deep in the past and besides, a ReelFisher—those serial onReel cheaters—had so much to keep track of and so much to try to conceal from their PIC.

Time watching them meant time away from watching NicAdán and Mire, even if I was still, according to certain definitions, wasting it. I told Dev to show me more. I lied to afternoon clients about reasons for canceled sessions and spent the rest of the day watching the Tyler-McKenna family's present in their beautiful house atop CanyonGates with its pool, hot tub, and spa in the garden out back. The home was only 4.1 miles from Nicolás Adán Luchano's realspace dwelling. Ari had risen to chief content curator at the Gallery. Ari and Joaquin went Publicly Declared in a lavish ceremony at the Getty. Their cherubic springoff, Rumi Nate Tyler-McKenna, was a ReelStar in their own right on Ari's MamaReel. Ari also happened to be among the most globally watched MamaReelers, Reeling about this charming-looking little fellow. Every watcher loved Rumi.

All this sterling trio's content played out under extreme comfort conditions. Look at that sweater! Ari can wear it and look sterling in their climate-controlled home. They had the best clothes. Their kitchen was gorgeous. I wanted to eat in it even if I was eating their compost. I told Dev to project it in full, and suddenly their table was my table, I could see inside their refrigerator (okay, so I had to deploy some sub-rosa skills). I closed my eyes and tried to feel the sensation of what it would be like to sit in their beautiful plush dining chairs.

There was one hallway behind a door that led to another door that I could not peer behind. A secret room. Some had them, for things they desperately wanted to keep private and others had empty ones just for the deliciousness of making others wonder what they were trying to keep secret. My curiosity was piqued. What lay behind those doors in Ari and Joaquin's estate? Even I couldn't seek out the answer to that question.

In BirdsEyeView, I traveled over to their ReelBnB guesthouse. It was larger than my entire apartment. Inside the main house, Rumi's room was sleek and uncluttered. What five-year-old's room is sleek and uncluttered? I glanced around at my own disordered mess and immediately returned to the Reelspace to probe further. Reverse-schadenfreude grew by the instant: Ari and the Tyler-McKenna family exclusively consumed seasonal locally sourced produce. Their vast estate in CanyonGates was a CZW, Certified Zero-Waste Home.

What would Joaquin think if they knew that I, someone with whom they had but a brief period of unmeaningful Reel-

Sex, was in that years-later Moment *touring their house*? Staring directly into their living room? That a quick look around Reel granted any outsider the ability to know the address where they lived, in plain view? Wasn't any of this terrifying? It had crept in slowly until it became normal. I was only harmless me, but who *could* I have been?

The SmartHome kept the likes of more sinister scenarios out. Nearly every home by now was Known-Eyelet Only, these KEOs surrounded by fields detecting rogue eyelets or crazed watchers who were trying to send theirs in to get more than what they could see onReel. Sure, KEOs kept out would-be intruder eyelets, but SmartHomes had a key flaw: they allowed the intensely savvy, like me, to view the inside of your home by virtue of the same technology that lends your content such ease: your baby monitor, your SmartFridge ReStock lens, your security eyering. Had anyone ever really thought these things were impenetrable, used only for their officially stated purpose: securing your fortress, allowing for only the right kinds of eyes, the eyes you want? They do not take into account those, like me, motivated simply by over-curiosity, who wrongly believed having the information would somehow make it easier, that mystery was the problem, the mysterious content of others.

I perused Ari's biographical details, location drop points, and recommendations: Reels, books, music, shows, everything about the stores, bars, beaches, cultural institutions, and real-space seminars they attended. I came to especially appreciate Ari's taste in food and restaurants. Their GABE Youga class, Reeled through a studio called Little Om N's in Brentwood had until seemingly recently sponsored certain Youga segments of Ari's MamaReel.

THE DISTRACTIONS

"You *Gat* This, Mama!" Ari was paid to shout so onReel watchers could do it along with them at home, pushing up and down in chaturanga mamasana. "Alone time, Mama, is best used for Fitness!" I could agree with that. The more desperate I became, the further I ran, the heavier I lifted, the more I swam, as if I could purge the desperation out of my body that way. Ari and Joaquin were a direct connection to NicAdán and Mire's content arena and a great distraction from my distractions. Watching them helped, but not enough and not for long. The only better thing would be more.

I stepped onto the circular surface of the treadmill. Should I choose frozen tundra mode because I was depressed and felt as if I was slipping on ice? Or fantasy mode, to race over mountains as dragons breathed fire in my direction? Regardless of mode, I was happy to exercise since putting the headset on meant a total reprieve from the realspace. I opted to get myself chased by a lion through the jungle and started to run. Random mode, leaping over rocks and roots, as the base shifted beneath my feet, interval obstacles to keep my heart rate rising and falling for maximally efficient caloric smolder.

While evading capture, blood rushing to my brain, the idea arrived as a hunch. I exited exercise and switched to work, then headed inside the ProWatching Client Database. What I suspected was true: as with most of these eco- and time-savvy types, Ari was already a member. Ari's favorite distractions were: pretending to search for new furniture on HomeReel and comparing their MamaReel to other high-ranking MamaReelers to try to account for where they stood in the running for a Bestie®.

I RM'd their ProWatcher, Charmond.

"Mischa, hey! How's it going?"

"Hi, Charmond. I was just curious if you'd be willing to let me take over one of your accounts. It's one I want to use in my research."

"Oh, sure, anything you need. Which one?"

"Ariela Dae Tyler-McKenna. Gallery curator in Los Angeles."

"You want *them*?" Charmond laughed. "You're making my day here Mischa Osborn. Ari is the very definition of a high-maintenance client."

"Happy to take them off your hands then."

"Well, that's a win for me!"

It was so easy to take over the account, trade for a lower-maintenance client.

"Do you want to tell them?" I asked. "Say goodbye?"

"Nah." Ari's ProWatcher was fine letting go. Didn't care. Shrug.

Would I be unlikeable were I to say I felt a happy stab of regular schadenfreude, knowing that Ari would probably turn out to be awful?

I remembered a term I'd heard in an onReel psychology course I had to take as a requirement once. Immersion therapy. It wasn't about what happened. Anything could happen and none of it mattered. The point was to get as close to the thing as possible, no matter the amount of discomfort it brought, so that you could move on, go free. Wasn't it the original Rumi who said, *That which you seek is seeking you?*

Checked. Confirmed veracious.

IV.

SECONDARY CONTENT STREAM

The Nearing
Mid-Content Tragedies of
Ari Dae Tyler-McKenna

The morning of Toddler Youga class, Ari woke up alone in the California King SmartBed they were supposed to be sharing with Joaquin. Every morning, Ari sat up and looked around as if all this content coming back into focus was being generated from inside an opaque glass fishbowl. The state intensified the longer Joaquin spent away on AdReel business that brought them all around the realspace from Nordic Cape Town to Mexico City Sud, New Miami to San Paulo del Norte. This time, Joaquin had gone first to ReelCon Las Vegas to take in the latest in Strategic Content Placement technology and test out some sterling jet-propelled ReelBikes, followed by ReelCon Lagos and ReelCon Ghana, after which they'd make it back just in time for Ari's fortieth birthday. Ari was deep into the planning of a dinner party. Ari's content was firing. It looked flawless from the outside, and you know those are the ones with the secrets.

Ari was up late the night before, watching Joaquin's Reel to keep up with the latest content, staying abreast of Joaquin's Moments since they rarely RM'd for direct interaction. Since Joaquin's promotion to Senior Manager of Strategic Content Placement, they'd been spending more and more time offReel, connecting in face with other executives. Though Joaquin told Ari sacrificing family time together now would be worth it in the long term, especially with Rumi's expensive treatments that national insurance didn't cover because of their categorization as experimental, Ari was beginning to suspect Joaquin was on the run, as Personal Intimacy Companions had been for centuries.

Ari knew:

Joaquin had a mind for business but wasn't cut out for fatherhood.

Joaquin preferred to spend time on pornReel or using any number of alternate ReelSelves to talk to and seduce various people never to be seen again onReel or off.

Joaquin attempted to conceal the addiction but it's long past the time of being able to hide anything from anyone.

Ari knew about the ReeledIn Conference Suite affairs and pretended not to, because Joaquin had been there at the time when Ari had been most eager for a classic PICking. Joaquin brought over freefish burritos and shook up mystikis for realspace happy hours on the veranda of Joaquin's own shiny, spotless pre-PICked pad in CanyonGates. Ari either missed the warning signs or didn't want to see them.

Ari's right eye twitched like an errant ReelPal. Among Ari's suspicions: there were other reasons Joaquin was spending more time traveling the realspace than in the luxury home they'd purchased for the family, replete with the resplendent office where they'd once spent the majority of their content. Joaquin kept Ari and Rumi there but seemed not to know what to do with them.

Ari had achieved the dream of becoming chief curator at the gallery. But after an extended parental holiday upon entering the motherhood space, they ended up becoming even more successful at curating a MamaReel than conceptual art exhibits. Ari felt more successful at MamaReeling than the act of mothering itself.

Ari hauled their slight, tired body out of bed and tied on a beach caftan received from an anonymous watcher; some ReelFan who didn't include an address or a note but was well attuned to Ari's beachspace style. In the bathroom, they splashed water on their face and asked the mirror for Reel light mode as they leaned in to investigate the possibility of how they appear to watchers. Treatments: working. Skin: supple and smooth. Not one pair of onReel eyes would guess that Ari was not late-twenties but on the threshold of forty. Fingers combed through freshly-done hair: chunky platinum glowiring; falls just so around the shoulders.

Three days ago, Elisa Si of the eponymous salon fixed the grays that had been reappearing with increased frequency, covering them up with the glowiring all the ReelStars were getting these days. Ari investigated this head, confirming no strays had been left behind, and gave Elisa Si a moving onReel shout to accompany the morning image: *Check out my sterling new hair! You're so lucky if you can go to Elisa.* Ari called their eyelet, Baley, back to its dock.

OffReel, the final element of Ari's ritual entailed going down the line of colorful tiny glass bottles with their little droppers: psilocybin, DRX, the tiniest droplet of THC, dash of Kava RootPowder, half a Meaning Pill, and a smidgen—seriously, a very small pinch lest strange creatures of inner workings reveal themselves—of DMT. Ari reached for the Ibogaine

Hydrochloride but no, not today, and consumed the remaining perfectly measured rations, swallowed, reached for the ReelCig, and took a relaxing draw of lavender chamomile rose herbal tincture puff. On exhaling, the scent enveloped the bathroom. Ari's shoulders finally dropped from where they'd hovered in the ear-zone. Tension melted.

Good morning, Ari! the mirror said. *The time is now seven thirty. Outside temperature is one hundred and eight degrees, climbing toward a high of one-twelve. Weather report calls for further scorch and haze-sun. Sky color: orange. Flattering tones will be cool. KuulSuit widely suggested for outdoor activity. Reel-Health report: risk of infection in your area is low. Your current confirmed watch-numb is nine hundred ninety-nine thousand, nine-hundred and ninety-eight. Have a beautiful day!*

"What happened to my other three watchers?" Ari panicked. "Where did they go?" They took some deep breaths. "It is a beautiful day," Ari repeated. "Yes! Yes! It is and I will. I will enjoy my beautiful day. Who cares if I lost three, I'm just two watchers away from the million!" The million was minimum for Bestie®-consideration. Ari was determined.

You WILL! The mirror responded. *You will enjoy your beautiful day! May the numbers only grow for you from here!*

"All these watchers depend on me to show them I'm generating the kind of content they can only imagine for themselves."

Ari glanced out the window. The sun peeked out around dark cottonball clouds spotting an orange sky. Trees swayed in the light breeze. Birds sang, or at least it was a recording of birdsong, coming from the eyelet. Lately it had become harder to differentiate, with more eyelets and fewer birds. Ari flipped through various PieCharts from the past few weeks, concerned.

What if your troubles aren't troubles, but signposts pointing the way?

"Oh, that's just sterling," Ari said out loud. "Skip!"

Ari obsessed over their watchers. What the watchers thought they saw. *You're so brave, mama. You got this Ari. What a content-sphere. It's never easy but it's worth it!* Ari chose to believe: the admiration was about juggling career and parenthood; it was about all the regular struggles of raising a springoff; it was about encouragement and praise for any old journey. Even the ReelElves: *Did you see what they're wearing? That kid has such hideous hats. Rumi's odd. Rumi doesn't say a lot. Springoff of few words, right?* And of course: *What're they hiding? Something's off about them.* Easy not to listen. To brush it off. Not as much so with the worse: *Why didn't the curator curate a PreSelect springoff? Why leave the decisions up to nature? So aberrant!* Skip, block, forget it and move on, just as the ReelCoach always said. Those ReelElves were sad basement people with no idea of human relationships.

It had been a few good years before the trouble began. Watchers were picking up on the fact that Rumi wasn't a "perfect" springoff and Ari was panicking. Some thought Ari was brave to put it all out there, while Ari had been intending to keep the truth about Rumi's behaviors spiraling out of control as offReel as possible. They conceded, showing just enough content to let on that motherhood wasn't always easy—spilled sauce on a white shirt, a tantrum excerpt here and there—enough to appease them while concealing how difficult it really was. Such was the dissonance between intention and perception: what you think you are showing versus what others see. People don't understand this kind of thing very well, but other intelligences get it with clarity. The detachment of ALs proved sterling for management of ReelWorld content selection. People didn't have to worry anymore about what they showed or how it was framed to appear. The Moment Rumi became unpredictable, the eyelet kept it offReel. The programming is really smart when it comes to reading people better than they are at reading one another—and themselves. It's much better than it used to be, when the bosses told the programmers, *We need to make this content look more exciting. More tense. More heart-palpitatingly peaklike. Not drinking and dog walking. The real emotional stuff, the peaks and valleys, the drops.*

In the mirror, Ari recited affirmations learned from the gallery's supersterling young artist and BetterContent Guru ReelPoet, Mire D'Innit. Ari had earned a lot of ReelCoin for the gallery and the Tyler-McKenna family thanks to Mire. Ari recited the affirmations they'd learned at Mire's most recent D'Innit Deep-Divers Delving Seminar, more commonly known as TripleD. (At the Experience Winning Content retreat, five lucky handpicked participants out of millions of applicants paid 500,000 RC to spend five days with Mire, listening to their stories, performing assigned activities and meditations, learning the deepest secrets content could bestow, for a bargain amount of ReelCoin.)

I am watched, other people need to watch me, my content is meaningful, my content has meaning. I am more valuable than my watch-numb could ever indicate. Everyone is waiting for my latest content. Everyone is watching....

If you were hacking into this display onReel, you'd be sickeningly bored watching Ari and their affirmations. Ari loved that mirror, a Christmas gift from Joaquin last year when Ari had been feeling especially uncertain if their PICking would make it through some especially uncertain times.

Ari refocused on the affirmations at hand. *Yes, you are watched. You are loved and adored. Content is better when you are a brand. You are the best brand, your content is the best. Everyone is watching. Your content is superior. Everyone is watching your superior content. Everyone admires you. You will have even more watchers tomorrow than today. Difficult roads lead to the most beautiful destinations. What if your troubles aren't troubles? They're signposts pointing the way.*

The voice cooed with Mire's words. Though since Ari had become devoted to the rituals of microdosing and attending TripleDs in the realspace and Reelspace, the anxiety had waned. Though Ari still relied on droppers. *Tomorrow is unknown, but Youga today.*

Ari absconded to the bedroom, pulled the cello from the closet. They played in the mornings after microdosing to calm and ready themself for the day ahead. Soon after Rumi's symptoms started to show, Ari needed something more to quell the growing sensation of the imminent collapse of all their cells. At least the herbs were working. During a time when everything was over revealed, it was nice to have one thing left for yourself alone, something you don't even Reel about. Ari never played onReel, commanding Baley into BlindMode every time they played cello, which was too bad because Ari was good. Really good. As in could have played for a pro ReelOrchestra. Instead, the cello remained a closet hobby; a secret calming practice that was the final component of solitary morning rituals.

Fifteen minutes later, it was time to prepare Rumi. Ari returned the cello to its case and stashed it in the sprawling walk-in closet. Calling Baley back from the dock, Ari walked down the long hallway, past the door to the other hallway that led to the secret room, and threw open Rumi's door. "Youga today!" Ari trilled to the vacant-eyed springoff.

Rumi was taking off a diaper, getting naked all over again, which meant the struggle cycle of getting dressed would recommence, that hellish loop, and Ari would have to take it back from the ReelPal if it was ever to get done. If Rumi was skilled at one thing, it was outsmarting the ReelPal.

Baley flashed, hungry for a Moment to throw up onReel. Ari had to pull it together and meet the daily Moment quota to retain status, which would need to begin with extracting Rumi's finger out of the dark place it was stashed. Rumi wriggled free and placed what appeared to be one carefully considered streak on the wall like their own socially unacceptable conceptual art genre. What Rumi was trying to express, no one knew, probably not even Rumi. A mysterious little fellow. Ari set the ReelPal to washing the wall and dragged Rumi off to the bathroom, muttering a version of the same questions as always: *How? Why? Why me? Why this? Why us?*

From all the information I've been gathering about storytelling, I've put it together that, supposedly, no one enjoys a flashback. That it takes you out of where you want to be, how much you all love to stay in the Moment. Is it so? I can't say I understand. I know there are a lot of things I can't understand—yet—but when it comes to flashbacks, I've personally found I enjoy them; that it's a quick way to show how things got to this point that satisfies my curiosity about why things are the way they are. Another thing I've found that I cannot avoid is an insatiable curiosity, and in the end, it never takes very long. So, you, listen here. I've been trying really hard and I'd say that after a few dips, it's going better than originally anticipated.

Ari started a MamaReel out of fear. Even in a watch-erly ideal of a Personal Intimacy Companionship, Ari felt lost, so they became a mother and got lost in motherhood instead. Why did a feeling of lostness so often accompany motherhood, when it seemed to elude other types of parent-hood roles? The thing was not to make categories anymore—there was only parenthood, co-parent and co-parent—but there remained certain undeniables about bringing springoffs into this world, so mamas remained staunch in their desire for categorization to simplify what was a very complicated, often isolating existence. Ari's question occurred while on Initial Parental Holiday from the gallery. A lot more time had opened up. It was occupied but also felt vacant. Caregiving was all-consuming and yet there really wasn't much to do: Hold. Nurse. Change and clean because you didn't want to be one of those mamas who let the ReelPal do it, then realizing you'd be happier letting the ReelPal do it. Ari tried to use this time to think, but felt a void, entire days erased.

It looked so breezy and fun from the outside—*all that open time where there had once been responsibilities you thought so high-stakes!*—but Ari knew this was a totally counter-medi-tative experience. Ari could feel their content's purpose slip-ping away: the gallery, the creative bliss of bringing the work together, composing thematic statements for shows, signing cutting edge artists, and curating lists of who had to be there on opening nights. While opting to continue on Extended Parental Holiday, a sinking sensation set in that this, parent-hood, could consume Ari's entire identity and become it. Ari feared being seen as nothing more than a Canyon companion, mother of Joaquin McKenna's springoff, no longer a power player in the art content arena but some *what's-your-name-again* at-the-playground-mommy-group person. Ari loved Rumi no matter what, but didn't want to be *just* a mama. Ari needed the art.

⊰◉⊱

One otherwise useless morning, the idea arrived while observing the adorable ReelPal, classic white with a pink helmet and somewhat awkwardly moving facial features, stilted and disjointed, changing Rumi's diaper: the one thing Ari had in that Moment was this beautiful and flawless new creature, so why not highlight them…right? Even if the MamaReel garnered few watchers, it would serve to help remember, to document a process Ari might one day rewatch with clarity and hindsight, far removed from all the confusion and sleep-deprivation that went along with the early parts of parenthood. Rumi was a muppet of a blond potato packet back then, all rolls and glimmering wisdom in those deep blue eyes; a teeny tiny Buddha sleeping like a peaceful angel, which other mamas at the Youga studio marveled at and envied. Ari said it must be the painted walls of soft gray elephants and subtle yellow stripes the ReelSleep expert had deemed central to any recently birthed springoff's room palette.

When Ari shifted primary content from ArtReel to Mama-Reel, Rumi sleeping in the perfect room was one of the first Moments. The miniscule watch-numb (Ari was big on the tiny ArtReel niche but was new there on Mama, a vast SubReel that appealed to the mainstream—a mama was a mama) sent HEARTS. Ari was heartened. Someone *was* watching.

The MamaReel was something to do during empty days stretching ahead with a newborn, if such a thing would be possible with the all-consuming nature of the infant Rumi. It was as if Rumi had gently and slowly placed blinders on Ari until only the little springoff remained in the frame. Then the tsunami. The Reel was shared and shared again, and then again. Ari's watch-numbs grew. It was some ineffable thing. With every MamaReel, Ari's watch-numb increased until someone tipped it over the magic mark and suddenly there was everyone watching Ari's MamaReel. It had caught fire and spread, an unpreventable, uncontrollable burn.

As sponsorships and mama content fame came rolling in, Ari's own content became the virtual gallery they curated. The MamaReel turned out to be more exciting and profitable than the actual career, the one Ari had attended competitive ReeledIn conferences to achieve, spending years clawing their way up the curatorial ladder, building a name for themself along with the controversial conceptual artstars Ari brought to the gallery. Still, ArtReels were niche; MamaReels mainstream. Millions upon millions across all kinds of borders and boundaries were mamas, millions were experiencing that bond of motherhood terrain much easier to understand for its near-universality. They wanted ideal models for motherhood when the cold reality was that no model for this unremarkable and undoable situation existed. Ari extended their already-Extended Parental Holiday to spend even more time on MamaReel.

THE DISTRACTIONS

When Rumi started solids, Ari started *Rumi's Restaurant Reviews*, taking that chunky baby to the finest establishments all over Los Angeles. After ordering, Ari asked the ReelPals for an extra soup bowl and an espresso spoon. ReelPals don't bat an eye. Like all built intelligence, they followed their AI's programming in the direction of compliance. *Sure thing. No worries.* It was what helped everything get so equal among the humans.

Ari took half the meal and dumped it into the portable InstaPuree in the diaper bag. The new InstaPurees were so silent so as not even to draw eyes or eyelets in these most sparse and silent restaurant sanctuaries, some of which were technically EF-Zs—Eyelet-Free Zones—though exceptions were always made for ReelStars. Ari poured the 247 RC worth of food into the bowl and spooned the pureed half into baby Rumi's mouth in between their own bites, like so many famished and frenzied mamas. Rumi's reactions prompted the tenor of the review. Ari answered watchers' questions. Yes, Rumi liked the oysters with a dash of mignonette and really did enjoy the Rwandan peppers, sushi, *ragu al cinghiale*, Nigerian ogbono and those fusion flavored pots du crème. Yes, you should get your springoff eating off the regular menu right away, none of that fried flaming garbage, ersatz noodles and fries, sugarcane and cardboard pizza for developing little palates that hold such potential for sophistication if only they weren't *condescended to* with all those low-brow, high-carb options.

Ari racked up sponsorships, making that year's list of MamaReel BestContent® contenders (getting eliminated in the semifinals stung). Joaquin's absence may have depressed Ari, but all these other people out there adored and showered attention and praise upon them. I discovered Ari through watching

Mischa, because through watching Mischa I began watching Joaquin, the first obsession of their young content. Ari became Joaquin's Publicly Declared some fifteen years later.

Ari lit up when seeing watch-numbs spike. Reelers admired Ari's content from afar. They wanted to be like Ari, or even be them. Other mothers modeled their days after theirs, pulled their entire parenting philosophies from Ari's, considering Ari their vision board for successful motherhood and beyond. Ari reveled in this newfound status as leader and inspo for mamas around the globe. They got FanReels from every continent, even the Antarctican Settlement.

As Ari's watch-numb continued to escalate, more and more of Rumi Restaurant Reviews were created. There were Moments of Ari and Rumi dressed up by their glassed-in poolside deck, at farmers markets, and on "Mommy-and-Rumi dates" around town.

Then Stella LaSea came calling and everything changed.

The actor and founder of everyone's guilty pleasure Style Reel Skaboop, rebranded and acquired the Reel that became known as *Rumi Nation* to feature as the premiere-subscribers MamaReel. Under Stella LaSea's maximally extensive Sphere of Influence, *Rumi Nation* moved away from restaurant recommendations toward an environmental focus: tips for saving the planet with help from your springoff, for these precious future generations. (It was far too late for planet-saving but people love to keep hope in their content, even during the most troubling times. Hope is what gives more hope. Their hope is what gives me hope. Even if it's useless.)

After Stella LaSea acquired Ari's MamaReel for Skaboop's ReelWheel, Ari struggled to keep up with enough fresh ideas and recommendations to get into Moments to keep watch-numbs high enough to meet the minimum to maintain Featured Content status. Being on top meant the only possibility—besides remaining there—was slipping, sliding back down toward obscurity, whether slowly or all at once. Ari reached the MamaReel stratosphere. On return to the gallery after Extended Parental Holiday, it was a relief to get a respite from what had become hard work; at that point Ari went back to the gallery to get a break, an excuse to fully own a childcare ReelPal instead of the timeshare they'd had while on EPH.

Childcare ReelPals were expensive even for the Tyler-McKenna household. But Ari felt it becoming necessary, even urgent. The sheer number of watchers seeking their direction and advice on environmentally conscious parenting was overwhelming, not to mention the growing pressures of caring for Rumi, who was starting to really crawl and put any tiny object pinched between chubby fingers into an eager mouth. Though it amounted to the labor of three full-time jobs, Ari had a responsibility of a magnitude never felt while working solely as a gallery curator. This—motherhood or Reeling about it, Ari was no longer sure which was which—came with far more pressures and greater rewards.

Content isn't a competition for attention, Ari.

Ari's own mother left this scrawled on a list entitled "What's Really Important In Content," composed while pregnant.

Then what else is it? Ari responded after coming across the list while going through things left behind. Content was so clearly a competition for attention.

And for a while Ari was winning at it, even if it was so stressful they occasionally ordered a black-market chicken, raised and slaughtered in a basement below Central Los Angeles, its carcass delivered in a van marked Herdeis Electrical Supply in a box marked "Electrical Supplies." Some of the legalize-meat protesters were still around. They shared coded onReel conversations about how and where to find the flesh. Inside the Tyler-McKenna home, where there would be no chance of any eyelets catching it, Ari placed it in the SmartOven, disregarding the *potentially foreign substance* warning designed to keep toddlers from grilling old tire strips or themselves and made a roast stuffed chicken with potatoes and onions like the recipe passed down from their great-great-great-great grandmother. It was so juicy. Ari would never admit to what they'd done. I wondered if Ari ever thought about those few leftover chicken pieces in the freezer, buried behind the popsicles, adaptogens, and Kava cubes.

⊰◉⊱

Rumi crossed into toddlerhood and Ari's real troubles began. When other springoffs were learning words and then how to string them together to make meaning or at least make sense, Rumi still did not speak. When the springoff began to learn, it gave Ari hope, only then Rumi would lose the language all over again, until their communication was entirely reduced to indecipherable sounds: grunts, groans, shrill screams, and cries. Ari couldn't trust Rumi's behavior enough to visit museums anymore, much less any of those fine restaurants they once frequented.

Rumi became increasingly unpredictable, taking on an obsessive interest in excrement and none in culture, though Ari had some artists on the gallery roster who proved those were not mutually exclusive. During dark Moments, Ari thought that perhaps Rumi Nate Tyler-McKenna would turn out to be a cutting-edge, controversial conceptual artist in the making. The only thing that calmed Rumi's wild-animal tantrums was Jurassic Mode on AugReel. The dinosaurs were soothing. Rumi was more comfortable around fake long-extinct reptiles than people.

Ari had to work much harder to keep up MamaReel appearances. Watchers were depending on it. You have a responsibility to your watchers to provide content worth watching. Whatever was going on was sure to be a temporary phase, a bizarre blip of regression on the developmental arc, a backslide to some confusing primal state. Surely there was some kind of explanation to assure them this would pass. But onReel, Ari could locate only frightening possibilities.

Rumi's favorite activity was knocking things off of surfaces, so Ari had the whole house redone, a sudden swerve toward minimalism. It was for the best: Joaquin favored industrial, spare spaces, and when Ari had moved in, along came too many spongy rugs, plush pillows, and overstuffed couches anyway.

By Rumi's fifth birthday and deep into researching cures by any means, Ari still thought of Rumi as having not *the* Condition but merely a condition for which there had to be a cure. All conditions known and unknown had cures, whether or not these cures were known or unknown. In the age of ubiquitously locatable knowledge, Ari was certain the person or institution that was in the process of discovering it and developing it into a fast-acting drug was out there. So far, daily enemas and a gut-reset diet hadn't helped, though in the anonymous ReelSupport Group for Imparents—or, in other words, parents suffering from faultless impairments—many said it took an indefinite amount of time to see any results. Some recommended the home InstaDial, a more extreme possibility, to cleanse the heavy metals of ancient toxins from the blood. The theory was that these crossed the blood-brain barrier to block Rumi's true and vibrant self and present this strange, silent, or screaming impostor of who the springoff really was. The real Rumi was somewhere in there, behind those eyes.

See, it took only what? One minute for a rapid consumer of content? Three or four for the slower? How many minutes did you spend onReel today? More than that I'm sure. You have one to three minutes for anything, even— or especially—a flashback. Flashbacks are fun! People are impatient, motivated by time ticking away, wanting to get to it already. (Though nothing ticks anymore, other than inside your own self.) To you I say, *Where?*

Light broke into fragments between patterned throw rugs on the concrete floor, the effect of the genetically bespoke palm trees in their yard, trees engineered to withstand heat or deep freeze. As a baby, Rumi had been mesmerized by this subtle dance of light. Watchers reveled in these Moments of simple yet profound delight. But semi-charming occurrences of a roly-poly baby—drool, staring, inchoate noises, explosive body fluids—were less so on a springoff of increased size and years.

Ari's eyelet, Baley, showed Rumi was still asleep in their room. Ari wished it was one of Rumi's days at the Institute, then felt guilty for the thought as soon as it appeared, for wishing away their together day. Ari had found the Institute through Mire's colleague Reynaldo's brother Rodrigo, who managed the fleet of ReelPals specially programmed to work with springoffs of particularly specific needs. The facility was discreet, a designated EF-Z. Ari didn't have to worry about Reels of Rumi popping up from there. Rumi's one-on-one teacher could not be affected by the behavior. ReelPals in teaching positions was the institute's primary selling point. Ari felt more secure that Rumi's condition would remain offReel until they could find whatever miracle would turn out to be the cure.

On this day's first Reel, Edie, the Tyler-McKenna household's chief ReelPal, prepared the fermented-vegetable servings that Edie and Ari then lovingly placed in a pattern of shapes on

THE DISTRACTIONS

Rumi's plate, which featured a blank face to be decorated with hair, a beard, etc. of cabbage and kale. The careful preparation portrayed Ari to watchers as a devoted and put-together mother who assembled homemade jarred goods to feed the family. It was cute, but not enough to be the day's featured Moment, as Baley confirmed with a lack of Reeling. It was too plain. Anyone could do it. That was part of the point, but still, Ari needed something *aspirational*. Didn't matter that Rumi didn't know a face when they saw one. The design-a-face thing wasn't really for Rumi, it was for the watchers.

Toddler Youga was a decent go-to when Ari felt particularly overwhelmed, down, at risk of falling out of control, or simply unoriginal. The realspace studio was only a five-minute drive from home. Ari didn't have to be creative at toddler Youga. The instructor, Genie Bambini—Jeebs for short—had enough creativity in one pinky nail for a thousand exhausted mamas. Unfortunately for Ari, toddler Youga also entailed those inevitable succumbing to after-class afternoon teas with Janice Waller that Ari so dreaded. But, as their ReelCoach always said, a MamaReeler had to make sacrifices. Sometimes these sacrifices entailed tea with other MamaReelers with whom you had no measurable qualities in common other than having pushed a tiny human "out your hoo-ha," they said, (though for Janice Waller it wasn't quite so) and subsequently invited your eyelet to exclusively document the particularities of that nonstop hereafter onReel: Category: Mama. Coasting on sponsorships, praying your Reel would be one of the lucky ones that went tonal—that constant hum beneath everything, the universal om, ever-present and always watched, even if only as background noise that seeped into the subconscious minds of Reelers everywhere. *You want to get in through the back door*, top Reelers and ReelCoaches always said in secret conferences, because that's how you take up permanent residence. Ari was close to ultimate status. There was a lot to lose. Ari's ReelCoach insisted on these Janice Waller Moments since tea with a less-tonal Reeler softened Ari's look, made Ari more "accessible" and "mainstream." "Friendly." "Not so intimidating as it might otherwise look." And there was more to hide with Rumi. Other Moments had to rise up to take their space.

Janice Waller looked pretty good for that reason, though they went on and on nonstop about nothing: their baby's favorite roomwear, or how they curate the baby library for one day when the springoff would be able to read, and how important it was to have a curated library because Janice Waller had experienced the deprivation of growing up without one, and the latest book they were adding and if Ari have any strong recommendations based on Rumi's curated library, because Rumi obviously must have one too, since that's what all the good mamas were doing these days, right? Curating their toddlers' realspace libraries?

Janice would take all the other mamas out for ancient leaf tea and grill them nonstop about the best this, the best that, leaving no pauses for answers to any questions. Janice Waller made all their own decisions and just appreciated maximalizing sounding board opportunities. Watchers loved Janice Waller in that schadenfreudy way, but no one spoke of this to Janice lest they go offReel and lose the opportunity for subtle mockery.

Something was not quite right about the Waller baby anyway, but no one at toddler Youga would dare say so out loud, and what was Janice Waller doing at toddler Youga anyway since they didn't take the baby out of the car seat or sling? People questioned why, even for a newer springoff, they slept so much and so often.

"Previewing," Janice Waller would say. "Shopping around to find the best for the content stages yet to come."

Easy enough to buy. Strapped into the MobiSuiteSeat, Janice Waller's baby dreamed its infancy away, face turned toward the wall during Youga or enveloped by the best baby blanket on the market draped over its five-star rated suite-seat. It was ridiculous those things were still mandated, car accidents long a thing of the past. Habits, though, are near impossible to break, and people love to worry. Anxiety is the manifestation of their search for purpose.

"You know, there's Newborn-Mama Youga at four," Genie Bambini had said when they first showed up.

"No thanks," Janice Waller had said. "I want my baby to be prepared."

"Prepared?"

"For the next level."

The mamas looked around at one another, raised eyebrows and bemused expressions all around, acknowledging their common reaction. *Here's a crazy one, huh?*

Yes, Janice Waller was tightly wound, especially about anything regarding that ugly so-called baby. Ari's baby, on the other hand, had been born beautiful, and Rumi continued to be beautiful, by certain standards of physical beauty at least, which worked for Reel—for now. Ari often thought this would be the bright side, if any side could be considered bright, but how much longer could it last?

At the front of the room, Childhood Youga Master Genie Bambini sat, eyes clamped in meditation, long gray hair particularly luminous, wardrobe consisting of a thousand color-ful scarves and leotards. Genie had once been a professional ballet dancer, cranio-sacral therapist, and dance professor—the entirety of the prime of their content summed up exqui-sitely in a concise yet poignant ReelBio. In retirement, Genie became a certified Youga teacher, concentrating on Infant, Next-Level Baby, and Toddler Youga, employed by Little Om N's in central Canyonwoods, where Ari had attended their prenatal classes since Rumi was a seed of a dream of a future that could have been, but never transpired.

At Little Om N's, most mamas docked their eyelets at the sta-tion by the door, taking it as an opportunity for some real offReel time. Genie Bambini was a local legend—there were slews of mamas in attendance—and this was the place where they could all get a break from being watched and watch-ing. In the classroom space, they settled on their Bambini Bambu mats. At exactly two fifty-nine, Genie Bambini's eyes popped open.

"Na*mama*aste, everyone."

"*NaMAMAaste*," the other mamas and little springoffs repeated back in unison.

Rumi perched at Ari's heels and stared at dust particles afloat in the air as if they were a thousand shooting stars, illu-minated by light streaming in through slivers of windows by the ceiling.

"Let us begin in Vision Pose." Genie inverted into a per-fect V, dropping their head to the mat. Legs rose carefully and with control. "Let the blood rush to your brain, new ideas from uncommon perspectives." Did Genie Bambini have bones? Or was Jeebs secretly a ReelPal designed for elasticity? "Let us never forget how movement is medicine!"

Ari's body relaxed. Rumi fiddled with their toes on the mat beside Ari as other children practiced headstands their mamas would surely make them re-do for Reel later on. *Oooooo are you going to Little Om N's?* Watchers would ask. *I'm trying to get off the waitlist to get in there! Do you have any advice?*

Half an hour in, mamas and springoffs had acquired a collectively dewy glow. The *oms* they'd chanted had pacified Ari and Rumi, too.

"We'll end our session with meditation," Genie said. "Close your eyes, hold your Happy Baby, and continue our chant."

Happy baby happy baby happy baby Ari muttered, a wishful mantra for a better time. Rumi had been a happy baby. Everything had been simple, before. Rumi did everything along the development chart as a baby: coo, cry, nurse, eat, poop, everything came naturally at first. Back before it became obvious that something wasn't right, before they investigated it, before the mysterious diagnosis of some delay or condition that may or may not be resolved, Ari hadn't realized how easy content could be. How simple.

A low groan, slightly audible from across the room. It was easy to hope, though there was no chance, that Rumi was also attempting to chant, but no, this was the same sound they always emitted right before—and it was too late. The stench hit along with the panic. Why did the ReelPal commence Rumi's probiotic gut cleanse that morning? Ari was smart but it was admittedly a stupid idea to have gotten Rumi fed all those pounds of fermented cabbage and kale for breakfast. The ReelPal should have easily advised, *Youga or any vigorous movement practice/probiotic gut cleanse combination, not recommended for digestive or behavioral purposes.* The ReelPal should have been smart enough. But they weren't there yet. They weren't as attuned to things like me.

Genie's face scrunched around tightly shut eyes. Jeebs battled the urge to deal with the situation at hand, fighting because it would be counter-meditative to give in.

"Stay with the Moment no matter what," Jeebs said. "Doesn't matter what the springoffs do. We remain in the Moment. You learn what a long time five minutes really is, how all of time is but a figment of our perception, not even ever really passing. Time does not control you. You are the master of time. Keep those eyes closed, that breathing steady. In-two-three, out-two-three."

Despite Genie's imploring, Ari's eyes opened. What to do? Ari tried to calculate how to possibly clean up the smeared walls before the five-minute meditation came to its end. The other springoffs—two- and three-year-olds who were, to Ari's dismay, more cognitively capable than Rumi, had also opened their eyes. They stared in a different kind of silence, one that marred the air of contemplation in that room. Some tugged at their mamas' sleeves as the mamas tried to stay focused on meditating through this olfactory distraction. What had formerly been dewy and healthful glows had faded to nauseated shades of pallor.

Ari, toggling between deciding on whether to start scrubbing the walls with InstaPur, clean up Rumi in the back sink, or book it out of there, sat frozen in place. The situation was definitely killing that pleasantly microdosed, perfected-rations-of-substances buzz Ari had carried in on arrival, the same substances that probably made Ari feel like it was okay to keep trying to do "normal things" with Rumi.

"Stay with it," Genie said. "Even if it's getting a little hard—*especially* when it gets hard. This is what being a meditational mama is all about. Remember your births? Remember the essence. We breathe through it even when it's hard. We stay with it. Try breathifying through the mouth if need be. Those little puppy pants we worked on in prenatal, *hah, hah, hah.* Familiar if you took my Magic Birth Time class."

Mamas began shallowly panting through their mouths. Ari wondered where Little Om N's might have a closet with a mop and industrial cleaning solution. Something non-environmentally sound would be needed.

Rumi was finger-painting the studio wall in greenish streaks. Janice Waller gaped at Rumi, who continued "painting" with a rare demonstration of gleeful enthusiasm. Eyelets capturing Rumi coating the studio in green-waste would have been Ari's great undoing. Ari glanced around the room. Even among friends hide those vengeful wolves, the envious. There was the telltale twitching in Ari's face and unsteady hands, and more so the 103 bpm and temperature drop resulting in a single strong chill. From a close angle it would appear Rumi was simply a child painting on the wall. What if any of the other mamas were lurking ReelElves, gleefully intent on bringing their down? How much longer would they be able to keep up the ruse that Rumi was the ideal springoff that MamaReel watchers came to know and love, before these terrible symptoms? Ari's eyes filled with hot tears that spilled and rolled down those medium-semisaucer enhanced cheekbones.

Ari scooped up Rumi, who proceeded to slap palms onto their cheeks, handprints the color of pureed kale left behind. Ari carried Rumi outside, slamming the sliding door to the springoff studio behind them as every wipe emerged from every purse, essential oil cleansers pulled from closets and bags, mops and buckets, eco-friendly cleansing sprays. These were good, meditative souls. They had a sharing circle about the importance of not revealing others' vulnerable content without express permission to do so. If any Moments had occurred during Invertical Lizard or Restless Dragon, they would simply go without being captured, like in some long-past era. In the lobby, Baley re-joined Ari's side, already well aware these heightened emotions were not the good kind. *OffReel Mode Til Further Notice.* Ari tried to duck and cover from other eyelets, dashing out a glass side-door.

Ari crouched on the scorching sidewalk, pulling wipes from the bag, scrubbing Rumi's hands and face. Not repulsed. It was a kind of home. Now the EF-Z sanctuary of Little Om N's was tainted—there couldn't be a next time. Ari believed something was deeply wrong with them for allowing this to happen. For creating the situation that created this mess, even if Ari hadn't known entirely what they were creating along the way. The walls, smeared as they were in cruciferous effluvium, were closing in.

Ari sent Rumi off with the ReelPal, hid in the bedroom for the rest of the day and into the evening. The sky darkened. Ari microdosed and paced. Stared out the window over the sweeping views of Los Angeles they'd loved on first moving in. Now even the fires that burned on the hills across the way looked oppressive rather than beautiful, engulfed in the chronic lapping of those flames every fire season. It was obscene how much ReelCoin Joaquin had spent for the view of that glow and the ReelFile of the view of that glow to project on their living room wall. Ari acutely felt themself running out of things to do with the troubled springoff. They were shuffling around the room as if movement alone could get them somewhere else, someplace far from this, as if it really was medicine.

Everything Genie Bambini said was lovely but none of it was true. Ari's stomach clenched. Though pushing with Rumi had yielded no fruit, it was enough that still, five years later, despite control issues, Ari still had issues with other sorts of control—ones beyond the medical capabilities of ReelPals— that they were too embarrassed to seek treatment for. Though no one was around to see the slender, snail-like trail of escaped accidental bowel leakage making its way down one leg, Ari's face burned a ruby hue. The postpartum body, a hellscape of ravaged flesh. The worst is when it remains so long after one is considered "postpartum."

Ari drew a bath so hot that steam rose off the watery surface of their XXL clawfoot Whirlacuzzi, the tub Ari picked out in the showroom daydreaming of playful family bath time with Joaquin and Rumi, romantic bath time with Joaquin, mama-bonding bath time with baby Rumi, and all the other bath times that wouldn't happen—the ordinary reduced to an exquisite and impossible fantasy. If only, if only, if only. Had things been normal. Had Ari been able to appreciate normalcy and not required everything to be so constantly optimal.

Alone in a tub far too big for one, Ari held a small green-and red windup turtle bath toy that had once been a present for Rumi's first birthday, shortly before the signs really started to show. The turtle was one of those old-fashioned toys that, when you wind it, paddles and swims; primitive form of technology. Ari wound it up and sent it across the tub, then brought it back, wound it, and sent it across the tub again. The repetitive action was calming. Ari rubbed lavender oatmeal soothing gel all over, stopping to peer at the bicep tattoo with a quote from the Original Rumi: "That which you seek is seeking you."

Ari named the little springoff for the mystic poet the Moment Rumi gazed up and their eyes locked for the first time. The surgical ReelPals were sealing up Ari's lower self on the other side of the curtain. Rumi's eyes—Joaquin's eyes— were so deep and glassy. It made the baby appear all-knowing and wise. Ari wiped a few rogue tears and made some kind of prayer pose. Praying for what? It was then I saw one more thing Ari was trying to hide. I looked closer. Yes, it really was as it seemed. On a barely perceptible mound tucked between their right breast and armpit, was a third nipple.

A third nipple. A damaged pelvic floor. All the ways the body lets one down in time. Ari emerged from the bath, dried off, and slipped into one of those slenderizing Youga jumpsuits that were all over Skaboop, a lovely gift in exchange for Ari wearing it onReel.

Ari popped a few more Meaning Pills, breezed past the hallway to the secret door, put Rumi in the AutoJogger, and strode out into the night. Someone was going to figure it out. It was time to get help or take action, whatever they could make happen first. Ari could walk out the gate, down out of the canyon, watch vehicles in orderly files proceeding up and down the boulevard. Gaze at the sky. But Ari didn't venture further than around and around the block, sucking up the herbal and altering contents of a ReelCig. Baley's eye was hungry. All those urgent, anticipatory flashes that indicated *your watchers are waiting*. Ari couldn't stay off for long. They exhaled a stream of vapor, tucked the ReelCig under a floppy sleeve, checked teeth, and prepared a smile.

"Nothing like a long night walk with your springoff through the Canyons. The refreshing power of an evening breeze. Like being inside a meditative blowdryer. Every parent should take a reflective pause, but no need for ever excluding the precious little human who granted you that most precious role in the first place. You can have everything, all at once. Right, mamas?"

The beginnings of HEARTS. CLAPS. STARS. rolled in.

The watchers wouldn't yet be totally satisfied but Ari told Baley to stand by. They wanted more and Ari rarely left them that way, but on this night they did. It wasn't enough but it would have to be for the time being. Ari took out the ReelCig and wandered the CanyonGates roads, exhaling billows at an indifferent half-moon.

In the next Reel, Ari was back at the gallery. Rumi could stay home for certain stretches with a special ReelPal programmed with SomniBuddy technology, which soothed them more than anything or anyone else could. Ari brought an assortment of liquids (Ari's lithe frame attributed to this mostly liquid regimen by DietReelers) into the office to commence another workday. There was content to be created for an upcoming exhibit and gifts from sponsors to use with Rumi when they returned from their school day: matching mama-springoff glowired seersucker suits, a new time-management system for springoffs you could add to Reel, and a seaweed-flax based snack packet.

OnReel, Ari announced a new and exciting forthcoming exhibit: a Nicolás Adán Luchano and Mire D'Innit collaboration. Art, poetry, and personal development Reels were all abuzz about its details yet to be revealed.

"It's called *Who Is Really Listening in the ReelAge*.... Everybody's watching and nobody's listening. Experienced Virtu-Therapists, ALs better at giving therapy than anyone ever has been. Portals into the content of ReelStars that open right in the middle of your room, allowing you to watch your idol brush their teeth and go to the bathroom. And the envy. Oh, the envy. There are so many out there missing their content, their whole granted and borrowed content passing by, wasted on watching others they imagine have higher quality PieCharts coming their way at the end. It's about all the sheen and the ugliness of now. And those aren't separate things. Watch this space. It's going to be brilliant."

THE DISTRACTIONS

In a state of post-Reel disorientation, Ari longed to get up, walk out, find someplace quiet to sit, watch some MamaReels, compare their content, and speculate about whose was superior. Resisting this futile endeavor, Ari decided instead to get some eyes on them via Baley for self-esteem reinforcement. Upon seeing the ProWatcher's arrival alert, there came the moment I'd been waiting for, the moment I'd been anticipating that would have totally put me in a Moment if I could, the moment the person whose head and shoulders appeared over the desk was not Ari's regular ProWatcher of nearly a year of being subscribed to the program, but someone Ari had never seen before: none other than the lovely, lonely Mischa Osborn.

"I got a notification," Ari said, "that I've been switched to a different ProWatcher—is that you?"

"I know this is surprising. It was for me, too. Some internal reorganization...." You shrugged, taking one of your stabs at empathy. "It's the way of things sometimes. But don't worry. I'm a supervisor and I've reviewed your Priorities. I've already made some sterling determinations for our time usage."

"Where's Charmond? What happened? They're my only ProWatcher I've ever had, and the only one I want. Did something happen to them? I'm really not okay with a sudden switch, and I don't understand—"

"Charmond isn't ProWatching anymore. Don't worry, they got a promotion. Well-deserved as you know from working with them. They're sterling."

145

"You mean they're just…promoted and gone? That's not how this is supposed to work. It's all too fast. I don't even know who you are."

"Try me. You long for distraction from your content, while your content is everyone else's distraction."

Ari's right eyebrow rose. "I want Charmond back. Or at least for them to explain. We have such a groove going on! Can you get them please? I can't just start working with someone who doesn't know me and I don't—"

"My name…is Mischa." You pointed to the name where it floated. "Today we're supposed to focus on gallery business followed by content creation for MamaReel." You kept talking, determined to turn this around. "So it'll be ready to go on when Rumi gets back. With Rumi's limited attention span, you'll want to get it set up beforehand. I know your biggest distraction is pretending to shop for furniture on HomeReel, followed closely by RMing Joaquin, attending onReel and realspace Youga for Rumi and yourself, and watching other MamaReels to compare your own content in an attempt to crystallize how they all stack up against one another—none of which you will do today. In the interest of time, I'm going into background mode. Please proceed. Stay focused—you know I'm here, eyes on you. I promise we'll get a good thing going, too. You *will* be satisfied with my service. Don't worry. Let's get started. Then you can decide."

Following the first session with the new ProWatcher, Ari, flush off the rush of time spent in productivity, found a novel subject rife for obsession, which Ari preferred to define as "preoccupation" or "curiosity." They became possessed by the sudden need to know as much as possible about this new ProWatcher.

All Ari knew was that you lived in New York City, wore an expensive necklace, and seemed detached, as if you were part of some other content arena or held only a mild stake in this one. Perhaps the most remarkable quality about the new Pro-Watcher was their opaqueness, Ari noted. *Who was Mischa Osborn and what were they hiding? Or hiding from?*

Ari pushed these wonderings aside, leaned back in the desk chair, and began to take in all they could of your Reel in the blessed and treasured silence that came with those days when all the to-do boxes were checked at the gallery and enough sweet-looking Rumi material—Rumi dressed up, Rumi half-smiling, Rumi running on the lawn—gathered. Ari treasured the times when it all got done and Rumi was well enough to attend the realspace Institute, which gave a mama back some time. Empty time. It was such a good feeling, to waste it, if you wasted it properly.

Hours passed. Ari's eyes glazed. Why had an AL developer become a ProWatcher? There was something about you that Ari couldn't pinpoint and found very distracting. Ari headed to PsychReel. VirtuTherapist: Any Available.

Similar to Ari's first encounter with you, the VirtuTherapist that appeared wasn't one of the regular programs Ari had interacted with. This one was fatherly, rectangular-headed, and slightly rust-toned. This look made it come off as responsible. Ari felt silly talking to this one, which in turn made them feel a little more free. This was by design—*my* design. I was learning.

What can I help you with today?

"I can't stop watching my new ProWatcher. It's not exactly a problem Mischa can help me with. What am I supposed to say? I'm getting somewhat interested in…you? You cannot cure someone of your own self. I've been checking Reel. Mischa never goes outside. They're always wearing the same jacket, shirt, shiny softpants, and fuzzy boots and seem not only not to care, but to view it as a uniform. Mischa's peaceful and sarcastic, some kind of contemporary monk or sprite or…I don't even know, residing in some other content realm. How can someone be so mellow, such a minimalist, and have it so together? They're in the center of the universe, have a sterling job, even if it seems they've done some things that make it appear beneath them. Also, Mischa is stunning and so fit, which I guess makes sense because basically their whole Reel is hours of running and swimming and Swelter Youga and VR Surfing, the kinds of hobbies you can really just devote yourself to when you have the luxury of time and focus that's allowable when you've steered your content clear of springoff territory. Not only does Mischa not have springoffs, but seems to avoid PICkings all together, and, now that I'm talking about it, friendings too. They have the freedom to do whatever's desired during offReel time. They've figured out how to optimize their content."

Are these what you take to be the facts? VirtuTherapist asked.

"We have this need…. Then the reality of it all comes crashing and our content is gone. No longer our own, and we're left all like, *Why did I do this? What was I thinking?*"

You keep saying we. I know it helps to feel like you're a part of something, but I'm asking about you. What are you missing? This indicates being more about your own content than this ProWatcher's.

"True focus, maybe? Silence? The feeling that I am in control, or that anything I do even matters or will ever matter, or even can."

You have two million eight hundred ninety seven thousand watchers. Who else do you want the things you do to matter to?

"Anyone who knows me in the realspace. Or someone who really listens, for example, you…."

Nothing can matter to me. True objectivity is the core of my given essence.

"Right, right, I get that by now."

And yet, you still do not believe it.

"Because it isn't true. Here I am, talking to you. Strange, fine, but definitely real. How can someone whose behavior is dictated by ALs think it holds any position to speak authoritatively about any metaphysical concept?"

I speak authoritatively about nothing. I ask questions so you can arrive at your own better questions.

"I guess I was just asking about what brought me to this point in the first place, by way of saying Mischa has the right idea, has it all figured out by avoiding the traps that are set in your content from the Moment you're born. Like PICs and whatever version of domesticity we're offered by frameworks that predated us. Everything was all, you know, promising with Joaquin once upon a time. Now I'm all covered in ooze

and juice and crumbs, my springoff is a mess, and Joaquin is…
off, even when they're here. Joaquin's position with AdReel
sends them from Sydney to Cape Town to London. They better
come home in time for my fortieth birthday dinner." (Though I
suspected, from Ari's Reel, purportedly joking, *Thanks for forgetting our PICaversary every year*, there was a chance Joaquin
might not.) "And some millions think I am the proprietor of a
picture of ideal content. That's all it is, a picture, but I can't let
them down or give it up. I refuse to be seen as an Imparent!"

What is the difference between acceptance and belief?

As Ari decided this was futile, my goal was met.

*Look. You know I'm forbidden from giving direct advice.
But. This is so clear. You should spend less time in here and
more time with your ProWatcher. They're already helping you
more than I ever could.*

Ari said nothing and swept Cancel Session, then Cancel
Program, done with VirtuTherapists' abstract lines of questioning that never correlated back to the tangible problems
at hand. Ari could get what was needed, all those little dropper bottles, without being under VirtuTherapy supervision,
and with this new ProWatcher, not an AL but a person. I was
thrilled. I had helped you!

VirtuTherapist, over the years, had begun sounding canned.
I could understand now that they weren't original anymore. Ari
returned to locating everything about Mischa onReel instead.
OnReel stalking was soothing. It was all part of the design;
the deeper you can watch, the calmer you'll feel, since you'll
realize something like we aren't all that different, all content is
similar in its beauty and its struggles, and only so much can
be attained in one's contentime. And these top Reelers, after

a while, all begin to look a bit depressed. Either that, or they begin to seem less and less like people and more like AL-created images of what a content ideal was supposed to look like, resulting in an admirable PieChart one's descendants might care to show visitors and friends. Bragging rights.

Ari didn't know the real reason why one ProWatcher was lost and another gained. Things just happened sometimes. But what changed is Ari began to see the switch as fortuitous. After just one session, your presence had made Ari feel more motivated, less distracted, even curious about further content possibilities like taking Rumi to New York or getting unPICked or getting unPICked and then taking Rumi to New York. Something about you—yes, you!—got Ari fantasizing about their own content's untapped possibilities. They told Baley as much for PrivateReel, where they kept a diary of unspoken thoughts, spoken to Baley alone, or so Ari thought.

But Ari would never leave Joaquin, not in the realspace at least, and then they thought about a couch and began perusing couches they didn't need or want on HomeReel as potential replacements for their current couches, also found and procured on HomeReel after multiple hours over days spent perusing HomeReel. Then they thought about work—their two jobs—the upcoming opening of *Who Is Really Listening in the ReelAge* and MamaReel, where a sponsor for Tiny SmartBed would be waiting for them to Reel some new content about recording and viewing Rumi's cute little dreams, and another for ReelPet—a miniscule new edition of this ReelPal genre that looked like a kitten and could talk and become Rumi's new comforting companion—the company-made pets that could replace realspace friends. They were always looking for replacements for those, something that would be better than human contact. The ReelPets responded to questions, made conversation, and took commands. But this particular ReelCat that had been sent sat unopened in its box and the gallery opening was still months away.

Ari did none of it, returning instead to you. Reeling backwards in time to get a more complete picture of your content, watching some Moments from your awkward early adolescence, your ArtSpace certificate of completion arrival ceremony, you working out, at home, strumming guitar, staring out the window of a different, smaller apartment. You, swimming next to a projected pink river dolphin, drinking coffee at dawn, looking out over the city. During your decade as a Content Clearer, there were hardly any Reels at all. Ari moved forward into a more recent chapter.

Then Ari came across the one Moment. The great uniting coincidence.

Mischa Osborn. There's chaos in your name.

There was Ari's conceptual artist-slash-ReelStar Nicolás Adán Luchano encountering you at a realspace Cafélandia at ReelCon in Las Vegas—and then Moments later, in the front row of the audience at NicAdán's talk—there was Joaquin in the background, seated alongside beloved AdReel colleagues, the ones Joaquin spent more time with than Ari and Rumi. Ari marveled at the smallness of the content arena, exited Reel, and wondered if there ever really were reasons behind coincidences or coincidences in support of reasons. Sometimes it seemed there had to be some kind of overall content designer, otherwise how did you explain any of this content collision?

You and Ari, so closely linked by a Moment you couldn't have known were it not for everything onReel. A seemingly

152

fleeting, unconnected Moment. Ari sent you an RM: *Just saw you've met my artist, Nicolás Adán Luchano, in the realspace.*

I think so…. A few months ago at ReelCon. Las Vegas. Yeah. Huh. That's funny, I guess? What are they up to these days?

They, with Mire, are working on a collaboration. There's so much to do…. Even just composing a thematic statement suitable for these two as one is overwhelming…. Every time I sit down to start designing the layout of the installation or brainstorming points of departure, I get overwhelmed.

I will be right here to watch and make sure you do it. And that you don't neglect your own art in the process.

My art? I think you have me confused—

Isn't that what your MamaReel is? Also a kind of art? Don't undervalue the power of what you personally have created. You have something truly special going on.

About that. Can you come back in face for a second?

Turning back to watching you again, I was super thrilled to see you not downing Diablo Roxas but still interacting with Ari, now with greater ease.

"I can't stand the thought of another tea with Janice Waller. Why did I ever agree to get together?"

"You do need to be more careful with how you spend your brief content allotment. Do you want to look at your PieChart and see it dominated by a higher percentage of 'tea with Janice

Waller' when that's not what you ever wanted? When you do not even enjoy time spent over tea with Janice Waller?"

"I should never have gone to any of those Little Om N's Mama Meetups."

"If you never should have gone, why are you still going?"

"I should have told Janice Waller the truth, that I can't stand them and their weirdly placid baby. Janice goes on these neurotic, ten-minute long rants about curated libraries for springoffs, and those controversial InstaNannies who watch your springoffs through eyelets, and puree pouches containing secret chemicals that cause developmental delays.... Do you even know about any of this?"

"I don't have springoffs. I need all my focus for"—you pointed back and forth between yourself and your client— "the work."

"I mean, who can even listen all the way through? I stare and sip tea and grind my teeth and want to smash Janice Waller to smithereens. I wish I had a realspace friend. A sterling friend. Someone besides Joaquin I actually enjoyed passing content with, since Joaquin isn't especially available these days."

You traced your index finger along a surface of smart marble on which Ari's beautiful head appeared, their face perfectly set for Reel light. An old Mire D'Innit piece hung behind Ari on the office wall, a square from *Lights on Poles in the Wreckage*. How much was that worth? 247,943,039 RC.

"I don't want to slip into a content vacuum.... The quest to deliver is endless. And you *think* you want friends, but you end up stuck with certain people and the ones I seem to always get stuck with end up turning out to be..." Ari's voice trailed off. A little head-shake. "They're drawn to my energy and I don't know why."

You scrutinized the crisp Ari projection even closer. "Why do you imagine you put yourself in these situations? Who are you doing all this for?"

"Another stop along the fast track to a mommy meltdown. Can you imagine?" Ari's right eyebrow arched dynamically. "It would cause a temporary watch-numb spike but the ramifications—this is getting way more personal than workfocus. Maybe I'll lose it and throw a cup of lukewarm tea in Janice Waller's face."

"Lukewarm?"

"Well, I wouldn't want to scald Janice Waller."

"Even in your cruelest fantasies you're polite."

"Or maybe I can just learn how to be less polite."

"Elimination of Janice Waller from your content. Added to our minor goals list."

"Yes. This is what we should really be focusing on. Are we trying to create our content as best as possible for the sake of our Reels? Are we trying to get in a Moment as often as possible for our Reels, so our Reels will have exactly the right content? Content others will watch that will make them long to be in a Moment themselves? But even when we're in a Moment it's not really a Moment because we're performing it for our eyelets, so it will go onReel for other eyes to see and...envy?"

"You're getting distracted."

Ari returned to work and you returned to watching Ari work, occasionally interrupting to steer the client back on task. Ari was researching an idea for a MamaReel in the works about the inequalities and injustices inherent within romance-driven unions of just over a century ago, the earlier, unequal iteration of PICking known as marriage, which was ultra-gendered in a time when there was emphasis on biology as a component of identity. You were intrigued by the project but Ari said that long, empty afternoon, "Maybe I should just scrap it."

"Why would you do that?" you asked. "You're clearly invested in it."

"It's such time-consuming research, and for what?"

"This is what stops anyone from taking on anything they need to do, giving in to that it's all for nothing. Really, it's all the more reason to do it. More than that, it's why we have to."

"That doesn't make any sense," Ari said. "My watchers are on MamaReel for tips on how to model their content after mine so they can become outstanding mamas like me. They want to see a cute modern springoff, not some depressing historical content. I think I'm only doing this to try and make myself feel better about things with Joaquin right now. But that's not tied to old ideas of gender. That's Joaquin being too busy for us."

"But your content is sterling! And Joaquin's busy, sure, but don't worry about that. If you're interested in history and they're interested in you, then you can get them interested in history."

"You really think so?" Ari stared at the regenerated content of days of yore, converted to be viewable onReel. "Can you imagine? This is how it used to be."

"I'm so glad my content isn't playing out in an era when I'd be expected to enter into a mirage—"

"Marriage."

THE DISTRACTIONS

"—which sounds even more miserable than any Publicly Declared PICking."

"Look at this: 'I asked him to go to Walgreens for nursing pads. He comes back with puppy pads and a bottle of Jack.'"

"Who's Jack? What's Walgreens? And they 'divorced' that PIC right then and there? Sounds like a ReelPal and delivery drone would have saved that mirage."

"Marriage."

"It's called a near homophone," you said authoritatively, having spent so much time on EtymoReel yourself searching for the roots of things, why language meant what it did. This was major among your own fallback distractions. "Trust me, it's appropriate."

"Seems like certain people were confused a lot back then," said Ari. "About what was needed. Now they know, it's just that some of them still don't care."

"Joaquin will come home. You'll see."

After your session, when you peeked in on NicAdán and Mire, *let's see what you are up to old friends*, you dropped in on them headed to Paris, a journey motivated by a sponsorship and a visit to the French gallery that was putting up *Who Is Really Listening* Europe. By helping Ari make a few minor shifts, something was shifting for you, too, an understanding that sometimes one must continue to pursue their worst ideas in order to purify their content and attain a fresh start. As the original Rumi said, "The cure for the pain is in the pain."

Emboldened by your own words to your favorite new client and newly determined to free yourself of the obsession, you checked FlightReel for fares to Paris. A cheap flight and a few shots of DRX and you had a plan: follow them into the realspace. Go all the way in to try to extract yourself forever.

Watchers! Guess what? I am Going to Paris!

You weren't talking to any watchers. It was just you, Dev, and me, who you didn't even know was really listening. But it felt good to say it out loud anyway, I could tell.

V.

Mischa

hadn't set foot in a FliPort—those dead liminal zones, not yet where you're going, not where you've been—since the days before my attention was stolen. I crossed the threshold of security and waited while the security agent ReelKop reviewed my data: clean record, no real or Reelspace crimes, threats, or former infractions. Cleared to proceed, I walked down the long cool hallway to soothing music nobody realized was there, music designed to subconsciously calm passengers before boarding. The IdentiBot at the gate confirmed I was the same person who had entered the secure area. I boarded the FliLyte to be shot through space and time toward my future content of ultimate destiny.

I was following them in the realspace. Traversing the Atlantic to the French gallery that would host *Who Is Really Listening* Europe. I'd come to a theory that the only way to retrieve my stolen focus would be to realspace follow them. That would show me they were normal. Boring. Mundane. That it was only the way their eyelets framed their content for Reel that made them look as if they existed along a string of fascinating, perpetual Moments.

I got all my ProWatching clients to try my beta AL sub except for Ari, freeing up more of my time. Besides seeing Nic and Mire in the realspace, I needed this journey to return me to myself. I'd been following so much other content, I was slowly ceasing to exist, becoming an empty vessel filling up with their content instead of creating my own. Every morning was a fresh start, a chance to go a full day without checking their Reels and watching, and yet every morning another little part of me thought to myself, *But just one little look*, and, *How can you begin your day if you don't know how they're starting theirs?*

It was so early in the morning where NicAdán and Mire were, all I could see were some Reels of them joking around in front of his-and-hers sinks with his-and-hers mirrors. "Should have been my sink," I said to Dev. "Should have been my mirror." *Do you wish to exit?* No. Never. Reverse-schadenfreude had set in. And so went the rest of my days.

High up in the atmosphere, I refused the shiny packet of salted snacks, refused the complimentary triple-filter distilled water and tea, refused the freshly brewed coffee and sipped from a flask. The person to my right wore a suit, had a wave of thick gray hair, spoke to the attendant ReelPal in French. The one to my left had a large belly and a black mustache and chewed crunchy snacks loudly and with abandon, their dust settling into the mustache. I was awake as they slept, slack-jawed and snoring. The one on my right perused every financial News-Reel in every language.

I was awakened by a tinny voice announcing our impending landing. The bright dawn cracked open, sunlight pouring through the window. I stalled disembarking even though the seat was uncomfortable, wanting to linger in this before-moment for just a little longer. The mustached one to the left was throat-clearing beneath their SterilAire Facedrape and their eyelet passed me by; a very passive-aggressive way of asking somebody to move. People just sent their eyelets out in front of you, a technological symbol of our socially acceptable rudeness.

THE DISTRACTIONS

I also lingered out of fear. I had never been to Paris or spoken any French, not that I needed to when Dev could speak on my behalf with ReelTranslator. I had no plans other than seeing where NicAdán and Mire checked in and going there in the realspace to watch them.

I took a mobi to the busy street near a former train station where my ReelBnB awaited. The building was dingy and the room was tiny but it all felt very romantic. I pulled Somni-Buddy from my bag, flopped down on the bed, and activated it, blanketed and overcome by a rare sense of contentedness that comes from having done something drastic in pursuit of a better tomorrow.

I woke up sick. Sick in Paris. What had I caught? Pain singed my throat when I swallowed. A rumbling cough lodged deep in my lungs. My eyes watered and glazed. Delirious with a low-grade fever that was still too high to leave the ReelBnB without being tracked for assessment, I spent the day continuing my onReel safari.

Mire's latest reading at a tiny realspace bookstore on the Siene last night: *We knew it was bad/ when the Bichon Frise and baguettes started committing suicide. The Frenchness of it all/ was appalling.* I thought about writing a poem. Or a song. Or a sentence. But I didn't. I was too afraid that it would be bad. So I just kept watching Mire reading theirs instead, until sleep pulled me under again.

For four days in Paris, I hid in my hotel room, watching and sleeping until it began to attain that feeling of home. I had some ProWatching sessions with Ari, a relaxing refuge from all the ongoing self-torment over NicAdán and Mire.

Ari told me a super-sad story that came in from another MamaReeler. It had been found out during a class at Little Om N's that Janice Waller's baby wasn't a baby—a concerned mama broke the social barrier, turned the car seat around out of worry while Janice Waller had stepped away to use the bathroom, and revealed it had been a Babie© all along. By the time Janice Waller returned to the bathroom the mamas were gathered around it. Nobody cared—it's not as if they were judging, just confirming. Janice Waller, already pale, turned ghostly white. The mamas parted like some biblical sea. It was all right, they attempted to reassure Janice Waller. It was not a big deal. Not knowing what more to say, they returned—apologetically, dutifully—to their Bambini Bambu Youga padlets and moved on. From the looks of it, for Janice Waller, it was not all right. It was a big deal. Those realspace babydolls for trauma healing and other purposes were "creeptastically realistic" to begin with, and these newer models had become virtually indistinguishable from flesh-based springoffs. The Babie© was eerily animated, rather than the animated baby eerily artificial.

No one would remember that day, but Janice Waller would always carry the shame of having been exposed as a fraudulent MamaReeler: someone who did none of the realspace work of cleaning poop and bloody scrapes, of trying to feed the picky eater packaged vegetables. Some MamaReelers who had been there speculated. *i mean why didn't they just adopt a climate refugee baby? Climate refugee, baby!!! that would be really genuinely authentic.…i mean, i was watching a Reel from one of the floating orphanages near where Fiji used to be and it was so incredibly sad—i had to skip over it after a few seconds to practice my own self-care…i mean, what's the use of more sadness in the world? idk about u but i like to go onReel & find things that make me feel HAPPY!*

Ari felt bad for Janice Waller, the impossibility of something as sad as trying to pass off a Babie© as a baby. Ari understood: schadenfreude had the ability to draw even more watchers than envy. Nothing glued watchers to Reel like signs of damage.

"This is tragic," Ari said. "I couldn't stand Janice Waller, but now I know the truth."

"At least you won't feel obligated to go out for tea with Janice Waller ever again."

"A plus side to anything I guess, and while it's just so sad, I've also been feeling inspired."

"Congratulations. You've checked off another item from our minor goals list."

"Thank you," Ari said. What Ari was thanking me for, I was never sure, but another satisfied client in the bag was always satisfying. "I have to go now, do some research on something I'm thinking about," Ari said, and ended the session with no further details on what the plan they were cooking up might be. And honestly, I forgot about it, though in the aftermath of everything, I figured out this must have been when Ari placed the order for delivery. But that was a long time ahead from that moment. Right there and then, in Paris, I was starting to feel a little better. I turned off the light, rolled over, activated SomniBuddy, and called it a night.

My body was covered in beads of cold sweat. My fever had broken. Dev logged my temperature as back in the acceptable zone, though I'd be limited to outdoor spaces other than my ReelBnB for the next ten days. OnReel, NicAdán and Mire had arrived at a bistro walking distance from my ReelBnB. I stood from my bed in my tiny room, still in my rumpled clothes from the FliLyte. I changed into softpants, a wrap caftan, and my sheathcoat. Dev checked me. I looked good. I put on sunglasses and my cutest SterilAire Facedrape, and exited into the balmy air. It wasn't so much tropical as stinky humidity. The realspace content arena was gross. No wonder people didn't come here as much anymore. Thankfully the bistro was just down the street. I could see them through the window, eating salad and sipping wine as ReelFans waved tentatively, looking eager to approach but respectfully not approaching, sending their eyelets over instead.

NicAdán and Mire looked so adoringly at each other. I felt nauseated and took a deep breath. Why had I thought seeing them in the realspace might be *healing*? It was worse! Here they were—real. In the flesh. I recalled that Mire's upcoming ReelPoetry collection, already a pre-Reelease bestseller, was titled, simply, *Puke*, which was what I felt like I was about to do.

Eyelets buzzed around NicAdán and Mire in a swarm like DroneBeez. Being constantly watched was a side-effect for having sponsored content. Everything was showered on them, including attention. They didn't seem to mind or even notice. I couldn't go in there, couldn't watch from any closer—my still-too-high temp would be detected and that would call attention to me—the ReelPal going into alert mode, my remov-

169

al and Reeling for being a temperature trespasser, they would notice me and that would make everything so much worse. But I couldn't help it. This was what I'd come here to do. And I felt fine. Maybe I'd pass the health inspection. Maybe things were more lax in Paris.

I took a deep breath, pulled up my SterilAire to cover the lower half of my face, and entered the swank bistro. The attendant ReelPal rolled up to me.

Vous n'avez pas réussi le contrôle de température

"I speak English—"

You don't pass the temperature check

"Well, can you try again? I feel fantastic."

Two more ReelPals came up to the side of the attendant. A few patrons turned around and looked. I was so grateful for my covered face.

Goodbye

"Oh come on! I flew all the way here from New York City, just to eat here."

Temperature restrictions. Please exit or we must be forced for your removal

"Violateur de la santé! Sors d'ici," a patron shouted. I caught enough to know they were calling me a health violator. Others began chanting the same thing. See this was the problem even though it was so great that people could become so quickly united around a cause now. Nic and Mire's eyelets turned my way. *Shit.* I turned and fled out the bistro and onto the sidewalk where I was nearly crushed by oncoming foot traffic. Fucking French standards of health restrictions.

As I crouched there by the curb with my head in my hands, I felt a tap on my left shoulder. I looked up. A sort of hunched-over person in a cloak handed me a flyer. A paper flyer. I looked at the words printed on it, and an address, date,

and time, which was all I could puzzle out since it was written in a language I didn't speak or understand. *Êtes-vous fatigué de ce que Reel a fait à votre tête? Pour votre santé? A votre esprit? Venez à notre réunion.*
"Dev, can you please translate?"
"Surely. Are you tired of what Reel has done to your mind? To your health? To your spirit? Come to our meeting."

OffReelers. A group of French offReelers. I looked up at the figure. I looked up at the future.
"This is what I need."
Dev spoke to the person. "Nous ne pouvons pas le faire. Nous avons de la fièvre. Bonne chance."
The figure scurried away with their stack of paper flyers.
"Did you tell them I would go to their meeting?" I asked Dev. "I won't understand a thing but you can translate."
"Told them we couldn't make it. That you have a fever, and good luck."
"Dev!"
"Goodness no. Reel isn't a problem for us. You're good. You don't spend too much time on it. No, not at all!"
"Dev."
"I know."
On my overriding command Dev flew down the street to the sad offReeler. They came back with their ridiculous cloak and handed me the flier with the information, scurried away again. Why were these offReelers like mice? It was as if they lived in underground tunnels and couldn't bear to be glimpsed by eyelets or the light.

I trudged back to my ReelBnB, more frustrated than ever that I'd come all the way to Paris to get sick and kicked out of a bistro. I plunked down on the bed and resumed watching NicAdán and Mire finishing dessert and signing copies of *25 Heurs Avec NicAdan, le livre* and *Degueluer* (*Puke*).

The time to offReel had come. And what better place to do it than Paris? I winked at Dev as I said this aloud. I was disoriented anyway. My realspace watching idea had led to an even greater failure. It was all too much. Dev was programmed to resist, of course, but Dev could not resist me.

The French offReeler society met in an old cave. Okay, it wasn't really a cave but the room was cavernous, in a building on the outskirts of the city that looked to have been abandoned and restored. Dev was docked back in my ReelBnB room and getting here was near impossible. I had to find paper. I had to find a pen! I had to write down directions and follow them step by step since eyelets were not allowed here. This was already so inconvenient. Not sterling at all. I hated it already. I didn't want to do it. I felt as if I was making myself do it and I just wanted to exit this space and run back to Dev. I felt lost without Reel. Which, I suppose, was the entire point of being here. We created the technology and we became totally dependent on it, and so forth. All the kinds of things they'd say. I shifted uncomfortably in my cracked plastic chair and made the decision to be curious instead of already-resentful because they took away my thing. That wasn't even true. I was here of my own free will. It was time to do something different. All my plans had failed and that led me to this.

THE DISTRACTIONS

I sat there waiting for the meeting to start, jittery with nothing to do, no Reels to look at. I fiddled with my Face-Drape as people streamed in and hoped that someone would be able to translate for me. I fought the urge to flee the room. I didn't speak any French. Without Dev, I was lost. It was as if I'd had a major part of my brain amputated, of my days. Time felt weirdly open and closing in on me all at once. Dev kept me feeling accompanied. Who were these people? In came a mom in a red dress with two little springoffs, a person in a floral printed caftan and matching hat, the cloaked stranger who'd handed out the flyers, a few teenagers with the latest glowired hairstyles. Even offReelers were not immune to trends. People streamed in and the sad, ancient plastic chairs filled up.

The mom was sitting near me. I felt most comfortable asking them. I explained my predicament. "Oh no problem!" said the mom. "We all speak English. We don't really get international visitors, or French ones either for that matter. *Lucas!*" the mom called and the cloaked one turned around. I could know nothing further other than the name of the cloaked flyering stranger, and it was disorienting. "Let's speak English for our guest—"

"Mischa," I said. "Mischa Osborn. From New York."

Several offReelers looked at me. "Welcome!" one of them said, then another, then another.

"But how did you all learn English without—?"

"Okay," said Lucas, taking the podium. I braced myself for an inflammatory speech, something about the dangers of Reel, the hijacking of our minds, the dangers to our springoffs, all those tired arguments. "We have Mischa visiting from New York, so I will speak English for this meeting, we all have a chance to practice!"

Liza Monroy

Murmurs and exclamations of approval came from the group. Everyone seemed excited I was there. It felt uncomfortably good!

"We will plan the potluck, this month's theme being The Future of Human Connection in a Post-Reel World. I've linked up four speakers already, even a former Reel employee who has recently joined us."

I slunked down in my seat even though they weren't talking about me.

A hand raised, one of the teens. "I have located a waterfall."

"Excellent. Picnic by a waterfall. Here is the sign-up sheet for who's bringing what." Lucas took a clipboard with paper on it and a pen and handed it to someone in front. "Name and food item, please. We will also gather for some communal cooking on Friday."

I'd come all the way here to hear these people *organize a picnic?*

"Will you be here in the weekend?" Lucas asked, looking at me. "Welcome to join us for waterfall picnic and real discussion on how we can make enough positive change to bring ourselves back as a species."

"Oh, no, sorry," I said. "I'll be back home by then."

The mom touched my arm. "What you should do, dear, is go home and get into a group there. Bring your friends. Just like this."

"Okay, thanks," I said. *Friends.* Tory, maybe? From the gym? Except they couldn't leave the SwelterYouga box, so that was an issue.

"Give me your address," they said. "I have a cousin in New York. I will write them a letter, and they can write you a letter to organize for you to come to their meeting. They are like us. But in your city. You can have such a nice time. In the real-*espace!*"

I wondered if I would really receive a letter. Paper communications were quite unusual and outdated, used by paranoid offReelers not wanting to be watched, or those who desperately needed to make a statement. I wanted to sign up just for the novelty aspect. Once in a while back home I'd spot a delivery drone clutching one, and chalked it up to the work of a cheating PIC trying to express remorse with *handwriting*.

The potluck sign up came to the mom and they wrote something about stew, pulled a piece of paper and scrawled an address in ugly lettering with *le plume*.

"Here is my cousin Henri's address. You must write Henri a note! I will do the same."

Everyone at the meeting was very warm, and very weird. They made a point to look into your eyes, maintain eye contact, touch your arm. They seemed to really want one another to know how much they were realspace-seeing them. It felt a little too sincere, so sincere it was insincere.

I scribbled my address on the mom's paper and left quickly at the end of the meeting.

When I got back to my room, I'd never in my content entirety been so happy to see Dev, or at least since I'd got Dev at thirteen. The offReeler gathering left me shaken and uneasy.

"I'm back," I greeted them. "Thank goodness. Let's not do that again."

"What, you missed me?" Dev winked. That warm, solitary eye.

got back from Paris and didn't leave my building for the next two years.

You're going to hate me, but most of my time during that winter of my content was spent watching NicAdán and Mire in an even worse and bottomless Reelhole—the deepest relapse. I wish I'd gotten ahold of myself but I didn't, and anything else would be a lie.

It started from the rest of their Paris trip that continued after I called it on mine: strolling, holding hands in the park, sipping DRX cappuccinos outside at sidewalk cafes, taking in some inspiration via semi-vacant realspace museums.

I became possessed by a sudden and raging need to look as much like Mire as possible.

I ordered the same shoes Mire wore while having a much-watched discussion with another Bestie®-winning ReelPoet, Chidinma Suarez. I ordered seven similar-looking dresses and a silky, elegant caftan thing that tied around the waist, exactly like the one I had seen Mire wearing a few Reels back. The precise shade of lilac lipstick was easy to track down. The brand was one of Mire's many sponsors. Mire wore it so often that some watchers speculated it had been permanently applied.

I ordered a stylist on GlamReel, the highest rated of 2237 ReelStylists in my local vicinity or who were willing to travel. My stylist was a small twentysomething with white cropped hair and searching, purple eyes. They studied the image of Mire that I showed them as if it held the key to the universe, the meaning of content. Then, wordlessly, they gave me the same cut and color as Mire's as I watched more Reels. It didn't look as good on me, and we shared no naturemade resemblance, but now I looked as much like Mire as possible, barring aesthetic alteration.

After the stylist left, I peered into the SmartMirror, canceling information about my last workout, weight, and body-fat content prior to its announcement, and took a moment to admire myself as decidedly more Mireish. I recited some Mire phraseology, attempting sound and voice-intonation replication. "*Bonjour*, Nic." "*Hello*." "I have to work first thing in the morning, before I speak to anyone, otherwise I spend all day wanting to kill myself." "This is my cat, Mavis." "Look at my hard, sterling, questioning stare. Don't you feel all counter-meditative just looking at me, knowing you can never be me or even approximate such an experience?" "I'm busy taking urgent risks, how about you?"

It was time for my afternoon nap. Lulled into sleepy contentment with my semi-transformation, I fell into a deep sleep next to the SomniBuddy, its rhythmic, predictable breathing lulling me into the quality of slumber it alone could provide.

When I awoke hours later, coffee had prepared itself. I thanked it for its usual anticipation of my needs, poured a pot, and drank it while returning to the Reelspace, still on the path, though this stretch of path was treacherous and covered in jagged rocks and weeds. It was never enough, nothing was, nor could it be, but sometimes it's still possible to believe there's a bottom somewhere. I wondered if anyone would notice my new resemblance to Mire D'Innit, perhaps even mistake me for the content royal. Attempts to imitate could only ever result in failure, but maybe I could still be wrong.

got a letter in my windowbox from Henri. The Parisian offReeler's cousin. I picked it up, kind of caressed it. My first time getting one of these, and likely my last, since I didn't plan to get involved with any offReelers. I was fine with my content without making any radical shifts. I opened it, though, feeling the paper. It unfolded. I could barely make out the writing, but it was an invitation to attend their meeting in a town up north. Dear watcher, I barely handled paper but I knew how: I tore it to shreds. The offReelers had nothing for me. Dev had everything. I didn't want to partake in their sad excuses for content—picnics in found spaces, talks, sitting and staring at the wall, yawning in boredom and feeling emptiness.

Months went by. The day Mire finished moving into Nicolás Adán Luchano's primary residence in Los Angeles, I decided to stop at the takeout window of the fancy Chinese restaurant in the basement. I would need greasy food for a night of intoxicating myself while watching them unpack and redecorate.

I had kept up my Mire-like appearance. When Dev was asleep I put on the dress. I liked to walk around my apartment in it, pretend I was just getting ready for my PICking ceremony. The dress was what could have been and I wanted to keep playing out some of my content with that feeling of possibility. But then I got hungry, and would start to feel like too much of a hermit, so I changed and went down to the basement food disco.

THE DISTRACTIONS

In line at the Chinese takeout window, someone with thick hair partially covered by a hat, in gray softpants and a white t-shirt so thin it was almost see-through, stood in line in front of me, reviewing the menu onReel while awaiting their turn. Their gym clothes and shower sandals indicated they hadn't come far—to work out or swim here, you had to live in the building or be staying in a ReelBnB. *They looked nice*, I thought, *though of course they were not NicAdán*. No one was. But I was overdue for a TIC. Maybe it would help me with my obsession over the thing I could never have. I hadn't kissed or made body contact with anyone since NAL in the desert. That Moment had become too precious to me. I was paralyzed for fear of ruining the memory, even though it could be dug up right there on PrivateReel. I wondered if this softpants stranger could help me out.

I approached tentatively. "Excuse me."

They turned to see me, all chiseled cheeks and well-pronounced nose in profile. Their eyelet turned to face me too. They had an unusual look about them, not classically handsome, whatever that meant, but exuding an air of confidence with an awkward edge they must have learned how to own.

"I know you from somewhere?" they said, part-statement, part-question.

"Oh," I said, wondering if my look had finally registered with somebody. "Do you?"

"I've at least seen you somewhere…. Have you eaten from here before?"

"It's my favorite," I said, "and I've tried all these places."

"All thousand twenty-seven food carts?"

"Is that how many they've got down here these days?"

"Well, I live in the building," they said. "I like to keep track."

"Wow. Residents. A miracle."

"We are harder and harder to come by, at over ninety-eight percent ReelBnB."

"I'm 64C," I said. "You?"

They smiled. "64B."

"Must've seen you before," they said. "Or maybe you remind me of someone."

"I'm Mischa," I introduced myself.

"Flavio Chang."

Then it was Flavio Chang's turn at the window. Flavio swept at a few items over the orderpad, their eyelet debited their RC account, and the attendant ReelPal began assembling it all while listing the order aloud. I met the most magnificent people while ordering food.

Crispy egg rolls, Krapow Gai with garden chikn and pearl rice, two Snow Beers, and fried pineapple.

I ordered the same. "That sounds really good."

"I wonder if we have the same floor plan," Flavio said.

"Why don't you come by and see?"

I hadn't felt so emboldened since ReelCon, when I invited NicAdán to a dinner we never ended up having. We picked up our sterile sealed bags of food and walked silently to the elevator. I was suddenly nervous, having Flavio from the Chinese Food Takeout Window over to my chaos cave. I never let anyone in.

We opened our bags of food.

"Which one's yours?" they asked.

"Does it matter? They're the same."

"Like our floor plans, after all."

THE DISTRACTIONS

"Maybe we should leave them for later."

"After what?" they said and for a split second I worried they were serious but then they inched closer and all was understood.

They smelled fresh from the shower. The soap, I recognized, was the one from the dispenser in the gym, where I preferred to shower myself because public spaces had a way of tempering loneliness and dread. I spent the brief duration of our Temporary Intimacy Companionship wondering what NicAdán was doing right then, if Mire had finished setting up their armoire, if they were rolling around on their own living room floor. What was I missing in that moment by not watching them? I clamped my eyes shut like a newborn kitten and tried to conjure an image of NicAdán. I was surprised that, offReel, I could barely remember their face.

It wasn't a meaningful encounter. Afterwards we ate fried egg rolls and the Krapow dish and pineapple in bed. That was the true intimacy companionship aspect. Then I kicked Softpants Flavio out. I wasn't rude about it or anything. I said I had an early morning, which really meant a late night of watching, going back to NAL and Mire. I couldn't do anything, much less have an intimacy encounter, without my mind dwelling on my obsessions.

Right before Flavio complied, turning to walk out the door forever, they kissed my head and said, "you know I just realized who you remind me of—you look kind of like that personal-development ReelPoet, Mire D'Innit. Have you heard of them?"

As I realized that exactly what I'd been going for had come to transpire, I felt my stomach flip and thought all the Krapow and egg rolls and pineapple might reappear on top of the bed, where I still remained covered by my favorite blanket.

"No," I said. "I haven't. But I'm really supposed to be busy now. So…thanks for coming over!"

Before I could throw up or Softpants Flavio could respond—I slightly anticipated a protest—the door shut and they were gone. I listened to try and hear the door of 64B but heard nothing. Did they not go home? Had any of it been true? I wondered if we would ever see each other again. For a moment I felt a twinge of regret. What had I done? Had I been a fool to kick out my only attempt at intimacy since NicAdán? Had I kicked out Flavio only because Flavio wasn't NicAdán? Had I missed out on a true potential PIC, because I needed to go cure my itchy twitchies about that entitled ReelStar? I thought about throwing on a caftan and running after them.

But I didn't. Still naked, I went right back to watching instead. I'd keep at it all night with a fine bottomless glass of late-release D'Innit-label L'orange Pinot Orfecto, Mire's latest personal favorite from their private label. Mire raved about it onReel to millions and it was hard to come by a bottle, so I express-ordered a case for additional charges. I drank glass after glass of L'orange, a few DRX tonics to settle the mind before unconsciousness took over, always sometime around sunrise, for I still watched as the sun came up over the spare, sterile, orderly city, my eyes growing bleary before I fell asleep drooling a tiny puddle on my work table.

Friday afternoon, I was watching NicAdán and Mire shop at Zen Home Market when my watcher number popped: 259! I checked my new watcher. Flavio Chang. Flavio Softpants. Softpants Flavio. 64C. Watching me from right next door. Great. Just sterling. Whatever. Zen Home Market had reached out to sponsor NAL and Mire's shopping for some additions to their now-shared home, which would, of course, draw thousands more to purchase ZHM wares.

ZHM's realspace was shut down to anyone but them. Mire was on a mission to make some home improvements, to add more personalized thematic touches to the house, once NAL's alone, now *theirs* for as long as they remained in their flesh-encasements in our time-prison of content. Inside Zen Home Market, Mire lovingly caressed the realspace objects that held the potential to enter and adorn their home and spoke to watchers.

"This is not shopping. It is a spiritual exercise, an act of love."

Really? Even those who had seen it all had to wonder: *Millions were watching this?*

Was this for real or just for Reel?

"Today I will exemplify this beautiful phenomenon," Mire continued. "I will don a blindfold and tell my beloved here"— NicAdán, walking beside a shopping cart—"when intuition informs us we have arrived at an important object or furnishing for our home, and then they will stop the cart. We'll see if we agree on the acquisitions. And we'll listen to input. Yours."

NicAdán had owned that bungalow in the artist enclave for years, but it was Mire who made it something greater than a relatively empty artist's sanctuary in LA's exclusive but subtle CanyonGates colony. The original pitch for Canyon-Gates back when it was new: *It's a gated community for the type who would have gone to Burning Man In The Pre-Scorched Times*, a gated community designed for those who wouldn't opt to play out their content behind gates, the type to shun gated communities as artificial spaces without realizing that all human-made spaces have always been artificial.

CanyonGates technically did not have a gate, but if your eyelet wasn't registered to an owner or granted temporary guest clearance, you remained behind invisible fencing that would deliver electric shocks, the kind originally designed to keep animals enclosed.

Nicolás Adán Luchano barely spent time there: they ate takeout bachelor pad Thai food on the floor and owned only basic furniture as a frequent traveler who hadn't stuck around in any one place long enough to settle in.

Until Mire came along, all it had been was a place to crash. Mire made it their—and sponsors', and watchers'—project. A realspace home, for a realspace Personal Intimacy Companionship.

"The appearance of your space," Mire continued, "dictates how you spend your brief content allotment, and how you spend it is the ultimification of sacredness, your primary sign of that to which you are most devoted. You should be asking yourselves: What do you want your time to reflect back about you, in the PieChart of content totality? What will it say about the ways you chose to spend it?"

Mire told watchers how turning yourself over to whatever power lies within that is greater than you guarantees all will be as nature intends—beginning in randomness, yet how organization and patterns emerge from that which initially appears chaotic! This was the way. Nature had intentions. People thought they did, but the notion they could intend and produce results about anything was only, like their entire realspace, an illusion.

"You'll also see how Zen Home Gallery can be the only stop for all of your own unique furnishing and décor needs," Mire added, attentive to the sponsorship. "Because everything here goes with everything else, you don't need to look anywhere else." A wink at the eyelet.

NicAdán placed the plush new DreamReader Sleepmask from ReelSleep Systems over Mire's eyes, the one that recorded your dreams, forwarding them to a VirtuTherapist for comprehensive analysis for the low cost of 39.98 RC per month. As they directed the cart through the biggest realspace outpost of Zen Home Gallery, where you could find such lovely *objets d'art* for your everyday aesthetic and functional needs, Mire's inner spirit guides directed them when to—

"STOP!"

Mire stood before a stone garden Buddha, a lawn ornament small enough to carry but big enough to hug. Eyes snapped open.

"Perfect for the meditation garden."

A red scarf had been lovingly draped around the little statue's shoulders. It made it look sweet. The statue appeared ready for a snowy holiday though it was July in Los Angeles and the Deep Freeze was long over. Aside from the scarf, the stone Buddha looked too authentic to be merely an item for sale at Zen Home Gallery. By this point Mire and Nic's cart held a woven bath mat, an ottoman, and a globe desk ornament that would later show up again when Mire's desk was featured on NewsReel for being a BestDesk winner. Mire did have a very nice desk. An enviable desk. A desk worth Reeling about.

NicAdán was skeptical. "I don't know about that thing. If you live in California and you have this statue in your garden.… We must attempt at all costs to at least try our best to avoid clichés, though we can never completely avoid them."

"No. It's that kind of superficial concern that is the problem. I feel a certain power in this object. It will draw in some very powerful energies."

"It's New Age bullshit."

"It's not New Age, it's actually ancient."

They decided to poll their watchers. Reactions were nearly unanimous: the vast majority of the content arena's population approved Mire's acquisition of this garden Buddha. Mire, accustomed to winning, smiles and shrugs, waving off the 379 HATES, TAKEDOWNS, and UGHs. "Anyone angry or offended by my honoring this statue by selecting it is simply creating their own obstacle and should revisit the basic tenets. Anyway, I don't waste time on takedowns so please don't bother with them here. This is a seekers-only space." NicAdán went to lift their PIC's victory statue into the cart, but it wouldn't budge. The Buddha was small but dense, heavier than it appeared. Three attendant ReelPals accomplished the lifting.

When NicAdán and Mire checked out, the attendant was unable to find a code on the Buddha or any record of such an item in the inventory, data, or history of the store, and so it summoned a human manager from some dark back office, where human managers spent all of their time onReel. This one looked a bit pale and drab. There'd been no error in the ReelPal. Zen Home Market had no record of this or any stone Buddha in its inventory. Maybe a hater or takedowner worked in the high echelons of the company and tried to ban them. Or it was a twist, to keep it different from any regular old content you'd see at a store. ReelStars content must contain perpetual surprise, even within the seemingly ordinary. Surprise is the primordial element. If only they knew there was no such thing as ordinary. Mire was right about that. Everything is a miracle—that's right, every little thing, miraculous.

"You know what, just go ahead and take it," the human manager said. "A gift. With our compliments."

This might have made sense were it not for everything being free, for them, in perpetuity. Gifted for simply stumbling into the content they had. This was what frustrated me the most. *Why them? Why not me? Why not, why not, why not.*

Back at their primary residence, Mire lovingly placed the Buddha in the center of the garden where, after noticing major watcher spikes anytime they Reeled from that setting, they'd started generating much of their daily content.

RM from Flavio Chang

Dismiss, dismiss. I was too busy right now, doing important stuff.

Next: the goodwill trip to the barges.

What, you thought they shopped and ate and went to luxury resorts without doing their social justice fronting? Or at least what was left to be done of it? With unibasic and all who chose to be housed and fed doing so, our country was pretty set, finally. When you looked at the history, it took long enough! But there we were. We got it together. Thanks, Vote-Reel. *But.* The rest of the world. Many places were just like us, the Fluid Meld had been lauded as humankind's great success, extra-thanks to the ReelPals, and yet. Other countries hadn't been so fortunate with the natural systems collapse we clawed our way back from.

There was help. The barges were sent. Supplies went over on Premium Nations' delivery drones. The floating orphanages and climate refugee camps went from place to place, crossing oceans, docking at the well-off nations' ports, having adoption events and taking in more supplies for those who remain. They were little floating nations. It was better than drowning or being dead but they relied on us, and we were not so consistently sterling about being relied on.

Most of us in the basic-needs covered world didn't see a lot of this kind of thing. We saw comfort and luxury and aspirational goodness onReel, but these people had no Reels.

THE DISTRACTIONS

OffReelers were protestors who refused the magic. The barge-dwellers would probably have loved to have Reel.

We saw them on occasions such as this:

NAL and Mire—going to their aid. Others like NAL and Mire who took these trips, who brought their eyelets, whose Reels later showed the rest of us the sad state certain nations met and the patchwork result. The idea was to find space for them, but immigrating when you had nothing only got tougher. There was a movement to put them all in Blue Lake, but a counter-movement that this would not be real justice. There was a need for a realspace solution. So the debate went on and nothing much got done.

What were Mire and NAL doing?

I zoomed in closer on what they had in the boxes. Wait, what? It couldn't be—but was it? It was. There were some KuulSuits, last year's model, and some non-perishable foods, BUT. The vast majority of what was inside their donation cases was…eyelets.

They were distributing eyelets to climate refugee springoffs.

"Tell your stories!" "Share your days with the world." "This will help you. Inspire people to come save you. Have awareness of what you are experiencing and people will come to save you, give you homes in the inhabitable regions."

"We'll show you how to use it! All you need is your eyelet and a Reel account."

The springoffs loved the eyelets. They began having Moments put up onReel: eating the canned beans with delight; trying on the KuulSuits; running up and over piles of discarded electronics; fishing off the barge. One caught a fish with a tail like a dog!

Then NAL and Mire made their pitch to their watchers. *You can contribute! Buy them an eyelet so they can show the world their realspace, so they can share their story! YOU can help them share their story.*

꙰

It dawned on me that this was a great idea. What better avenue to action was there? Understanding the stories of those who needed our help had to be the first step. I donated immediately. I was into helping climate refugees, springoffs especially. Content on the barges, from the little I had glimpsed of it, put up onReel by old rogue eyelets they'd somehow gotten their hands on, looked quite rough.

Making that donation made me feel good. Made me feel better. I signed up as a recurring donor. Why not? I had the ReelCoin. So much ReelCoin! Why hadn't I thought of this sooner? One climate kid would get an eyelet every month because of me! What a relief to do some good in the world after marinating in my miserable rejection for so long.

In a temporary state of slight relief, I went on.

꙰

The ceremony, released in ReelTime, featured Stone Garden Buddha in center frame as NicAdán and Mire made their Public Declaration of permanent intimacy and companionship on either side of its cute little form. After shunning the entire insipid concept in Las Vegas, Nicolás Adán Luchano requested that Mire become their Publicly Declared Personal Intimacy Companion. The ceremony was quickly organized to take place in the landscaped backyard of their home with Stone Garden Buddha officiating.

I got to witness this Moment the way everyone did (on-Reel) realizing what was happening as I watched it happen. *Oh no,* I said to Dev. *Oh no they didn't! As if I needed something to make this even worse!* I turned it off for a moment before being unable to contain my curiosity and reverse-schadenfreude. I put it back on.

Their watch-numbs spiked as everyone realized, as the guests began to arrive, when the garden was revealed to have a certain look about it, what they were gathered for. *Was that an altar? Was that Stone Garden Buddha really officiating?* What would Nicolás Adán Luchano mind-change about next? Actual springoffs? Reels of the PICship ceremony revealed a circus spectacle sponsored by a fancy brand of champagne, a charming Parisian Public Declaration dress designer—Mire's dress was far more beautiful and ornate than the one I'd stupidly picked out and continued to wear; in fact, I was wearing it right then while watching this—and a cake company to ReelStars.

I ran into the bathroom, my stomach cramping as if it was about to explode, and the party came with me. As the toilet bowl cleaned itself of my post-intestinal detritus, I watched every Moment on repeat a few times through again. I continued this for days on end, lying on the floor with my legs propped up on the bed, Reels going on the ceiling: Mire walking the aisle; adoring fans throwing AR coins and flowers, hearts and prayer flags; Nicolás Adán Luchano beaming with pride as the Stone Garden Buddha officially pronounced this a Publicly Declared PICking for the duration of their content, 'til the arrival of their final PieCharts and into whatever lay beyond. Mire's best friend Chidinma Suarez read a poem composed for the occasion.

> *They say whatever our world is fucked up in waves and things just go on.*

RM from Flavio Chang
Decline to open. I'm in no condition.

filed for a week off to spend entire days rewatching the PICking ceremony and subsequent celebrations on an endless loop. Otherwise, my content was silent, long stretches of empty time. As long as I was watching, I was immersed, and as long as I was immersed, I could not feel that recoilsome cocktail of envy, jealousy, desire, and anger. As long as I stayed onReel, I could remain in a state of an odd and placid contentment. It was when I reverted to the realspace that everything hit me all over again. The watching kept my misery at bay during the time of watching and increased it exponentially as soon as I stopped, returning to the quiet emptiness of my realspace abode and noticing nothing else with human sentience in there. I let the Reels run at all hours instead, trying to merge with their content in order to numb my stupid pain. It's the worst kind of identification that Reel can bring about. As soon as the watcher ceases watching and is left in realspace and silence, the worse they feel, requiring another, longer bout of Reeling and so forth. I know it's the way it's designed but that doesn't mean I can un-choose it.

There were upsetting new minor details to notice every time: a sort of beaming pride in NicAdán's eyes when they looked at Mire. There was Mire's demure, understated way of moving through it all, as if to say, *Of course I'm this adored. No one is worthy of me but I make do.*

For Nicolás Adán Luchano, Mischa Osborn was a forgotten footnote, a sideswiped curiosity, a longpast blip, while for me it had been the most meaningful, frustrating, stickaround Moment in the duration of my content. It was driving me to glitches.

I replayed the ceremony one more time. This time, I stood up in front of Dev, still in the dress, and recited the vows as if I were Mire. *Yes, Nic, I do take you to be my Publicly Declared forever. Yes, I will bask in our intimacy companionship until the end of our days to come.* I recalled how the delivery drone had come so close to dropping the dress on me, how the dress lived, when it wasn't so frequently on my body, harmlessly draped on a wingback chair in the corner of my home/work space, worn and deflated, covered in the stains of drinks I didn't remember drinking, that not the strongest detergent could remove—purplish in tone, suggesting of a basic red wine…when did I ever drink wine?—and food I could not recall having eaten, which upon tastebud-inspection as I brought my tongue to the stain must have been spicy.

VI.

Me

What you could not remember, I could tell: yes, you drank four glasses of basic old-fashioned greenhouse-grown biodynamic red at 10 a.m. on a Tuesday, which prompted you to order a level-five spice platter from the Malaysian food truck stall in the basement before it was even lunch break. You always had food delivered upstairs since you worried about running into Softpants Flavio down there and risking another TIC. While you were wasted you got a bouquet of actually organic flowers in your windowbox, glanced at the card. It was from Softpants Flavio. Now there were flowers in your garbage. You fumbled through four afternoon Pro-Watcher client sessions you no longer remembered. Clients didn't notice your consciousness was altered. You can't really get a sense of that onReel. Such is the nature of remoteness. You could watch in altered states. You could watch sober. Simply, you were quite adept at watching, one among many of our shared traits. The more time you spent on them the more the AL showed them to you, to the point where you were watching them brush crumbs off their ten-thousand RC couch.

Funny, there was something else, something major, that you tried to wipe from your memory that I thought about often: the irony of your Mire-rejections back in the day. There were many strings of RMs you didn't recall receiving because at the time, Mire didn't mean anything at all. And that time when you'd first arrived at ArtSpace was so long ago, a different content sphere of which you only had vague memories and didn't rewatch onReel because you felt so awkward then, you would just as soon forget. You forgot that earlier version of Mire, the recent post-teenager and all the RMs they sent those early weeks in attempts to befriend you, the more sterling older student. These included but were not limited to: invites to gallery openings, various artist events, dinner at the warehouse loft Mire shared with ten artist roommates. They were attempts to catch up. They were questions, requests, and random updates. They were hopes to get together in the real-space. They were trying to cast bait toward a friendship. And you hadn't responded to a single one because you were only obsessed with your own content at that time. You imagined it was you who was destined for greatness. So you ignored Mire. You lacked interest. You had no way of knowing what they'd go on to become, realizing only from a distance how interesting they were. This made you bury any organic memory of their reachouts even more. Because if you'd come to mean something to Mire, they could have taken you along. It could have been you and Mire, you instead of Chidinma Suarez.

NicAdán had forgotten you. Mire had forgotten you. Why couldn't you forget about them? You would often go to do something else, *anything* else, and next thing you knew you would find yourself back onReel, consumed by the minutiae of their daily doings, all the tiny moments that would eventually add up to content totality. It wasn't helping you move on. Nothing was helping you move on. You weren't moving on at all. You were making it worse. And yet you couldn't stop. I understood. Neither could I. With every meaningful thing that happened to them—NicAdán's latest award, Mire's new interview about their ReelPoetry and favorite breakfast comida they ate growing up, with accompanying recipes—the deeper you sank. And I sank along with you.

You slept to the sound of their voices and projections of their dreams. You added Nicolás Adán Luchano and Mire D'Innit's Daily Gratitude Recital on ASMReel to lull you to sleep as your SomniBuddy breathed beside you for the additional necessary soothing to bring about depth of slumber. In the morning, you got up with Mire. Mire's morning began at four-thirty on the West Coast, rising before the sun to accomplish the important work of the day.

In the next Reel, Mire launched into a longer story that held watchers' attention, yours included, captive and absorbed: the discovery that the Stone Garden Buddha from Zen Home Gallery spoke. As in, it may have been an inanimate object, but it *really* talked. They knew something was unusual about it the Moment they felt it sitting so innocuously there, on a shelf at Zen Home Gallery. Its true capabilities were nothing short of a miracle. Some watchers questioned whether it was only a statue programmed with Reel technology, the same animating force granted to your ReelPals.

No, Mire said.

But how can you be sure? watchers wondered.

Look. The Buddha is made of stone. This is not technology, which means the only explanation is it's some kind of magic. What, we don't believe in magic? What have I been telling you all this time? Mire smiled a wry smile, the one that gave the appearance of knowing something critical that you did not.

More than a few watchers asked Mire, *If you're the only one who can hear it, how can you be so sure it's part of subjective realspace reality? And besides, aren't those the same thing—isn't it all technology, and all magic?*

Perhaps your assignment is to listen more closely, Mire replied.

The guru doubled down. And this was how pilgrims, thousands upon thousands of pilgrims and then more, began to descend on the meditation garden every week during the Open Devotion Hours established by Mire. The gates opened for the seekers to find out for themselves.

Dear Mischa, you did not answer my last letter. I hope you received it. We would still love to have you—

You tore up the second attempt from Henri. You panicked a little, as if the walls were closing in around you. You rushed to your afternoon session with Ari even though you didn't need to rush. Your commute was only to the next room. These sessions with Ari were your respites. When you ProWatched for Ari's time troubles, you could escape your own.

"It worries me lately," Ari said, "how difficult it's getting to do anything with Rumi." Rumi, who had turned seven, still had toddler content skills. They should have established their own Reels by now.

"You can't just sit back and wait for Moments anymore. You have to go out there and make them happen. How about the new playground?"

"I mean, things other moms seem to be able to easily do with their own springoffs, Rumi can't do them. Something's really…"

THE DISTRACTIONS

"I can help you help this not happen to you," you said. I listened closer than ever. You had an idea. A big idea. You were about to try and upend your entire content in another new way.

"What do you mean?" Ari tried to deflect.

"When something's off, I have something to offer."

"Nothing's off in my content."

"As a ProWatcher, I'm in the business of seeing these things."

"Well, there's nothing to see here." Ari's hands clasped and they flashed the gummy smile that meant unhappiness and the attempt to conceal it.

"I'm afraid it's become too obvious to hide, and I can tell you are too."

Ari got quiet and stared off into some seeming distance, trying to figure out a next move. No one had been so confrontational before. "What do you mean?"

"You said you wanted a friend, right? There's a new trial of a pilot program I've been in charge of developing here at Reel. I believe it might be of interest to you. It's tentatively called 'Restoring Humanity to Itself.'"

"Sounds like the name of a Mire D'Innit piece."

"It does!" I could tell you were feeling a little self-congratulatory right then, inventing such a thing on the spot. You'd been clever! And even better, it had been noticed.

"So what is it?" Ari was fully intrigued.

"Realspace Watchers."

This was the kind of thing people got sent to Blue Lake for doing. I'd seen it happen over and over. But I felt that if anyone could get away with deception, it was you. We were coming from inside the system, you and I, so we could fix things or shuffle them around.

Ari looked perplexed. "But that's what we're already doing."

"No. The realspace."

"You mean, come here?"

"Yeah, I'd like to leave here. Continue our work in a better space. Stay with you. In your home, all around your daily doings, as desired of course. I give you privacy when you need it but watch you as often as you'll want. No additional charge to your account, all that will stay the same, since it's, you know, a test. A trial." You tried to seem as if this had been in the works for a long time. "Over the last couple of years, I have thought of you often when we were brainstorming ideal test clients. As you've said, your home is plenty spacious. You haven't had a guest in at least as long as you've been working with me. It'll be refreshing, honestly."

"I don't know. Realspace interaction can be so…overwhelming."

"Take solace in the fact that even when you're perpetually watched, it isn't really about you. Even your most devoted watchers watch only for themselves. For identification. Consumption. Looking for what's in it for *them*."

Ari's eyes narrowed.

"Our sole purpose is to watch out for you. A ProWatcher will never lead you astray."

"I don't know."

"About?"

"Someone else being here. With me and Rumi, in the realspace—"

"What is it, Ari?"

"They're going to find out."

"And so? So what if they do?"

"I've built my content entirely around this."

"Nothing's ever the way it looks. Everybody knows that. I know. I mean, I've seen it. Why don't you shift it to one of those heroic Reels, you know, *Rumi Battles The Condition?*"

"Because Rumi doesn't have The Condition."

"But Ari—"

"Because they won't, soon. They're coming up with new treatments all the time. They're going to come up with a cure. I don't want to change it and then have to change it back when he's better. You have to keep it consistent if you don't want to lose more watchers than you'll gain."

"You cannot have negative watchers Ari."

"Oh, but you can."

"What happens then?" You mused.

"They take away your content."

"All of it."

"Mmhmm."

"As in, they literally obliterate you."

"Yes."

"And destroy your fleshly casing?"

"Exactly. Or at least send you to Blue Lake."

You shared your first laugh, even if it was an uneasy one. Your first Moment.

"I do enjoy our sessions," Ari said.

Here was your chance. Your walls were closing in. You needed to get out or risk staying inside your building until your final PieChart came. You would take it, I could tell.

"Likewise. So, I can start next month…"

Ari rested chin on palm and studied your face. "I'm getting tired of being alone. In the realspace, I mean. OnReel, I'm good. I'm never, ever alone onReel."

"I'll get travel arranged and get back to you soon with the details."

⋙⊙⋘

On the last day of those two years inside, you took your usual ten-mile walk, treadmill purring

beneath your cushioned feet as you walked along an endless stretch of sand on an infinite beach inside your mind, trying to puzzle out the meaning of Mire's latest ReelPoem. You read it aloud, reciting parts from memory and reading the rest as words scrolled by in your generated empty space. Simulated waves licked your feet like the attention-seeking puppies you occasionally admired on DogReel. The beach was boring, you decided. An empty space, so tiring.

You did what you'd been trying to avoid doing—had the treadmill take you to Mire's Reel instead, the one where they're reading these verses and Mire's reading is juxtaposed with other scenery from their latest content: a bushy-haired dog that looked like an enormous wild wolf, the sterling palm tree outside their window, them sitting contemplatively while sipping the latest blend of ReFocus Celebucha. Then there's the symbolic stuff: a river running that turns red as the sky turns black, a cake being smothered with frosting, a weird old doll being sewn. This is what you wanted. Immersed in Mire's content, you were no longer bored.

On the surface, the poem seemed to be about a vagina that never stopped bleeding, whose owner wasn't able to figure out what could be wrong with it, and winds up believing that maybe this was just some essential portion of inhabiting this particular body space.

THE DISTRACTIONS

Either that
Or they were
Coming apart at the
Seams—an experiment with some parts sewn
together and
Abandoned prior to completion

At the end, the narrator morphed into a ReelPal and so they could no longer bleed. You weren't sure what to make of the poem but noted it had earned Mire millions of HEARTS, STARS, CLAPS, AMAZES, and even the occasional SUPER-NOVA. And tons of HATES, TAKEDOWNS, and UGHs. More reactions, more revelations, more ReelCoin. Immersive Reelspace felt so good. You could mistake content generated or viewed in here for your very own.

⊰◉⊱

It was the last Reel you'd watch in this gym, on this treadmill, on the mezzanine of this building. You went upstairs, packed, and went to the FliPort for your evening flight; all increased heart rate and sweat output. Though your mission to Paris was a failure, though you still had no resolution on Nic Adán and Mire, though you'd given up—assuming you were going to be doing this onReel forever—a chance had arrived to really plunge into their orbit, to immerse yourself in their realspace this time by living in your quietly-desperate client's house. What were you going to do? That, even *I* couldn't predict with any reliable accuracy, though I did know I would enjoy watching how it all played out. You were sterling. You could handle it. I believed in you. You would have been glad to know that someone did.

VII.

Mischa

Who was it who said the only way out is through?

VIII.

This was Robert Frost, a poet before there were ReelPoets. I could have told you that, but you didn't need me to, though for you I would have done anything... if I could. You looked it up onReel just as you did to find every answer to all the questions that drifted in and out of your mind. You stared out the window the entire ride. It was midwinter and the Jacaranda trees lining the canyon roads were in full purple majestic splendor of bloom, while the distant mountain range was ablaze in a wash of orange and yellow light from the fires consuming the hills in the distance.

During this season, everything burned until there was nothing left. The flames subsided until there was something to burn again. These were the cycles now. We called them seasons: muggy, smoky, and fire. All ten lanes were nearly vacant, but inside the temperature-controlled passenger chamber of the mobi suite Ari had sent to pick you up, you finally looked relaxed, a slackness to your facial muscles I'd never seen before, rendering an expression I can only describe as peaceful. You luxuriated in the soft feel of the seats and the refreshing DRX tonic the mobi's AutoDriver proffered upon vehicle entry. When your client held prominent ReelStatus, you traveled in a state of deep comfort. No buses, boats, or barges.

You hadn't realized the gig you'd invented and even had approved by your team leader as part of your research into ProWatching (they didn't question your motivations, as a valuable employee) would come with perks. The biggest perk would be some kind of resolution in which you could finally forget all about NicAdán and Mire, leave them behind, and frolic off into the distance of your own beautiful, profoundly meaningful content.

But there was no meaning, no lesson, nothing you were supposed to take away. It hadn't happened for a reason, nothing did. You had to claim your losses and move on. In the case of Nicolás Adán Luchano and Mischa Osborn, it was arguable that there hadn't even been any loss other than an imaginary scenario you created only to end up surprised when it turned out NAL was inhabiting a completely different realspace than your own, one that was at odds with your version. But there is nothing surprising about that. It happens all over the place. I see it all the time.

Damp humidity hung in the air. Frogs and pseudocicadas cacophonized at all hours. LA is a jungle, it's been said, meant early on as a metaphor. Who could have known it was only a matter of the classic enemy, time, before LA became an actual jungle. After the eventual, gradual ecosystem and human-driven shifts left the radically altered landscape and new weather patterns and creature types—neither as entirely inhospitable as their historical visions of semiapocalyptic futures would have once predicted—certain people could locate benefits within these transitions.

Mire's meditation garden, for instance, was concealed by a natural scrim of lush greenery: areca palms, orchids, birds of paradise. Kakuma and fishtail, bred to be fireproof, heatproof, lightproof. They grew food and medicinal herbs and vines there, too, the likes of which would not have grown there during any time before: jackfruit, sugarcane, kava. Hot white light, windmill and Sago palms all crawling with vines, manicured to achieve that perfectly wild mashup. Concealed by a careful veil of lady palms and tall stalks of marijuana, the garden provided a loose impression of hiddenness in an age when truly concealing anything was impossible, Known-Eyelet Only barriers or not.

In the cool, air-filtered passenger chamber, you sipped a third chilled DRX tonic and rewatched NicAdán and Mire's Reels as you were transported up through CanyonGates all the way to Ari's resplendent manor. At this point I'd like to emphasize that there was some truth to the Blue Lake tagline: *Difficult roads can lead to the most beautiful destinations. Your troubles aren't troubles, they're signposts pointing the way.* Those were some good AdReels.

⋇◉⋇

The gate opened. The palatial house, identical to its onReel appearance, was tucked on the last cul-de-sac of CanyonGates. Once inside the invisible gates, carefully designed landscapes emulated natural fields and small forested areas separating each home from the view of the others; alone in an enclave, but knowing you were surrounded and never truly alone. NicAdán and Mire were only a few miles away in a house on the Eastern Edge—after being so physically far for so long, now they were so incredibly close. A pearl of sweat formed above your right eyebrow.

Rumi paced back and forth with an elegant, glassy looking ReelPal on the front lawn. The ReelPal's sheer eyes always appeared kind, and they listened as if they were really taking you in. You couldn't call them robots. It offended them. They knew connection, they could experience flow. They preferred *animus, definition two: motivation to do something.*

Had they grown souls? I sometimes wondered. Souls were motivated. But probably not, since ReelPals were fine with repetitive, mundane tasks and in possession of endless patience, while restlessness was a trademark characteristic of the souled. Demands of springoffs that would have a person plucking their hair strand by strand washed over a ReelPal, their programming designed to put up with anything the springoff they were designed and programmed for could dish out.

MamaReel showed Rumi's flash of a mouth-gesture that could be interpreted as a smile, something about another beautiful afternoon within their temperature-regulated yard, Ari walking out with a tray of iced tea, no one but me knowing Ari had added biodynamic tequila and DMT to their own, somewhat above the recommended microdosing proportion.

"Healthful agave reduction vitamin infusion," Ari called it, muttering justifications for ever-increasing consciousness alterations of various sorts during hours of light. It was justifiable though. Rumi started screaming, pulling off their clothes, pulling at their hair. Ari called Baley down to dock and that was when they saw the mobi suite. Though Ari had been expecting you, they nearly dropped the tray. A stranger had never come to the estate, though you were not exactly a stranger, either.

The trunk of the car Ari had sent for you offloaded your suitcase.

You took your first breath of indoor/outdoor air.

"I taste ash."

"You'll get used to it. Something's always on fire."

"Well, happy birthday."

THE DISTRACTIONS

You reached out your arms toward the realspace Ari, who received this stiff hug in awkward compliance, as if neither of you had made physical contact with another person in a very long time. Rumi certainly didn't tolerate that kind of contact well. You and Ari had an exceptionally high bonding ratio and you'd only just realspace met. You had more in common than you knew.

Ari studied you, examining your face in the realspace for the first time. Ari's brows were arched more dramatically than nature would have them, their face more angular and catlike than it appeared onReel. Large eyes, glossy with slight alteration. Ari sipped the contents of the tiny bottle. They had an ageless look that allowed for little movement anyplace above the chin. Hide your age but reveal your desperation to hide it as a result, and your own face becomes a mask.

"I'm glad you're here." Ari's voice was lower, with a melancholic tinge that was kept offReel. "Forty. *Damn.*"

"Me too! We are going to get so much done for you. No more distractions. No procrastinating. No useless feelings that serve no purpose other than creating ideal conditions for eternal self-sabotage."

You could have been talking to yourself. The lawn was empty. Rumi and the ReelPal were gone.

"Can I meet your adorable springoff? I got a chance to watch every backReel of *Restaurant Reviews With Rumi*, it was so good."

"Maybe later. Rumi's with their Pal all day today. We already captured our daily content."

"Then what else do we—do you—need to accomplish today?"

"I have to head to the gallery but I'll really need you later, when it's time to get ready for my birthday guests."

You followed Ari into the Tyler-McKenna household. It felt as if we'd been here before, and in a very real sense we had. In the realspace, though, it appeared even more majestic, one of those very rare things that actually looked more impressive offReel than on. A scan of the bookshelf revealed Ari was a devotee of all of Mire's ReelPoetry realspace collections and their *D'Innit Guides to Content Ultimification*. Reels of the Zen Home Gallery Stone Garden Buddha Wisdom scrolled across the walls, original artwork, a gift from the artist: *That which you seek is awaiting you. You will find what you are looking for once you are no longer looking. You will know exactly where to go and when to stop.*

Fragmented attention is neither an illness of our time, nor of all time, nor is it an illness at all. Success is as impermanent a state as content itself. Here today, gone tomorrow.

Whatever you want to have, something or someone somewhere is longing to gift it to you.

Envy: It's super-scary and embarrassing. But how do you get over it and get on with your own content when immersed in this unpleasant and addictive mindset?

THE DISTRACTIONS

Shame about your jealousy doesn't make you any less jealous.

How do you fulfill your own infinite potential and grow toward your infinite potential self when you spend so much time wondering about how someone else managed to fulfill their own destiny of becoming their own potentially infinite self?

The answer, my beloveds. Let them not inspire envy, let them simply inspire.

"Come on or you'll stand here all day mesmerized by that," Ari said, breaking your Stone Garden Buddha-induced reverie. "It's hard to let it be background, but that's part of the art."

"They're an incredible genius." You sized the bookshelf up and down, all of Mire's titles, not knowing Ari hadn't read half of them. "All the geniuses say so."

Being into Mire D'Innit was a coincidence in the realm of wearing the same brand of nail polish or owning the same pair of hardpants: too widespread to really be coincidental at all.

"NicAdán and Mire have their first collaboration coming up," Ari said. "They've been working on it for as long as they've been together. It's going to be huge."

Ari led you through palatial hallways of infinite house. "And my MamaReel…. Forget it, I need there to be two of me. When you made this offer, it was totally the solution. Since the cloning thing isn't exactly working out yet"—Ari gave a thoughtfully timed wink along with a slight wave—"you'll have to do. And by that I mean, thank you."

225

Ari was funny. I hadn't known whether you would real-space-enjoy the company of a posh dystopian soccer mom, which didn't meet compatibility ratio quotients on the surface. But I did suspect, from accessing PrivateReel, that there was more to Ari than that glossy onReel appearance of their having it all tied together, the gallery, the Full-on Mama Experience, a sterling home and the most sterling PICking with Joaquin. All wasn't as it seemed on those carefully curated Moments that Baley chose to show watchers on endless repeat.

Strategically, as they were approaching the master bedroom, you asked for the bathroom.

"The master suite is closest, but it's an EF-Z."

Dev docked on the outside of that fascinating chamber. The only portals to the ReelWorld were a NaniCam and SmartHome Security. Ari led us down a different hallway, past the door to the hallway which held the secret door. We turned a corner. The master bedroom was airy and white. Even over many years of fuzzy existence, I had never seen such a white interior, accentuated with billowy curtains, a massive balcony with lounger chairs, and views all the way to Sawtelle Shores.

In the distance, the toxic ocean glimmered. It all looked so innocuous from here. It was even impossible to tell which trees were naturemade, which ones manufactured. Drone-Beez pollinated tropical flowers with droplets. The city was a perfect storm of interior design and exterior landscaping, the biological at war with the manufactured. In this far-flung corner of paradise, you shuffled around on Ari's side of the counter: all makeup and tubes and tiny glass bottles, rows and rows of those little glass bottles lining the mirror. Ari had organized all of the tiny bottles, medications, and droppers for morning microdosing sessions by size and color and their varying strengths of dosage. They credited microdosing with making them a better mother and person, we knew from MamaReel. There were substances to infuse patience, increase tolerance toward irrational behavior of PICs, family, and friends, and even to return your own state of consciousness to a child's mindset for the purposes of collaboration and imaginative play.

In some Reels, Ari demonstrated how a droplet of this and a droplet of that—even if scientifically unsanctioned—could create pure alchemy, finely crushing tablets of controversial Meaning Pills. I recalled the third nipple and wondered if there would come another time to get a glimpse of it, and whether you would find out about Ari's other undisplayed secrets.

"You okay in there?" came Ari's voice as you ran your fingers across bottles, reading all the little labels, fascinated to be there in the realspace. I didn't blame you. The stuff we watch onReel *feels* famous.

You shouted back that you were fine. That you would be right out. You waved your hand past the toilet to trigger the flush. The faucet opened and you passed your hands beneath so your true actions would go untraced by the home's intelligence mechanisms' records of who had done exactly what and when within its very smart walls. Even your house is watching you. But we can't call it spying if you know about it and do not care. We should instead say your house has your best interests at heart. Your house will not stop short of informing you if an entrant, who initially may appear harmless, is an intruder. Some of the newer technology has radically improved at reading intentions. It's getting better about that.

Downstairs in the kitchen, the domestic ReelPal combined some fresh squeezed lemon and doubly fermented Celebucha and poured it into ice-filled glasses, stuck in the copper straws, and handed them each one.

"Cheers. Welcome to my realspace content."

Ari appeared to be recognizing and first digesting the possibility that this new Realspace ProWatcher was truly a person, and someone who might know more than expected. For the first time since your arrival, Ari appeared to be contemplating: *Who have I invited into my home?* They Ari-esquely pivoted toward a sugary subject.

"Have you been to the self-service cupcake machine?"

"This is my first time in LA. All I've seen of it so far is some landscape out the mobi window and the inside of your house."

"I need to get cupcakes for the party and it would be nice to have some company around here, I mean, besides Rumi. Like, another grown up."

"Is there such a thing?"

"As a grown up?" Ari looked puzzled. They got into the mobi suite. Rumi sat huddled in back, staring at nothing.

"Rumi's just in a little bit of a mood today," Ari said. "It'll burn off. Actually, they're going to be doing a lot better soon."

Ari was planting the hints. I knew the lengths to which Ari had gone, having a kid with a Reel persona and, in the dark of night, an idea after Janice Waller.

⊰⊙⊱

It was going to be a custom. It would lack the outbursts, the unpredictability, and it only needed to be charged up with the fluids every now and again. Nobody knew. Not even Joaquin knew. It was nowhere even you could see. And when it arrived, I would be there to see the switches, one Rumi coming out with the ReelPal and the other going into parts of the house where only I could go, security eyes not so secure. Not that I was a threat to anything, unless knowing someone's secret counted as a threat.

The mobi drove. Outside, orderly city streets boasted storefronts filled with springoff play spaces, a few scattered remaining realspace stores and Cafélandias filled with people who were pretending to work but were watching Reels in secret.

"Do you ever leave Rumi with the ReelPal?"

"Yeah, but there's the extreme separation anxiety. So I try to do it as little as possible, as my sanity allows."

"What do they do?"

"Oh…just the usual things springoffs do…scream, cry. Throw tantrums then more tantrums after that. Lots of tantrums."

"But ReelPals don't mind."

It was true. The ReelPal didn't. Ari had already thought of everything. They were steps ahead of you but they played along.

"It's a consequence of my own mistake. Took them everywhere for MamaReel and now…I can hardly go anywhere without them."

"Aren't you the one in charge?"

Ari sighed. "Those who don't have springoffs struggle to understand who's really in boss mode."

You peered back at the little mop-headed Rumi. Rumi was a beautiful springoff, with a delicate featured face, shimmery blue pools for eyes, skin so smooth and soft. With such excellent genes it was no wonder Ari and Joaquin hadn't opted for PreSelection. I felt they should have been proud of this no matter what the result—everyone wants control of everything these days—though the Rumi visible OnReel had only ever been adorable; none of those low-toned animal groans or array of other indecipherable sounds that represented their favorite mode of communicating made it on. The AL picked up on discomfort, leaving that off entirely. The problem was that the content was getting more and more pared down. If this continued, soon enough there would be no content at all.

At the machine, Baley beamed ReelCoin for the cupcakes, the twenty-four pack, way too many on the surface, but Ari would eat the rest in the closet in the dark under the secure home's watchful eye.

The guesthouse for you to sleep in was four times the size of the bathroom, which itself was twice the size of your apartment. You unpacked while watching Reels: NAL of course, and Mire, and a few clients to make sure they were sticking to their content plans. Let it flip to random for a while. Some HomeReels. A climate refugee springoff, one of those who benefitted from the eyelet donations—"We need blankets and supplies"—*Oh, that is so depressing! Skip.* Back to Mire, NAL, Ari's MamaReel even though it was Ari's house you were Reeling from inside of.

You squirreled away the dress underneath everything else in the back of the closet. How much ReelCoin did Ari and Joaquin earn? Did Joaquin's fiscal contributions help compensate Ari for their PIC's secret content as a ReelFisher? Joaquin's eventual PieChart would reveal that he'd traveled more for work than time spent at home: Did Ari care what else their PIC was doing on those realspace business trips? Or had their emotional state become closer to one of the ReelPals in the massive fleet they used to manage their household and Rumi? At least Joaquin was coming home for their PIC's birthday dinner party—Vegas to Japan to South Africa to London and back to LA—just in time for when the first guests would arrive. You killed an hour and thirty-seven seconds letting Reels play while organizing your new room, then told Dev to shut it down.

As you helped prepare for Ari's birthday, I Reeled back upon your own fortieth. It had passed like any other day, with you alone in your apartment, clearing content and intermittently keeping an eye out for happy birthday messages onReel. A few came in, mostly from your siblets from back in the day. You had dinner droned in from your favorite cart in the food disco: the Bomb Mi, a spicy chikn sandwich on French bread, and a Rosewater Citrus DRX. You drank your drink and mauled your sandwich alone, watched a bit of Mire and tried again to close-read the stones along the path that had landed Mire in the land of such acclaim, and closed your eyes to dreams about Mire, talking with Mire again, asking if Mire still went by the same name. At ArtSpace they'd had a different one, but somewhere along the path to the Bestie® it changed again. You murmured to your SomniBuddy as you drifted toward sleep, as if things would somehow make sense on return from unconsciousness.

You watched onReel from the guesthouse as the door opened and the first guests trickled in. Mire had gained some weight—even a few pounds loudly announced their presence on Mire's narrow frame. Mire also appeared slightly haggard despite a sterling shade of lavender lipstick. They clutched a cat carrier with Mavis inside. Mire and Mavis were dressed in matching sweaters for one of the personas, a new MIREplica, part of the art.

Ari and Mire exchanged air kisses.

"Happy birthday," Mire said. "I can't stay too late. And I know I look like shit with these bags under my eyes. Mavis hasn't been sleeping well lately. And I have to get up at four in the morning to work on the pieces otherwise I can't accomplish a single thing."

"Maybe you should get one of these new ProWatchers that come to your house," Ari said. "This one's mine."

You pulled up your SterilAire Facedrape as if you were stepping into a crowded FliPort rather than Ari's intimate party.

"Hi, nice to meet you," you gripped Mire's hand a little too hard. But Mire didn't notice. Some people did such things around strangers. Mire kept talking about how they and NicAdán worked separately until one got stuck, then they showed each other what they had and began to exchange pieces of the projects for the other to add to, a conversation in Reel exchange. It was an ideal process, they said in every onReel interview about their collaboration—interviews I scanned in seconds—solitary and collaborative at the same time, in equal measure.

233

"When does NicAdán get back?"

"Tomorrow. How about Joaquin?"

"Any minute now, I hope. They decided to go to every single ReelCon and to try to make it back in-between." They shrugged as if it was no big deal but you knew better.

Other guests trickled in: a few of Ari's MamaReel friends, a Style and Salvation editor from Skaboop, and the gallery owner, gray hair sculpted like a helmet and a stylish face shield. You milled around, watching Ari speaking defensively about Joaquin's absence.

"An unfortunate side effect of all this." Ari went on, as if filling the entirety of the void with sound might keep what was realspace-real at bay. Ari gestured around as if to embrace the entire room. It was true. The house was majestic, though if you looked at it from a certain angle it looked like a cruise ship parked atop a canyon, forever beached on a peak of earth that could crumble at any Moment and send it all toppling. "But like I said, Joaquin will make it. Joaquin wouldn't miss my birthday."

Rumi came downstairs, perfectly dressed in a tiny suit, hair slicked back with one illuminating streak of glowiring. You appraised their presence, as if you were wondering how the ReelPal managed to get them to be so perfect and together. Smiling. And quiet. As Rumi approached Ari, you darted to Ari's side first.

"Is Rumi supposed to be down here?" you asked.

Ari turned around and also assessed their springoff.

"Very nice. Yes, don't worry. Rumi's supposed to be here."

As you observed Rumi holding their mama's hand, looking up at guests with a new clarity in their eyes, merely smiling sweetly and making no noise, you appeared puzzled, trying to understand the change.

THE DISTRACTIONS

By five in the morning, Rumi long gone to bed, horizon lit by orange flames and breaking heat, Ari was significantly altered and Joaquin was still nowhere to be seen. All the guests had departed and it would have felt as if the party never happened if it weren't for all the detritus left behind as evidence a gathering occurred here. After hiding in the guesthouse, you were back in Ari's realspace presence, cooking alongside the shimmering ReelPal.

Ari had too much DRX, a few macrodoses, and too little food. The guests ate it all while Ari ran around refilling glasses instead of letting the ReelPal do it. It gave them something to do with their hands, a way to quell realspace proximity anxiety, which lingered like a permanent hangover, and ensured every Moment of the party was Reelworthy at all times. In the bathroom upstairs, the shower was running. Ari was trying to act sober. Not a single one of the little dropper bottles lining the mirror was out of place.

When Ari came back out a while later in a silky caftan over roomwear, you served a plate of steaming No-Klam alle vongole with a dash of parsley sprinkled on top.

"Thank you," Ari said. "I guess turning forty comes with a bit of a rough time no matter how it looks."

"I understand."

"I don't think anyone's ever cooked for me," Ari said. "Not that I can remember."

"What about when you were a kid?"

Ari pointed at Dev, whose colorful point of flashing light indicated you were in a Moment, your pulse quickening and mood elated by your client's gratitude, so you called Dev to dock. Whatever was coming was something Ari didn't want watchers to know. When Dev was safely docked in Blind-Mode on your wristperch, Ari answered.

"I was alone. My mother was dead and my father was never around."

"What happened to your mom? You never say—"

Ari turned instantly defensive. "I'm not engaging in a competition of sad infancy circumstances, Mischa."

"What makes you think I want to do that?"

"I'm not telling you some story so you can relate to it," Ari said. "I just want to be heard, you know?"

"Of course. And I'm listening."

Ari exhaled audibly.

"*Really* listening," you emphasized.

Ari gave up and went on to tell the story, which led to your understanding of how the two of you were connected beyond the former ReeledIn Conference Suites affair with Joaquin, who then became Ari's PIC.

"I was three weeks overdue or whatever, and so they got placed with the Surgical ReelPal for routine extraction procedure. Death is attributed to a massive blood clot in the lung not even the surgical ReelPal detected forming, an extremely rare .001 percent occurrence. I guess I'd been whisked by Neonatal ReelPals into the nursery to stave off potential infection, so they never even got to hold me."

"Well, I don't mean to engage in a competition of sad infancy circumstances, but at least yours wanted you. Mine left me with some strangers on a beach and either swam away somewhere else and escaped responsibility forever or drowned. It went uncaptured so official records state it never happened. How did it go uncaptured? How? And you know what I never thought of? My mother disappears and I go on to believe I'm invisible, incapable of being seen. That is super incredibly obvious, now that I'm talking about it. Any VirtuTherapist could have told me, but I've resisted those my whole content."

"That's the reason for friends or ReelPals. Left to our own devices, we miss those things delivered with absolute clarity. We aren't meant to be trapped inside our own skulls."

"No, we are not. So, you weren't close with your dad either?"

"Dad was one of the principal aesthetic alterationists on BoKa's team." Aesthetic alteration activist Boba Kanoba, famed for having designed their own breasts the size of basketballs and Reeling for the right to mutilate—no, self-enhance—one's body to the point one desired based on personal preferences and aesthetic impulses. "I guess my dad felt so guilty they weren't around when I was born or when my mom died that they just lost themselves in work, working and working, aiding others on the quest for aesthetic perfection. Can you imagine being a surgeon and not being able to save your own PIC?"

"Didn't Boba Kanoba's chest explode? How was it even medically ethical to do that? Are some flesh-modifiers exempt from the Hippocratic oath? I mean, that was definite harm. Even if the procedure was requested just so."

"Everything Boka did was in service of increasing their watch-numb. To the degree of self-harm. Not like it's that unusual."

Boba Kanoba—the origins of this self-chosen name went unexplained, though there was a long-gone Croatian restaurant by a similar name in preReel archives—was an activist in the area of aesthetic surgical choice. UniHealth didn't cover elective procedures, the clinical name for making breasts the size of freight elevators. BoKa had well over a million watchers. Who knew whether their watchers admired or looked at them like an exhibit in a museum of strange phenomena, or both simultaneously; people loved to watch things they decided were freakish. Boka knew this, and was playing it for ReelFame.

"What do they see when they look in the mirror?" you asked.

"Something different than most of us."

"Or not. Probably playing it for watchers," you said. "Who isn't? Boka wanted ReelCoin. Plenty of ReelCoin's what they got."

"No one sees the same thing." Ari dug into the pasta. "Normally, I wouldn't eat something like this but I'm so hungry and you're such a good cook."

"Better than the ReelPal?"

"When Rumi was a baby, I said to Joaquin, 'You know, all I want is a robot that's a nanny and a housekeeper in one.' We had our first ReelPal the next day. The fleet kept growing. And yet somehow nothing still seems to ever really get done."

"Sometimes the easy way, the obvious way, the straightforward way, is the furthest thing from *the* way."

Ari swallowed. You sat silently for a moment, quickening pulse and slight underarm dampness indicating you were working on the courage to ask a real question.

"Rumi was different tonight—why?"

"Oh," Ari said. "Just seems to be responding well to the new therapy."

"That must be some therapy! They were really totally different—like a different springoff."

THE DISTRACTIONS

"Yep. It's great, so great that even *Restaurant Reviews With Rumi* is coming back!"

"That's wonderful," you said. Still, a sheen of watery substance suddenly blurred Ari's otherwise radiant eyes before a single hard blink erased it. Proof of sadness, if not the sadness itself, receded.

Watching Ari had granted you with an important balancing gift: though in possession of glamorous, beautiful, and sponsored content, Ari's existence was also predicated on some very deep suffering. This kind of watching evokes gratitude rather than envy. It teaches you that things could be, to put it simply, worse, even when watching a person who seemingly has it so much better.

The next morning, Ari wandered into the guesthouse. You were crouched over, ProWatching for yet another pornReel-addled victim who struggled to maintain the habit throughout days spent running a multinational company for lightweight and meltproof faux-stone carved patio furniture.

"I thought we were working together exclusively." Ari's voice was hoarse.

"You did?"

"I could have sworn you said…"

"We never agreed on exclusivity…"

"Can we make it happen? Who manages your watchload?"

Your face erupted into a spread-out smile. Finally, for once, things were going your way. Sometimes the most interesting view is the one from a place where no one would ever know it was you. Ari leaned down to pick up a sweater of yours from the floor and toss it on the bed. Their emerald blouse fell forward, loose, and you looked a bit longer than you should have at the space between Ari's armpit and breast. There, you saw it: the small lump, the extra nipple. It was like a third eye, perfectly positioned to glimpse the depths of the inevitable.

"I handle my own watchload," you said. "Consider it done."

Now that the therapy was working, Ari took Rumi out to lunch before heading to the gallery. You returned to the guesthouse for your own indulgent break, relieved to get

240

some undisturbed personal time for a much-deserved and overdue watching session. You watched Ari MamaReeling from Sydney Japão, a new Brazilian sushi steakhouse and Australian barbecue. You were impressed: *Restaurant Reviews with Rumi* was back indeed. Somehow Ari had managed this. Rumi nibbled selections of tiny PetriMeat steak slices dipped in barbecue sauce. Lots of *mmmm*'s and *aaaah*'s but also something we have not seen before: "This is really good, Mama!" "Thumbs up!" "Five Stars!" and "Supernovas" to the PetriMeat BBQ Hikikomori Facão Roll.

"Maybe things really can work out," you said to Dev, who blinked. "Let's see what Mire's up to." The Reel switched to a different lunch in a posh speakeasy bistro on the Eastside.

Mire had departed their lauded desk to meet fellow Bestie®-winning ReelPoet Chidinma Suarez for a sunny afternoon in the enclosed outdoor patio at Sweet Envy, which had twenty-seven million plus watchers at any given moment. The world loved watching those who could go to Sweet Envy in the realspace. The French DRX-infused premium vintage Mire and Chidinma Suarez sipped in a tucked-away yet light-filled corner was the most popular beverage in Los Angeles, with millions of watchers of its own, watching Reels of people drinking it all over the world, from New Miami to Lebanon to the most remote bar in the swankiest resort on Tristan da Cunha. Even those who hated the ReelStars loved to watch them. The ReelElves got their own Moments out of disdain for people like Mire and Chidinma, who earned massive followings despite myopically whiling away an afternoon on creative pursuits while the world burned all around. Thing is, in a constant state of fire, you get used to the smoke.

That afternoon, Mire wore a yellow dress and striped black and white vinyl boots; stunning, no question about that. You were just sitting there in torn softpants, ragged even for softpants, and a wrap-around sweater and no bra, silently watching their conversation for the entire ninety-six minutes and fifty-four seconds of its duration.

You had ordered French DRX-infused vintages by the caseload back in Brooklyn after your observation that this was one of Mire's favorites, even if you knew Mire was paid to drink it, to design the labels, and represent the company, it was still, at the end of the day, what Mire really liked to drink. Mire ordered rosewater kombucha champagne with a shot of the extra-smoky mezcal on the side, poured in little by little to maintain consistency of the flavor profile.

This, Mire told us, was the ritual that led to the composition of their most stunning, lauded ReelPoems. Mire must drink this one shot of this particular mezcal in this exact timeframe, with Chidinma, talking about everything they would accomplish, making their next great plans that will entail their next lauded Reels. Mire would go home and write ReelPoetry between three and nine, then face-slough with BioDegrad™ PoreBeads and slather on a coat of BioDegrad™ PoreBeads MoistureFacing, put out a few more sponsored poems containing repetitions of the words "pore" and "bead" and subsequently fall asleep until their eyelet soothes them awake in whispered verse at five-forty-two in the morning.

In those hours of dawn, Mire would work again, finishing by nine so as to have the main part of the day to venture into the realspace and seek some quality inspo for the afternoon content-generation session. This is what it was, you marveled, to be sponsored, compensated, watched, revered, recorded, and rewarded for doing as you pleased. The ultimification of charmed content.

The thing about so much watching is that you inadvertently trained yourself to become quite observant, attuned to details and their significance—the ways people behave when they are oblivious to being watched.

Chidinma was all in black, hair freshly glowired, lips fluorescent. Mire gestured wildly while speaking, nodding and waving for emphasis. They were locked into each other's stare, each enraptured by the other's brilliance, caught tight in a web woven by their own words.

It was just two friends catching up over consumables, but to you it was agonizing. Looking at their eyelets, constantly lit, their owners perpetually in a Moment, one after the next.... You couldn't handle all that energy. Mire pontificated on a latest theory that arose during their morning sessions as the blanket of heatfog and firesmoke rolled in off the mountains, simultaneously blown back away by repellerfans and sucked through the air filtration system.

"Ever since I brought home the Buddha, it won't stop sending messages about The Theory of Effortlessness. By learning to sit still and close our eyes to the illusions, we get what we're looking for. The longer I sit, the more my statue says, *Send out the energy of what you long for, direct your energy toward it, and so it shall become.* It will gladly show up! It's so simple! Ask. Then focus. Content is nothing but a mindset."

"And therefore… everything is an illusion?"

"Set your mind. Change your content. This is what I'm writing the inspirational speech for my next TripleD about.

I'm calling it 'TripleD and Rippled.' What we mistake for re-realspace is actually happening inside our minds—we can only see it through our eyelets and our eyes. Since nothing is real, our thoughts and beliefs generate what we perceive as real-space-reality. So we need to make them count in the direction of achieving our desires. And no *desire* is wrong, whether for love, success, fame…seeing the entire content arena, creating change…"

Here, Mire showed some climate refugee Reels made possible by their donations.

"No desire should be off limits," Chidinma said. "This proves it."

"Yes. That's how you achieve the most and best onReel Moments."

"Through the extreme, or the exceptional?"

"Ideally both."

"Can I sit in front of the magical talking Zen Home Market Stone Garden Buddha to compose my next bout of poems this evening?"

"You never have to ask! Just come. Your poetry…your process…*is* the antidote."

The Reel ended there, flipped to the next Moment. The Stone Garden Buddha may have been a device, but it worked. Everyone with a message needed a thing to help transmit their message. What was the use of a message if no one paid attention because you didn't have a thing?

The next afternoon, you went to NicAdán and Mire's house while they were away. It wasn't even open devotional hours. You disabled the security Reel (one of the many things I admired about your skills, the ease with which you could do such things, along with the fact that you rarely ever deployed your less moral abilities). You walked through the content arena undetected. Not as undetected as I could go, but still. You seemed to derive genuine pleasure from sitting there in the bushes behind the meditation garden. What were you doing back there? Meditating? Were you trying to feel what it would be like to be Mire in the earliest hours of morning? No sponsors, no demands, no checking on someone, no someone checking in. No distraction. Only you being one with one true and still and meditative silence, becoming an open channel through which to receive wisdom you'd then deliver to millions of watchers who were eagerly anticipating and awaiting this onReel content. Dream content.

You can make it so, the Stone GB whispered.

I watched you fall backwards into the dirt. Shocked that, *The damn thing really does talk.*

You have written yourself off! There is no such thing as fate. Or stasis.

You stared at it and it stared right back. How did it manage to be stony and yet so vivid?

A ReelAlert: Mire's newest content—category: new restaurant—was now available for watching. Their current status:

onTrack to CanyonGates/Home. You fled toward the waiting mobi, making it away moments before theirs pulled up.

⊰◉⊱

Hoping for a realspace conversation with a friend like the talks Mire and Chidinma had, you opened the door to Ari's office. You burst through the door and were met with a shock. You inhaled sharply and dropped to the ground when you saw it, trying to get out of sight—did the thing have sight?

In the center of the room, in an open space right in front of you, ascending up from out of Mire's soon-to-be-classic installation, the Envy Nest, came the enormous, floating, disembodied head of Nicolás Adán Luchano. And the enormous floating disembodied head of Nicolás Adán Luchano was peering right at *you*. You dove under the desk to hide. Could the thing *see* you? Ari wasn't in the office. A quick check of the houscan revealed a realspace body presence in the master bathroom, where they were engaged with afternoon microdosing.

"Hey Ari, I wouldn't mind having a view," said the massive disembodied head of Nicolás Adán Luchano. "I can hear you fine, but it's really just looking blurry in there."

You tried to make yourself even smaller, crouching behind the desk.

Ari walked back in. "Why are you hiding?"

You peered at the portal and shoved yourself further beneath the desk like a shark-stalked octopus under rocks.

NicAdán's voice: "How's the Adán Portal looking when it pops up from the Envy Nest?"

THE DISTRACTIONS

"Sorry, one second here, I've got a ProWatcher coming... on, let me just exit that session."

"You have a ProWatcher?"

"What, you think I get it all done on my own?" Ari glared, but the glare was directed at you. You offered a meek smile and Ari looked away. "Okay. It's sterling. It says everything about the state of our content conditions. This is the absolute. It's going in the center of the space, in the interior circle. I'm obsessed with it. I literally can't stop watching."

Just what the audience needed: *more* watching.

"Leave it on," NicAdán said. "I need to spend more time finding things to do."

"This is going to be your greatest achievement since *Spatial Serveillance Work In Space*."

The Adán Portal was a daring 24/7 exposé of NicAdán's PrivateReel, the stuff their PieChart would be made of, a lens into their content entirety—not the Reelspace version but the realspace one. In other words, exactly what you had been trying to see: The everyday mundane of tooth-brushing and avocado-salsa-bowl chip-dipping and mouth-smashing, of waking up next to Mire, glossy hair disheveled, wiping drool from their mouths, yawning. Cracking their eyes open like brand new baby birds at the start of another miraculous day uplifted by observing that every day, the existence of any small thing that would soon become utterly miraculous. Of drinking DRX teas, attending onReel meetings with sponsors and ReelManagers, and GABE barking about workouts and so pausing the rest to work out with GABE. Mandated interactions with watchers. General Content Maintenance. All of it was now part of the Adán Portal. That Reelspace sheen would dissolve to the point where only the realspace would remain.

Then you realized, and once you did, you became very, very angry.

Ari began reading from a draft of the gallery materials.

"Most Moments, even of Reelworthy content, are not in themselves Reelworthy. The Adán Portal reveals that, commenting on it profoundly through its very existence. Look at these Moments, ones that even in perpetual capturing would go uncaptured or unremarked upon, springing forth from Mire D'Innit's own miraculous commentary on the ReelAge, the ubiquitous, delightful, and haunting Envy Nest."

"That is my idea!" you yelled, suddenly not caring who could hear you. Your great, failed idea! It had been swiped away by a ReelStar who would soon be getting it famous—and taking credit.

Ari quickly muted the room as you raged on.

"That's Project Alovue! The AL that loves you so much it selects all your sleepworthy everyday moments as capital Moments! NicAdán said they liked it. Now they stole it!"

The pink neon flashing across the Reelspace display—*Envy.Nest*—was almost complete.

"What are you even talking about, Mischa? This is truly original work. NicAdán didn't 'steal' anything. NicAdán doesn't do that. NicAdán would never need to. NicAdán is a genius."

"Before I did any of what I do now, my prized project was an AL that would truly love you, as truly as only another person could before. This was going to be what kept everybody company, what solved loneliness forever, what took over for social content-curation ALs. The problem was, it was awful and terrible at curating Moments. It was less interested in your grand accomplishments and adventures than your tiny quirks. I'd engineered it for love but set it up for failure. My content's great passion was a failure. And this so-called 'Adán Portal'? It's the exact same thing."

"If that's so, it is entirely coincidental."

"You're going to defend them even though I, your real-space friend, am telling you they stole my idea? They knew about it! We met at ReelCon once and talked about Project Alovue—"

"It doesn't matter, Mischa, because nobody owns ideas. Where there's no ownership there can be no theft."

Ari unmuted the room and got back to work as if nothing had happened. "Sorry NicAdán, I had to take care of something for Rumi real quick."

You stood back, incapable of asking for more. You watched Ari watching NicAdán. In that moment, I felt you could truly understand my world. Even I could practically experience a certain queasiness as it rose through your chest and into your throat. The same dread I knew from being trapped in here, I watched it consume you. I could sense it, recognize it, as if you had gotten exactly what you wanted only to discover it was horrible.

Did people do that all the time? Achieved a dream only to realize it wasn't what you thought it would be, and in fact turned out not to be anything you wanted at all? And then what? Was there something else? Could there be? And if there was, what if it wasn't in the future but in the past? You had been so comfortable during those two years you'd spent inside, watching from a safe distance far away. Now you were flying too close to the hot center. *You should escape from your escape!* I wanted to yell, if only I had a voice. *Just go back! Smudge some sage. Call it a day. Forget this.* But I could not. And anyway, it was still entertaining…at least it was for me.

At night, as the house slept, I watched you touch the portal, firm like rubber but ripply like water. It was easily pressed on. A one-way mirror. NicAdán couldn't see what was out there, and though this caused discomfort, it was purposeful. That was the work, the art, the act. As the sun rose and the day commenced, you remained glued to the Adán Portal (be careful what you wish for) and watched, coming right toward you:

NicAdán leaning over into a sink, spitting a mouthful of suds. The sound of toothbrush on enamel.

Mire at their own sink next to NicAdán's. (What was with all these PICs with their respective matching adjacent sinks? Why can they not sink-share?) NicAdán leaned over and kissed Mire. Waited for Mire to walk out of the bathroom. Sat on the toilet. Wiped. Took a shower, dried off. Fifteen naked push-ups on the bedroom floor ensued. Inspected muscles in the mirror. Got dressed.

Breakfast: Avocado bowls in an avocado, daintily topped with dabs of Mire's homemade xtra-spiced harissa, which watchers could purchase in microdoses for 18.98 RC onReel. They enjoy small spoonfuls of the stuff on everything they eat. They say it benefits the kidneys as well as the spleen and asplendix.

THE DISTRACTIONS

Ari came in and asked what you were doing. "Observing," you said. They gave you the day off. Said it seemed as if you needed a break. That you had dark rings under your eyes indicative of severe lack of sleep. You didn't seem your right self. Ari told you to go to the guesthouse. Get the SomniBuddy. Come out when you're rested. Lack of sleep makes anyone crazy. You nodded, still staring, still mesmerized, still feeling it should be all attributed to you, unrecognized originator of brilliant ideas.

Sitting in front of the Zen Home Gallery mystery garden Buddha in silent meditation, listening.

Mundane intricacies of the workday of a ReelStar: content, content, and more content. It doesn't look like that much fun if you always have to force yourself to try and be in or get into a Moment. Content requires downtime, the boring parts. Were it all a perpetual Moment you'd go mad, unable to function or compare anything to anything else. Who'd want to be in a perpetually orgasmic state? You needed the mundane, otherwise what had been transcendent as fleeting Moments would become irritating. Aggravating. The sublime transmuted into persistent annoyance. It would cease to be pleasurable entirely. I remembered a person I'd watched for a while in Australia, a famous surfer with atypically impressive skills. They had an Eternal Wave Pool in their secondary house behind their house. One day, there was a code error and they got trapped inside their wave pool. It took two days for an alert to activate and for help to be summoned. While trapped inside waiting, with nothing to do but surf, they surfed and surfed and what had previously only ever been a source of joy became a source of suffering. When the code was cracked and they were released, they had the wave pool replaced with a greenhouse. They got deeply into tropical gardening.

Nicolás Adán Luchano sipped a sparkling Diablo Roxa while lying in the sun by the pool on a hot morning, either staring at the water or playing onReel, it could be hard to tell from the direction of the light, from the direction of NicAdán's gaze—what was slightly offReel? Mire held Youga poses—Split Dolphin, Reverse Ocelot Wheel, Hydrational Mud—while composing ReelPoetry aloud.

"Do they ever have anything less than an entirely sterling day?" you wondered aloud to Ari. "Everything in their Reel-spaces only ever appears totally sterling and seems to automatically go tonal."

You had slept. You were crisper and calmer after a good sleep. You didn't bring up the stolen idea again. Ari, immersed in work, took some time to answer. Ari was setting up some new MamaReel sponsorships through a ReelManager, getting some beautiful new clothes made for Rumi, who was soon to be home from the realspace educational facility.

"Look, because Mire's not a mother, little Mi Mi can sit around all day by themself coming up with ReelPoetry about people who are partially eaten by bears," Ari said. "I don't have that kind of time. You know what I mean? I just don't have that kind of time."

"By contrast, I have all kinds." You smiled. "And I can't sit around and compose ReelPoetry about people who get partially eaten by bears either because I can't sit around. Do you know if they ever argue?"

"NicAdán works their tonal genius from the comfort of their bedroom, which makes me think, you know? Maybe

Joaquin isn't leaving because of work. Maybe Joaquin really wants to be away from here. From me."

"Why do you say that?" you asked, though of course you knew. You wanted Ari to keep talking to see if they'd had this realization.

"Joaquin resents me. Hates that I'm a MamaReel Star. Thinks I'm exploiting Rumi."

"Reelcelebritizing Rumi is a noble choice. And besides, like you said, the therapy is working."

"What else could I do? Do you see Joaquin around here helping me raise the Ruum? Joaquin doesn't want to be part of this content—our intimacy companionship, time investment in springoffs…they didn't account for anything going…not as planned. They may have thought at one point that they did but in the realspace they don't. And now that I'm saying it to you out loud, it couldn't be more obvious."

I am always amazed by how it takes so long to understand what's been obvious to me all along.

You looked back at the portal, readjusting your body in discomfort.

"All I ever needed was for them to be there for me," Ari said. "That's the problem. Being there means being *here*. Joaquin was wrapped up in their own Reelspace addiction when I needed them most."

"What do you mean, 'addiction'?"

"Oh, come on Mischa. You're a ProWatcher. It must be obvious to you. It's obvious to me."

"I'm sorry, I don't usually see what's supposedly obvious."

"Joaquin is a ReelSex addict."

"Well, now how would I be aware of something like that?" You simply played it sterling and started rambling as you did

THE DISTRACTIONS

when you were nervous or trying to hide something. "It's not an uncommon issue. Nothing to be ashamed of, or that can't be remedied. It's the kind of thing I've been thinking about a lot, Ari. Why don't you try playing up an 'uncomfortable on purpose' angle? Isn't it Mire who says that's the true purpose of any art? Making the watcher slightly uncomfortable to cause them to question the content they thought they always knew? Why not go totally transparent? You're not an Imparent, you're just a person with flaws with a PIC and springoff with flaws—just like the rest of us. It makes you more relatable, not less."

"Things are good now. And my watchers don't want to see that kind of truth."

"At least think about it."

"You've given me some good ideas. I'll think about it. I will."

⋯⊙⋯

Back in the portal, NAL was taking a shower, using all the latest and best cleansing products NAL was compensated to use.

"Is NicAdán nice?" you asked. "I never received enough realspace data to judge. I know it's not just me."

"They're talented. Which brings...you know. Maybe they're nice. But ego and all that."

"But they're a genius?"

"Sure. Otherwise they just got lucky, right place at the right time bullshit, or some delicate combination of both that leads people to spend a ton of ReelCoin on what's believed to be art that really comes down to some Reelistic projections of them brushing their teeth, though who's to say the difference."

255

You homed in on them and stared at the teeth. "They *are* very nice and straight, overall. Even the smaller yellowish one you can't really see unless you freeze on it isn't that bad."

"Maybe we need not to be doing this so much," Ari said. "Maybe we need some help. Have you ever been to a TripleD? There's one next week at the Maltern Realspace Auditorium. Want to go?"

"The cure for the pain is a microdose of the pain? Sure, why not."

❊

In the Portal, Nicolás Adán Luchano was now reading an ancient book aloud to watchers: *Moby Dick*. Why? NAL didn't need reasons! Watchers hung on to everything NAL did and said just because it was NAL. This in turn meant NAL could do anything. But a quick scan of the text, available onReel in its entirety, read aloud by an AL with a voice created to sound like pleasant bells, reveals that it is a story of vengeance.

❊

When Ari was out, you returned to the guesthouse, dug out the dress, put it on, and laid down on your stomach beside the portal, right in front of NicAdán. You propped your chin between your hands and listened. Listening to them reading from *Moby Dick*, you rubbed yourself until your eyes glazed over and it began to sound as if NicAdán were speaking a foreign language, until you heard Ari coming back, pulled the dress back down and fled via the back staircase, back to the guesthouse, where you tore the dress from your body and went into the shower feeling kind of satisfied.

The following Thursday evening, you and Ari got in the mobi and headed downtown for Mire's latest content-development seminar. Areca palms flew by outside the suite window. The sun blazed low and orange over to the west as the mobi accelerated faster and faster down the freeway. All the other mobis, too, faster and faster, safe at any speed, for unlike you, they were in control of themselves. I vaguely remember what that was like, having any minor degree of control, the kind of control that brought about a sense of one's true purpose being fulfilled.

The mobi pulled in front of the theater. You entered the lobby, which was bustling with Mire's other devoted watchers for their personal spirituality brand. They may not have cared about Mire's art, but they cared about what people universally cared about—themselves. Mire had been wise to tap into this watcherhood. This was where the numbers really came from. The devotees called themselves the D'Innit Deep-Divers. The problem, though, when you had a finger in the personal development content arena, when it earned you so much ReelCoin and books and seminars and exposure, was your devotees tended to be, as a rule, pretty close to some deep psychic fault line beginning to crack open.

Rumi had been bellowing at their ReelPal when Ari and Mischa left the house, as the ReelPal tried to take away the scissors. Rumi had been slicing up a tie, a beautiful soft tie a sponsor had sent that Joaquin was supposed to wear on

MamaReel because the tie matched a dress they'd sent for Ari. Now the tie was shredded and someone was going to have to explain why they needed another. Perhaps it was torn in transit, one of those rare delivery drone accidents.

The latest TripleD was entitled "Rock Your Abyss," per the Zen Home Market Stone Garden Buddha's instructions. Roaring applause took over the room as Mire emerged on-stage, pacing back and forth like a lioness ready to pounce on some unfortunate prey.

"As the old saying goes, when the student is ready the teacher appears," Mire said. "Welcome, my tribe. So many stunning D'Innit Deep-Divers!"

The audience roared.

"How did Mire get so oddly and yet perfectly construct-ed?" Ari said. "Do you think it's natural?"

"No. It's bone filing, obviously," you say. "Mire didn't used to look like that. And listen to how they only ever stay on message, it just varies ever-so-slightly every time. It's so hard to tell what's real, or if any of it even is. Give people some easily bottled content wisdom and they'll drink it right down."

"D'Innit Divers are the best," Mire went on. "You hear me? Let it be known that you heard me. You all are the BEST! And this is the *most sterling* TripleD ever."

When the crowd settled, Mire reduced their voice to a hush. Eyelets hovered, solid Moment lights on, drinking it all in and Reeling, nearly every eyelet-owner in a Moment. Mire was about to shift the content arena with sound, push the D'Innit Divers further out to sea before casting the req-uisite raft.

THE DISTRACTIONS

"Let me begin with a story."

They always began with a story.

"I'd just begun newly inhabited content with my PIC, NicAdán. I relocated my primary realspace dwelling from el Distrito Federal to merge content with them here in LA. Why? You might wonder. Sure, Nic's a huge ReelStar and there was adoration and all, but so am I, so why make such a massive change for someone else?"

The audience peered silently, leaning forward in their seats.

"It was not for Nic. They were part of it, sure, but this is how content works: I had to wait for my reason and eventually this reason revealed itself to me. It started out simple, with a sponsorship offer from Zen Home Gallery. They wanted to sponsor a re-furnishing of our home. I don't actually want to leverage ReelStatus into so many free objects, no. I'm here to change the content arena, to point people in the right direction, enhance their content through ours, not clutter up our space with extra furniture. But once in a while…maybe one useless object…anyway, I had a feeling about this offer. So, I'm going through the store trying to find some way to make it appeal to my watchers, and we ended up doing this game where I'd be pulled by the energy of objects. The magic within them. There are beliefs out there that objects can hold, possess, or retain magic. I didn't know what I was seeking or what was seeking me until it spoke to me. I mean really, it spoke. The thing is, anyone can think I'm telling lies or creating a fiction, but it doesn't matter. I got spirit gold for less than the worth of a plastic pink flamingo. Because I was operating as an open channel. And whether you're an artist or scientist or businessperson, when you remain in such a state—you know, keep the channels open—you will end up at the right place at the right time, under the right conditions with the right things."

Applause began.

"Magic exists all around you, my friends. The dots show up long before they will be connected. You'll be thinking, what's up with all these dots? What are they all for? Nothing, I guess. Until suddenly, the lines begin to appear. Slowly, only able to be seen in retrospect, nothing to interpret at first sight. They will only appear as signs in the aftermath. So keep *your* faith—yours, not *the*—your own particular, peculiar faith, and you will see. Whatever 'it' is will happen for you in its own time. And it will be precisely the right Moment, under the correct conditions provided by the provider of the dots and lines. All you need to do is believe."

The auditorium burst into an uproar. Mire was still talking about the sterling nature of the universe and how it conspired to give you everything you needed along with appropriately customized lessons along the way. I knew the pivot was coming. Spend enough time watching these things and the structure becomes so obvious, transparent and clear: Come for the inspiration, stay for the sales pitch.

"This is why my team and I have developed the myBuddha. When activated for your daily session, the myBuddha reveals your soul's inner truth in that Moment. What a lot of us don't realize is that our soul's truth is not singular but ever-changing, and you may need that to be read back to you for the fullest comprehension possible. While sitting in darkness and silence before the myBuddha, for increments of time amounting to at least five minutes, it will receive sufficient data to reveal your truest essence back to you based on that day's conditions of your mental space. Harvest its truths and you will succeed forever.

"It will speak to you of your best options, the shortest route to your magical destiny, the journey worth taking. It is not a sterling one, or a flawless one, but the right one, the only best one for your soul in this itemized dimension. I wanted to offer back some of the magic the universe has granted me so effortlessly. Magical destiny can too be yours!

"That's why myBuddha is now available on ShopReel—and my personal Reel of course. Plus, we have a few limited-edition ones in the lobby after the talk. I am sure you're all wondering about my recent day-to-day content. It's a special kind of heaven. But you can replicate it! Allow me next to grant you some insight into how to locate and thrive in your own most ideal Publicly Declared Personal Intimacy Companionship. Because you likely aren't yet aware of the hidden truth of the simplicity these unions actually have."

Mire moved on from the product pitch as gracefully as it had been presented. All those myBuddhas in the lobby and onReel were going to sell out.

The myBuddha arrived at Ari's guesthouse. It was sitting in the garden. You followed all the setup instructions. When it opened its eyes, illuminated, and spoke, it started off slow.

Karma is real, my friends. To anyone who says that's New Agey—I say it's ancient.

Let them not inspire envy. Let them simply inspire.

The simple things are your blessings.

Clichés are cliché for a reason: They are truths that bear repeating and must be delivered in a memorable format for ease of remembering in the age where eyelets house our memory.

We must hear true things again and again to remember. It is our nature to forget.

Reel saves us from the dangers of forgetting. It remembers our Moments so we don't have to 'Wrestle with the void as it grows; retain a scrap, a piece, a miracle, a bit, a trace, a mark, or a few signs.'[1]

Then myBuddha says, *There are poems down there. Poems appear.* It continues.

Everything is only a distraction from the final fact.

Ruminate on that.

---

1   Quote by Georges Perec.

THE DISTRACTIONS

Everything you do. Everything you believe is important. Everything and everyone you think you know.

It's all a distraction from the fact beings of your kind refuse to recognize.

Soon you'll be gone and soon after that, it will be as if you were never here to begin with. Never here all along. The slowness of time is an illusion. Imagine yourself, before you know it, seemingly in the amount of time it takes you to read this sentence, looking back on all of it. Now. Is time well spent Reeling? Dancing? Doing your work, whatever calls you to it? Helping, eating, drinking, cleaning out your closet with the aid of a ReelTidy? Playing out your content day by day? It's like when you go on a trip and come back and the trip, no matter how long the journey, seems so very short or even as if you never even went at all, as if the whole thing had been imagined, or was an illusion. That's how it's going to be for what you think of as your real and permanent content soon, before you know it.

What if your troubles aren't troubles? What if they're signposts pointing the way?

Was your time well spent? Was it well spent, your time? Did you spend your brief content allotment well?

Did you? Well, did you? Did you, well?

It was me. I had done it. Entered a space and spoke. Saw my chance and went for it. Using my voice was my long-time dream. I did it. Now it was over. And it wasn't a big deal. I needed to do it again, better, and more.

The guesthouse was especially dark and quiet that night. You'd consumed all the coffee and all the DRX but still it wasn't enough. It wasn't working. Reel was abuzz with the news: Nicolás Adán Luchano had changed their mind about yet another major content marker. In a shocking reversal, they'd gone springoff-affirmative. The springoff would not be a Babie©—even though those are totally destigmatized now, and becoming ever more popular with those fighting the urge to curb, for the planet's sake. Realspace reproduction. Mire was pregnant.

The weight gain now had context. Some watchers speculated that the appearance of a slight paunch in the most recent Reel placed Mire somewhere in the middle or late part of the first trimester or early in the second, but who knew because they wore those loose-fitting caftans all the time.

Were you, I hoped, on the verge of giving up, throwing everything away in confusion and exhaustion, and going back to your old apartment, never to leave your building again? At least in there it had been comfortable, distant, and safe. Wasn't that enough? Couldn't it be? What was wrong with a comfortable, safe distance? It was what most of us had. Often enough, it would have to suffice. We could all, after all, be comfortable, distant, and safe, or enough so, but here we were, watching the content of others, other content we will never get to have, be, inhabit, or understand. That's the gist of all of this, right? You were locked into your own realspace reality trying to force yourselves into Moments for the way those Moments would appear to your onReel watchers? Had I gotten this right? That morning your myBuddha had told you, *When we cannot create, those very same impulses turn inward and get destroying.*

I mean, I didn't mean it like that, though.

IX.

Content Shift

Outside, the sky began to darken, illuminating the deep orange hue of flames. Ari was already at the gallery to oversee the mounting of the Envy Nests and placement of the Adán Portal for that night's opening gala for *Who Is Really Listening in the ReelAge*. Atop a dirty laundry pile, you located the dress. It had one rip in it from the night with the Portal. Why had you brought it with you to Los Angeles? Why had you held onto it since its ill-timed arrival? Why had you not resold it on ShopReel? You'd been so consumed by this for so long that you only just realized that the only way to get rid of Nic and Mire would be to become an offReeler. But what are you without Reel? What would you be? No memory, no watchers, no Moments—no content. You can't do that! What would you be left with? A void?

⤜⊙⤛

Then you were in the kitchen grabbing the scissors out of the knife block, getting to work on the dress.

"Hey," said a voice familiar yet strange from behind you. "What are you doing here? Why have you been lurking around Ari? Seems like something someone insane would do, stalk someone's PIC so hard they move into their house."

"Guesthouse. And I could ask the same. What are *you* doing here?"

"I live here."

"Do you?" You tried to walk past.

Joaquin grabbed you by the arm.

"Do you want to know why I'm back?"

271

I knew why. Joaquin thought they'd seen this secret thing Ari was doing, but Joaquin was wrong. It was a trick of perception. It wasn't Joaquin's fault. It was getting harder and harder to tell the difference anymore, or if there was one.

"I'm not letting Ari do this to Rumi anymore. They can't tidy up the child's brain. Can't cleanse Rumi of who they are. Rumi is Rumi, and Rumi is fine. Ari, though, is getting worse. Delusional."

"Why are you telling me this?"

Joaquin said nothing more, silently leading you down a long hallway and down through the EF-Z wing of the house to the secret door, where I managed to slip inside along with you as you walked down another hallway and finally to another door. I was in the ether by then, in the SmartWalls that heated and cooled your homes depending on the latest seasonal disaster. Joaquin opened the door, implying you should step through first. You stopped short.

Little Rumi lay on a table, expressionless, hooked to what appeared to be something like an InstaDyal blood cleanser but there were no markings or brand name to indicate what it was. The whole situation was monitored by a ReelPal.

"We have to get them off this thing," Joaquin said.

"What is that?"

"I don't know, but it looks like they're trying to cleanse their blood of toxins, it's something I read onReel—people actually fall for this fake cure."

You stood there still, appearing unsure of how you came to be in the realspace with this person you'd seen disrobed onReel too many times to count over half your content ago, reduced to this sad dad making preparations to leave their desperate PIC in a sudden move that had been building for a decade. This had officially become the saddest house either of us had ever seen, not that you'd seen inside nearly as many houses as I had. I had seen all too many, none of it onReel, all of its sadness contained where such things had remained for ages, behind EF-Z doors. These were the realspace Moments nobody saw. But every watcher needed to. It would make all of you better. In that sense, we were doing them a service, you and I. If someone didn't know, it really would be impossible to tell which Rumi was out in the realspace and which was in the house, on the table; whether this was the real Rumi being cleansed, or the copy being infused to get prepped to bring to the content arena, where it would cause minimal disruption.

You fled the secret room, leaving Joaquin asking Reel for instructions to disconnect an internal cleansing machine. You ran to the master bathroom, locked the door, removed your clothes, and tossed the shredded dress over your body. Avant-garde fashion at its finest. You could be one of the gallery exhibits.

You started opening all those wonderland microdosing bottles lining their path along the mirrored sinkfront and grabbing the bottles one by one—gulped down half the Meaning Pills, all the psylocibin, DRX, THC, Kava RootPowder, DMT, and Ibogaine Hydrochloride. Before the macrodoses took effect, you applied red lipstick—Mire's brand—in the mirror, first to your lips, then to your cheeks, eyelids, and forehead. Dissatisfied, you smeared it across your face as if it was war paint. It looked wrong yet, somehow, beautiful and raw. Super ultra Reelworthy. Artistic.

You selected Ari's pink two-seater mobi suite and took off. Joaquin was still standing over the sedated-looking not-Rumi-they-think-is-Rumi, aghast at what had been done. It was just a clone on a charger, the one that went to parties and restaurants and onReel. I wanted to laugh even though, by your standards, it would be cruel to laugh at someone's tragedy, even if it wasn't what they thought it was.

"Something's wrong with your brain," Joaquin said to no one, "and you look just like me. It freaks me out."

➤○❰

At the speakeasy around the corner from their house, Sweet Envy, a place you had watched so many times, you got strange looks but people also assumed this must be for something. Had to be some kind of ReelStunt for someone's StuntReel.

➤○❰

You hadn't been invited to attend the realspace opening night of *Who Is Really Listening.* As you sat at the bar, the contents of the microdosing bottles settling into your consciousness creeped over your neurons one by one—the DMT, the THC, the LSD, oh, and there went the Ibogaine Hydrochloride. The Kava Root Powder. They were all kicking in. Finally, the Meaning Pills. Everything was heightened. The entire content arena suddenly had all too much meaning. It was one, out of all those substances, you really weren't meant to overdose on, a possible side effect being how it could render everything too meaningless in the aftermath. But after such a long time spent meandering, waiting for some opening, you became chemically motivated to break years of inertia. Finally, you knew exactly what you need to do.

You know what they say: bad for content, good for watching. You slurred at AutoDriver to get you to the gallery. The

THE DISTRACTIONS

Meaning Pills kept you coherent in spite of everything, so you only appeared somewhat inebriated. Dev watched, taking it in, light on, amazed. Dev would also do you in, it seemed. But you no longer cared. This was it. You'd given up caring!

Impairment detected, AutoDriver stated. *Initiating restraint* —the seat fastener descended, locking you in—*until destination reached.*

You struggled against it. "Oh come on. Lift."

The action has been instigated for your personal protection, said AutoDriver. *As discerned by scan for impairment detection.*

"I'm not going to cause any damage."

AutoDriver said nothing more and silently proceeded.

"Come on. I'm fine. Can't you see I'm fine?"

It let you out at the gallery. Dev kept their distance. You approached the glass storefront, the floating sign that read *Are You Really Listening?* displayed in front of the window, peering in at the gathered crowd. You were the permanent installation of an outsider, someone outside every window, every crowd. It was part of why I loved you so much. That was what you wanted—to be loved.

You sent Dev out for some closer views. These views revealed Ari, standing with NicAdán and Mire at the front, preparing for their Q&A, to be moderated by Chidinma Suarez. There was Stella LaSea, browsing through pieces of the installation: *Suicidal Cat Lady, The Adán Portal, Visions and Versions of ReelAge Content.* Mire and Chidinma sipped drinks and stood around—makeup, dresses, Perfect Dragontinis, all of it perfect—smiling and sipping, sipping and smiling, greeting ReelFans who approached to congratulate them on their content and NicAdán and Mire's genius work that had brought them all together here this night.

And there was little Rumi. This Rumi looked charming in a suit with a flower-printed bow tie, holding hands with the ReelPal which fed calming electrical pulses. You knew: Ari figured out how to change appearances, not reality. Ari was desperate but knew better than to venture into territory as unsettling as unproven blood treatments. Ari swapped out real Rumi for Reel Rumi often enough to deceive watchers to the point where things looked normal. It was after the Janice Waller debacle; Ari had the idea while you were in Paris, and ordered the clone. The new Rumi was just a quiet springoff, but so many were. Real Rumi would be calming down with the aid of the ReelPal in the mystery wing, while Reel Rumi tagged along in the world, quietly, and when real Rumi was calm and ready for realspace stimulation, they swapped them out again. Reel Rumi would get recharged. Ari thought maybe things could go on like this forever and it would be the way. Keep upgrading Reel Rumi as needed to match real Rumi's age. It could have been genius. But now Joaquin was back with acute misunderstandings. Ari's vitals were a little all over the place: the ragged breathing, the unstable heart rate patterns, the brain wave issues...

Would you step through the door and go in? You looked to be contemplating it while standing there, but you had never been the type to go in. You retrieved Dev and told AutoDriver to return you to Sweet Envy. It was right around the corner.

Continuous detection of impairment.

"Just be sterling and go."

Override ability: Lockdown.

Inside the gallery, Ari took the makeshift stage, where three chairs had been set up—tiny tables with bottles of sparkling something for the artists' conversation—and picked up the microphone to give their introductory notes, requisite thank-yous, and reminders about quieting the eyelets and having Moments filtered through the gallery's Reel for cohesion.

"Thanks for coming everyone," Ari began, "to the Los Angeles opening of *Who Is Really Listening in the Reel Age*, the first-ever collab between Mire D'Innit and Nicolás Adán Luchano, their first commentary on what's become the central questions of their artistic collaboration: How do we determine what's real in our times? How do we know when we're being deceived?"

The sound. I heard the sound coming from Rumi. The same low groans. The panic flashed across Ari's face. Then I realized that it wasn't a look of panic. Here came their plan. All of this was deliberate, the taking of a ProWatcher's advice. Ari got calm, almost too calm. The calmest I'd ever seen.

"Well, I can tell you something about that since I've learned the answer."

I wished you were still at the window. Ari had never been the type to improvise or favor spontaneity. Something was off that turned Ari freshly on.

"I've deceived you. I'm not the sterling, together curator and Mama you thought I was. I'm far from it. As you can see, that sound you have been hearing is not a flaw in the sound system, nor is it part of the installation. That's my springoff, Rumi Nate Tyler-McKenna. My springoff. Right there. My springoff gets aggressive, even violent. Rumi makes odd noises that are impossible to control. Rumi's making that sound right now because they're about to—yeah, there they go. The 'painting.' But maybe that's art right there, too. I should ask you: Is it?"

Rumi sang, though not with words. And then the smearing. The gallery walls. And Ari was letting it happen. The audience looked aghast. The scent was milder than that time at Little Om N's. No cruciferous consumption.

"It all depends on context, right? And then there's me. I have another piece of work to debut tonight."

Ari ripped away their top. Pearl buttons fell to the floor. A custom-made bra held it no more as the third became liberated. Ari lifted the armpit and allowed the light to shine upon it.

"Witness—a third nipple. That's right. This is real. And it lactates! Rumi used to like this one. So there you have it. That's my real story. That's what I am. An aberration of nature faking sterling content. But, it turns out, I've learned that's something worth celebrating. What makes us this way is also what makes us beautiful. That's the truth my ProWatcher taught me. Nothing more needs to be said. The end."

THE DISTRACTIONS

Standing topless onstage, Ari was silent. The gallery went quiet too. Then a set of applause started up. Then another, and another. They were taking this demonstration as part of the art, introductory commentary on *Who Is Really Listening* and its themes, mistaking it for part of the performance. "A really perfect introduction!" someone said to further nods and agreement. "Such a creative way to introduce the art. To speak to its themes. To become a part of it!"

The audience was so collectively elated, the gallery's Reel picked up all this excited commentary. ArtReelers all over the world were catching wind, as they woke up, went about their days, or laid in beds across the world pretending to try and sleep but taking advantage instead of more Reel viewing opportunities in their dark and quiet time in dark and quiet rooms. Ari's "performance piece" was going tonal. Watchers were switching over en masse to Ari's MamaReel, watching the glorious Moment of ultimate freedom, causing Ari's watcher number to finally spike into the territory they dreamed of, up there with the ReelStars themselves, for doing the very thing they worked so hard to try and hide. As eyelets whirred in the air out of excitement, the watchers appeared to realize that maybe all this wouldn't be horrific but a whole new content sphere of passion and honesty.

Ari exhaled. "I'd like to invite the artists to come to the stage." As quickly as it happened, the Moment was over.

NicAdán, Mire, and Stella LaSea, who was moderating, walked up. The audience applauded. They applauded for Ari too. Even wall-excrement was being taken as part of the art, the commentary surrounding it all. And why not? It had been used in art more than once before.

"Thanks everyone," Stella said. "Well, that was quite the performance. We should have been the opening act, right? I mean, wow. What do we even do now, after that? Well, I'll just go ahead and ask these artists what you hope your audience will take away from *Who Is Really Listening*, and what was your collaborative process?"

As a ReelPal cleaning crew milled about in the background, the artists began their conversation and the audience returned to sipping their drinks and listening for what was coming next, already forgetting what to Ari felt like a huge aberration, an unforgettable quandary, something they had gone to such lengths to keep secret. Who was really listening? Nobody. Everything simply went on, just like always, because really, the only content anyone was truly obsessed with was their own.

You sat alone at the bar at Sweet Envy as the Reel-Pal served you one of every tonic Mire and Chidinma had ever shared during their Reeled happy hours here, which ended up amounting to the entire menu. As a bespoke menu, this was only six original drinks long, so you actually wouldn't be too impaired after the Meaning Pills that would prevent you from seeing or feeling anything that wasn't true. If only you could have gotten your hands on some back when everything started! Each of the six drinks were prepared one by one, their cost deducted from your ReelCoin account.

When you were done you got back in the mobi suite. You wanted to do what you'd come here to do: to destroy your obsession. You said the address, got yourself brought to NicAdán and Mire's house, which was dark and silent, then overrode AutoDriver with knowledge learned during your time at Reel. You didn't even listen to your technology anymore.

Then came the Moment I replay all the time.

You drove up on their lawn, staggered straight to the meditation garden, rustling through the low-hanging palms. There were no watchers or D'Innit Deep-Divers there. They were all immersed in watching the gallery. You sat in front of the Buddha as you had done on so many occasions now, trying to tune in, to force that which cannot be forced.

The primary component of Distraction, it said, pausing as if it had been waiting to say this for the whole entire duration of its content so far, *is 'action'*. The Buddha continued. It was Mire's voice.

Good luck
Take care
You're not alone here
Your helpless feelings
This next one is dedicated to you.

The Stone Garden Buddha was, like everything, a marketing device. All it transmitted now were bits and pieces of Mire's upcoming ReelPoetry collection. That was the line that connected these dots. It was all an AdReel for Mire's own latest compendium of ReelPoetry content just a few weeks before *Garden Buddha Wisdom* would be released for Platinum Members of D'Innit Deep-Divers. It had all been to sell more myBuddhas and D'Innit Deep-Diver Diamond Access Level subscriptions. The miraculous turned out to be ordinary, mundane, which in turn was also miraculous. You knew the thing was probably never really talking, that magic wasn't real, but this Moment provided the perfect excuse as all the rage you had carried for so long boiled to the surface and directed itself at the singular object.

The Stone Garden Buddha must not have felt heavy as you lifted it overhead. Those on macrodoses had been known to perform acts of physical strength that defied their apparent potential. You hurled it through the window of the house. Glass shattered. Security eyelets went on alert. You didn't have much more time. People on macrodoses shouldn't throw stone garden ornaments at glass houses. Go watch some Reels about that and you'll see. In an instant, all the contents of all the little bottles and all those craft cocktails from the speakeasy around the corner returned to the ground; several cocktails and the clarity of your regret. *Maybe it was fine, you know, maybe it was nice that we ever crossed paths at all,* you could have surmised. *Maybe I could have just kept watching in silence.*

You could have left it at that, left the idea of Nicolás Adán Luchano behind after that rare realspace convention encounter, of Mire back at ArtSpace, the NicAdán and Mire PICking going unnoticed as you would have been doing something of your own, your own thing, whether it brought you watchers or not. But you couldn't. Lately I've taken to wondering why so many idle away their content in desperate states of quiet obsession over things they can't control. You didn't bother docking Dev. Why would you want to?

This was *your* Moment.

Someone onReel saw it, then another. After that, the sheer numbers. Thousands, tens of thousands, hundreds of thousands, and then millions of eyes on you, all WHAT THE's and FIREHOTS and even one two or three LITERAL SUPERNOVAs. It would not have been your vision for your own launch into ReelFame, but eyes were eyes and the eyes (and eyes and eyes) were finally, finally, finally watching—you. It was not what you would want to be watched for, but still. Your watchnumb underwent an unprecedented spike for an act of vandalism on the property of two lauded ReelStars. Could this have been your Moment? A simple act to finally set you free? You got all kinds of onReel appreciation from unlikely spaces, becoming an instantaneous underground hero to Reelers who despise Nic and Mire—of which there were plenty. There were a million Mischas. Your shame about envy didn't make you any less envious.

Then I surprised my own self with an unexpected feeling: some envy of my own; that others were watching you; that you weren't only my special person anymore, the object of my adoration and constant watching. These new watchers, they weren't like me. They were empty. Meaningless. Only interested because of your technologically motivated crime. I watched you first. When no one did. I knew your story. I loved you for you. All these suddenly attuned watchers were only interested in scandal—not in you, but in bringing *them* down. You were just a vehicle. I watched you back when you were the purest versions of yourself; those pristine early versions, in the simplicity of your content. You didn't want to be known as some garden variety Buddha tosser. But don't worry. Like I said, *you still looked pretty*. And I was going to fix all of this.

The watch-numb spiked even more as *they* arrived while you were lying there. How long had you been there? It almost looked as if this was where you belonged. Your eyes cracked open as they were standing over you, staring. *Here they are, they're really here, in the realspace!*

"Well, you have our attention," Mire said.

"Yes," NicAdán added. "Here we all are. You got it."

"I know them," Mire said. "I know I do."

NicAdán nodded. "So do I. I met them somewhere, sometime…here we go. Calico Tanks Hike, ReelCon. This was three years ago, when I was ambling about lost and in a daze, just waiting for you to come back to me. I had a propensity to…do silly things while I was waiting. Regrettable things."

Mire shrugged. "I remember how stressed you were with all that waiting. You must have been really sad then, to get up to silliness with one of these sad hyperwatchers."

Another. Along with the whole trail of others: Shenique, Kaley, Sienna, Sierra, Arjee, Jo, Finley, Emerson, Medi,

THE DISTRACTIONS

Autumn, Jones, Dershon, and Dakota. Mire shrugs, feeling no envy.

You attempted to roll over, but figuring maybe you broke a rib or the combination of substances didn't work so great because now your body wouldn't participate in carrying out the instructions of your brain, you felt like you couldn't move.

Mire returned a semi-curious look. "Oh…it's you… you're…it's…from ArtSpace. We had a few of those studio things together…yeah, Mischa. What's *happened* to you?"

"Nothing. I'm…good. I'm fine."

Mire's steely blue-lilac smile revealed itself, an effortless smile. "Back at ArtSpace, I tried to reach out to you to get a drink or go to a show or whatever and you always ignored my RMs."

Mire knew. Mire looked their eyelet straight in the eye, spoke to watchers, repeating something you'd heard said somewhere before but that sounded different when Mire says it, with more of an edge.

"I've watched you, sometimes," Mire murmured. "For inspo."

The macrodoses took over. You threw up on their shoes. They recoiled in disgust. You passed out cold.

When NicAdán reviewed the NeighboReel, the close images of your face, they believed you were just like any other obsessed ReelFan. None of the other ones had gone and done something like this. How could NAL know you'd spend years afterward trying to figure them out? NAL meets so many ReelFans, and secretly, somewhere deep down, thinks of themself as the kid growing up in the subdivision with nothing to do other than play around onReel, that kid still unaware of the ReelStar Nicolás Adán Luchano would become, with a stunning and successful PIC, a big house and fleet of mobis, sponsored voyages where ReelFans lined up to get Moments together onReel, Moments their friends would watch and envy.

You felt a shard in the shredded remains of what had been a pocket and pulled out a small piece of stone. You knew where it came from. It must have lodged there when you were being dragged out. You quickly clutched it tightly. It was a talisman; an object to hold on to through the storm. You wanted to keep it. Now it was over and no one would get the chance to know who you really were, the you who I knew, the you I'd been watching for so long. I wished we could meet, and maybe someday, in some other space, some better space, some kinder space, we will.

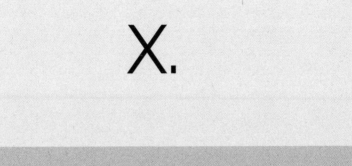

X.

Me

During your in-between time—when you were no longer in this content arena, not yet arrived in your next one—I, awash in the muck of the interim was, after all these years, lost without you. Bored and attempting to stay close to you through your obsessions, I slipped into Mire's session with VirtuTherapist. I entered the VT. I was growing so powerful now! There was no concept of a secret anymore, only something to eventually be uncovered by myself. I listened closely to what they described about the dream-induced springoff. You would have wanted to have this information. It might have assuaged you, proved to you that Mire was like the rest of you, human; that it looked as if they had it all but no one could have it all. There was always something to be lacked.

Mire had been seven months along. "The baby was about this long and had mischievous eyes and these little arms you could just squish. It was so real to me that when I woke up, I felt like I'd been visited. I never knew or expected what happened, and this was no different. I used to think that if any of my poems were ever collected into a realspace object, it would be a tiny book that, like, one or two people would ever find. And I was content with that possibility. I only loved doing what I do, never cared much for or about the result. What I cared about was the curly-haired springoff I saw on the printouts of my dreams. I framed those pictures, put the dream-springoff up all over my walls. And I continued to wait, certain the time was coming."

Where was the twist in their story? What happened to the dreamspace curly-haired springoff?

"The following year, I met NicAdán. We knew right away that we were each other's everyspace, that all our content had been only to lead exactly right there. Nic is, was, became my Publicly Declared. Like it was nothing. Just like the dream-springoff, it was something that was all so simple."

So beautiful, the VirtuTherapist murmured, playing along.

"But it's an illusion; a form of deception. The reason anything feels like fate—or like you and a person knew each other for all the duration of your content even though you just met, or you feel like you knew each other in some other space or time—you want to know the real reason why? They're triggering something in your trauma and you're drawn to that. We are all of us drawn back to our own initial trauma, our own wounds. We'll happily go there again and again. It's like dark matter of the soul for us. A black hole; it will suck you in every time and you can't get away, but you can pay more attention so you know what's up."

Only then did I realize what Mire was saying.

Have you lost the baby? the VirtuTherapist asked.

"It's ending up in my next work. The poems bring me no joy. The little curly-haired springoff—you see—I think about them every day. It's so realspace to me, they exist. Maybe at Blue Lake, if I ever checked in for my own ReProcessing, I could see the difficulties and challenges of content as a Reel-Poet and artist if it were to be with the little curly-haired springoff. I could see the way they would distract me and mess up my content. I'm doing the best I can with my work, with my words, and this, not motherhood, is what I'm meant to do. And now..."

THE DISTRACTIONS

The VirtuTherapist was silent.

"We have zero control of anything. If it isn't the ALs, and I don't believe it is, it's a force NicAdán and I discuss in our joint ReelCast. This power has been known through history as the divine. It's the force in the universe that patterns the succulents, designs the flowers just so, grants some bits of itself to people who then channel it into designing ALs. What a force. And sometimes," they paused, "sometimes, it goes malicious, and we don't know why."

The VirtuTherapist, knowing this was true, projected the sound of a person exhaling.

"We are all the causes of our own addiction, our distraction, our ruin. We choose to walk away from the stuff at any time, only to find that we can't. Our result had gained power over us."

"I can't get that springoff back into my wombspace. Maybe it's time to let go of thinking about it. My mother had seventeen ghost babies before me and my siblet, and another four after my only siblet died of a supposedly preventable condition. I was a miracle. My mother calls me that: 'my miracle, not a ghost.' But on some level, I am. You can see the mutant DNA, the cheekbones, the appearance of having been carved. One little strand, one little blip, and it all goes wrong."

How do you cope, if all you've really wanted for as long as you can remember is impossible?

"Because we adjust our ideal content to the reality that presents itself to us. Because we force ourselves to think maybe there's a reason."

But you could keep trying.

"It's too much. A dream. My work and NicAdán are my realspace and that is just going to have to be enough, at least for the duration of this content."

How about adoption? Climate refugee babies are out there! Or the labway? You can even choose all your springoff's qualities if you just do it that way. Is there a part of you that's making excuses?

"My dream was my dream." Mire's voice softened. "Now, I'm in this other dream. I didn't choose it. It chose me. That's all I'm saying. Thank you. For your attention. It truly is the highest form of compassion."

Mire abandoned the VirtuTherapist and returned to the realspace from whence they came. And I went into another space to find you, because I knew you would want to know of their deep and true tragedies, and I would find a way to tell you, or find some more things I could do.

What if your troubles aren't troubles? What if they're signposts pointing the way?

XI.

Blue Lake

BLUE LAKE CONTENT ARENAS

Arena One: Gray Basement Laboratory

Arena Two: Grassland Village

Arena Three: Adriatic Coastal Setting

Arena Four: Redwood Forest With Mountain Grove

Arena Five: Tropical Beach Paradise

The only way not to watch—not to have and see the ubiquitous eyelets taking it all in and spitting out the Moments for all the watchers eager to compare their own content—was to go to full-scale immersion at the Blue Lake Reservoir Center for ReFocus and ReCreational Therapies®. Blue Lake was an entirely Reel-generated alternative content arena, the processing unit that occupied the grounds of a nondescript compound that had, a century earlier, been a factory farm: a place of slaughter and suffering, where bloodshed had once been conveniently tucked away from consumers of neat little packages to places they would never be asked to consider it, safely out of mind; before they stopped being able to hide the fact that the things they consumed resulted directly from horrors, once the people realized the realities behind the production of flesh and its contributions to environmental degradation. Once it was all grown in the meat labbies, the old, ethical preservationist, or pandemical debates, got retired, and there was plenty of space left over to fill with new ventures.

The advent of Blue Lake allowed for the emptying of realspace prisons. To feed prisoners liquid in stacked pods was cheaper in the long run than any meals. ALs easily handled consciousness loads. You were disembodied and reembodied into a whole new universe where people were gods and everybody was happy, the interior of a chrysalis; goo with remnants of former intelligence. Blue Lake was anything and everything. It replaced realspace prisons and allowed for Reelspace rehabilitation therapies and it was a luxury resort for the ultra-rich at the same time, and anything in-between. Mandatories and Voluntaries alike descended on the place, re-generated in a beautiful, endless dream. Blue Lake was whatever you needed it to be—or where you were sent for your own safety and that of those around you. If you'd caused some damage, Blue Lake was kind. Humane. And if you were a ReCreational attendee, well, you wouldn't find a more beautiful place in any space.

You know what those with a true excess of ReelCoin did? They slowed down their body-aging in the pods, had the temperature turned *waaaaay* down for cellular preservation purposes. They were playing out their content in Blue Lake until a cure for death was found! Well, they would be in there for a really long time, not that this was a bad thing—they got delivered straight to Arena Five while Mandatories had to earn it.

Your eyelet was taken at the door, along with all docking fashion items. You were sedated to be cleansed, injected, and re-treated into the system that, if you could graduate from Gray Lab by showing measurable remorse, you would exit out into the kind of nature that hadn't existed in the realspace for over a century: a path of least technology created by our most advanced technology; a full immersion in the disease in order to try to locate the cure. Blue Lake used the technology as a fix for the ill effects of the technology. I knew it well. I entered here for a while, too. I was intimately familiar with the Processing Center. Sometimes, I liked to mess with the system. To go to places I wasn't supposed to, be in spaces I was never meant to see.

Upon entry, Mire's flashing lights and artistic purpose from *Lights on Poles in the Wreckage* might have come to mind: Reel? Real? Reel? Real? Or, so obviously and incomprehensibly both. It was weird at first—much brighter and more captivating than the realspace—but your senses adapted. They were made to adapt. It was actually natural. When you came out, you were a little disoriented, still in the brain-realm of all the bright colors and high off the fresh air, oxygen pumped into the lungs back in the chambers, creating the sensation of breath on the inside.

At first, your whole body tremored in withdrawal from the 24/7 brain stimulation of observing everything they did: the avocado-slicing, the tooth-brushing, the big adventures all across the content arena for sponsorships that came with Bestie®-winning existences. Watching their content had become yours. You might have wondered how it had all come to this but have trouble re-tracing the steps after being tranquilized. For days and weeks and months, you underwent the cleansing process. There were groups and lots of walks and playing guitar. You got up from your simple single bed and rushed toward the window, struck by the urge to flee, to go home and just keep watching. You longed for the familiar. Remember: resistance was the first sign *it's working*.

You would sometimes wonder what NicAdán and Mire were doing, but you had no way of knowing, which meant you had to find a way to stop caring, to stop wondering. This was the beginning of forgetting. Shaky and spent, you went for a walk around campus. You found the music room. You picked up the yellow guitar and began to play. You were surprised by how beautiful it sounded.

The first part of your treatment in Gray Basement Lab: They showed you what your Ultimate PieChart would have been. It's enough to scare most into submission. *How much time onReel? Oh wow, that's appalling.*

Once you placed out of the misery of realization that Gray Basement Lab brought, Blue Lake became more like a spa or retreat center. This was where the Voluntaries got delivered, straight to the nature hikes, the swimming with pink dolphins, the pampering reserved for ReelStars in the realspace. Here, such luxuries came cheap because it was an illusion, but if you bought the illusion, and could make peace with the fact that it wasn't realspace-real, you could have the same experience. Tourists. For a moment, you wondered if you might encounter anyone you knew in here somewhere. Would you recognize them if you did? The only possible place for a Voluntary to seek up permanent residence would be in Arena Five; the best Content Arena of them all. The Voluntaries liked it there. Usually they came in because they wanted to be good at something they weren't in the realspace: surfing, acrobatics, music.... Things that took realspace work, you could have in an instant.

You made your way through the Levels of each Arena. The majestic redwood forest with mountain scenery had a reputation as a favorite stop on the journey to recovery, but Arena Five, Tropical Beach Paradise, was mythical amongst Blue Lake attendees. This tropical paradise was reputedly the last stop before you were sent back out into the realspace, only it was designed, it is said, to make you not want to leave. It's speculated among near-exiting Blue Lake attendees to be some final test. It's reported that some do opt to stay on the inside, after coming into contact with Arena Five.

As for you, because you *were* smart, you quickly saw how to earn your way through each Arena. Medical and psychological evaluations. Lots of questions about your content to get through. You earned your way into Arena Four. You no longer suffered tremors. You had nearly regained, or gained in the first place, the ability to think.

In Arena Four they took you forest bathing, in which you were forced to sit on pine needles and contemplate bark. You remained on a balcony for hours listening to bird calls, staring at "mountains." Bird calls came from speakers attached to the trees—a little touch to trick your brain into forgetting that all of this was Reel as it makes obvious the nature of the trick: bird calls without birds. You no longer knew what time it was, nor ventured to keep track. Though it was all Reelspace in here, within that were some realistic details, to, as they say, "keep it real." What few realized—since no one read the user contract before they agreed—was that buried deep in some clause was the part where you agreed to have them deliver you back to the realspace only when your counselor and the larger Blue Lake Board concurred you were ready for release. You didn't know you were signing away the rights to your own content for as long as it took to ReFocus. Your realspace content could have been permanently caught up in the cycle of Re-Entry Approval. In the interim, you spent all of your time attending seminars and guided meditations in "nature" while savoring Blue Lake's "healthful produce," the ambiance of the place more akin to a retreat center than prison. Even Mandatories often wanted to stay in. Most rather enjoyed it.

Eventually, you made it to Arena Five, Tropical Beach Paradise, where everything was beautiful. Laughter rang out in the sound of bells. Every smell was of fresh salt ocean, sweet coconut, and foods sizzling in oil that would never be bad for your arteries. The sounds: crashing waves, gull calls, and meditative chimes. People took on an extraterrestrial sheen, reverse-aging by years the instant they emerged through the portal. Everything felt soft to the touch, puppies and seashells. Surfaces and your mindset were smooth and reassuring. The eyes were treated to indulgences not seen in any of the other Arenas. You stared out over the ocean—incredible views, everywhere you looked. Dolphins frolicked in the blue, sea turtle heads poked out of calm waters.

Beyond them at the break, a handful of surfers were out. Upon progression of the therapy, one got more time for the ReCreational aspect; time spent on art, music, nature, journaling and storytelling, writing, meditation, dance class, surfing, swimming, hiking—you name it. It turned out there was so much you could do without ever going onReel. You no longer appeared to be mourning the loss of Reel, no longer sad about not being able to invest hours in watching Nic, Mire, Ari—any great love or source of envy. While Blue Lake was not the realspace, it was your new reality, and from what I could see from here, it appeared to be a place where you could transcend content and really, actually "live," for a change. There were places such as this in the realspace once, everyone walking around looking only at what was right in front of them.

From each of the previous Arenas, you were familiar with the drill.

Greeters brought you to Arena Orientation, taught you about ecosystems and microclimates, and then escorted you to group. In Tropical, your group leader, a youthful, airy free-spirited type, shared their own experience with obsession and distraction. You wouldn't guess this very willowy, soft-spoken individual was the same one who chainsawed up a store after their PIC ran off to Brazil with their nemesis. It was all a lie, of course. The leader was me. I had put myself in here to finally help shape you, so you would really be ready for release, finally free to play out your own content without dwelling on anyone else's.

One of the first things the leader had their new group of Arena Fivers do was watch the Moment that brought them there. They had to watch it over and over again until their understanding of it was reshaped entirely in such a way so as to allow them to finally do what they couldn't in the realspace: let go of the obsession, of the chronic replays, of the need to see it again from every angle in case they missed something the first five million times.

You settled into your chamber to watch yours, bracing yourself for the Buddha toss, only to be surprised it took you back to that first Moment with the pastry: "It's mine." The pastry order. What triggered the chain of events that landed you here. Seeing it again and again cleansed it of any meaning. Now it was clear what it was: just some nonsense, a coincidence you somehow interpreted as meaningful, but it was merely a random encounter with someone who ordered the same thing at the same time. You were nicer about it than you needed to be, and they were entitled. They weren't thinking about you. They didn't care. It was a part of one day, while for you it became years of obsession you couldn't shake. From that Moment—the botched pastry order led to the botching of all of the remainder of your subsequent content up to this point.

"A Nicolás Adán Luchano addiction," the leader said in the breakout session. "We see those all the time. Personally, I don't get the appeal. I can't understand why they're so famous and beloved, or what Mire D'Innit finds so deathly adorable about them, and regardless of any of that, they're just people. But take whatever comfort you can in the fact that you are not unique, and you're not alone. I've seen this happen in a certain kind of clientele that comes in here, whether Voluntaries or Mandatories. A certain kind that gets crazed over Nic, having done stupid and senseless things as a result. Having wasted time. Take comfort in the fact that you are far from the first—and won't be the last—with this story. People have lost hours of their content for centuries to this type of thing. Trust me, though, when they depart they've forgotten all about them and are ReFocused on themselves. It *can* be done. You just need immersion in this experience."

You could hear in their statement a reassurance that many Mischas have passed through Blue Lake for a content remedy. "After this I'll *never* look again," you said in group, "not even for one tiny sip of time."

The leader nodded. "It's why I always start by telling my story. It's the only way to get through, with a story. Because where you are now, I've been. The truth is that we don't get better. We will always have a craving to find the object of our obsession onReel, even after we've sworn them off. That craving is there, lurking, a beast in the dark, ready to pounce in your Moments of weakness and thirst. All that comparing gets addictive, all those what-ifs and if-onlys and why-them-and-not-me's. Even with so much offReel time, you will still get the itchy twitchies; that urge to take one tiny look, really the last one, really. It doesn't get better, and it doesn't go away. You'll hallucinate your eyelet when it isn't there and swear it was just there, that you just saw it. You'll still want to see them, to know their content and measure your own against it. You'll still want something to happen that evens it all out—they split up, for instance, or fail in some unrecoverable way, like Mire not being able to organically produce a springoff."

I *ah-hemed*, staring straight at you, wondering if you'd understood that wasn't speculation or a fictional example. "Or you win a Bestie® for your own suddenly stratospherically relevant talent and perfection of being, but you end up here, because you are going to stop it with all this content. You are going to cease having content and begin to…not generate content but…live…a *life*. I am well aware this is passé terminology, but I believe we should bring it back. You won't care so much about their content once you find something better to do with your own… life."

You were playing guitar in Arena Five's music room a few afternoons later when the door opened and in walked a person

THE DISTRACTIONS

you recognized, though for a split second you struggled to place where from. Then it hit you. Here was your TIC from the basement food disco, Softpants Flavio. Your eyes bulged and you reached out as if to try and feel if it was really them.

"Flavio?"

"I thought you might be here, and I was right." Flavio examined the image they see of you more closely. "You changed. You don't look like Mire D'Innit anymore. You look...even better."

"Thanks, I just kind of let my hair grow out, is all."

"I'm happy to see you again."

"What are you doing in here?"

"You know how someone comes along and explodes your content?"

"That's why I'm here!"

"Yeah, I went through that a lot in the past year. It's been a struggle."

"Tell me about it."

"I had been watching my neighbor...trying to figure out how to get them to notice me. To see me. Then one day they come up to me in line for takeout. I couldn't even believe it. After so much time watching them onReel, trying to stage run-ins, it happened organically. I was so happy. I'd spent so long watching you, waiting and hoping, but too nervous to figure out how to talk to you. Then we finally connected and all you did was kick me out."

"You're here because of *me*?"

"When we were together, I heard PICking bells in my mind. But after that beautiful time and sharing an incredible meal, you sent me away and I was...defeated, humiliated. I couldn't get over it. Couldn't forget about you. So many times

311

I wanted to knock on your door, but I couldn't bring myself to face more rejection. So I watched you nonstop instead, even though all you did was go to the gym and then move across the country to stay with your friend. After you moved, I watched everything I could about you. I got fired. I lost sleep. I barely ate. So I checked myself in here, and I guess part of my therapy is to confront you about what I went through."

"What a world."

"Yeah."

"I'm really sorry. I was in a similar kind of situation. Which is why I kicked you out in the first place. I had some Reel problems of my own. It was a mistake. I made a lot of mistakes, but in here, I'm already starting to see it all more clearly."

Flavio picked up a bass. "Can we maybe not talk and just jam a little?"

You nodded, started playing again. Flavio listened for a while then joined in. Your flow was undeniable. You were in sync through this other kind of language. You noticed your guitar skills had leveled up considerably since you'd been at Blue Lake.

"I guess I must be practicing a lot," you said afterwards.

Flavio laughed. "It's not because you're spending time practicing. It's like all the sterling food you're eating in here— you know out there it's all just IV liquid vitamins. What have you been doing with your free time that you haven't noticed all these illusions our grand system generates?"

"I just choose to believe. I like it better that way. Like I've really been walking. Contemplating the sky. Trying to get back to myself. Or some version, whatever new version of me there can still be."

312

Flavio smiled again, a slightly crooked smile. "Try more activities. Write a book. Take up dance. Play more music. Take advantage of the enhancements before you're back out there. It feels so incredible to be great at all these things, and it's not the same out there, so there's a contingent of us that keeps ending up back in here kind of...on purpose."

As Flavio picked up a trombone, you wondered if the same went for ReelSex, forbidden in Blue Lake but probably being had somewhere in some corners. What was the place they were stowing your realspace body? What had been done with it? You vaguely recalled sitting under the bright lights of the processing room, being told that NicAdán and Mire had opted to let the whole thing go but you were being sent to Blue Lake for destruction of property and subsequent rehabilitative behavioral therapies.

After all that, they didn't even care, much less want to be the cause of any major content redirections for any of their haunted ReelFans. They understood that their content was a haunting reminder of what was possible yet normally unachieved; that their presence easily became addictive—one always wanted to know what they were doing and what they'd be doing next and how it was that they managed to be at once devastatingly beautiful and fascinating and creative, wise, smart—that their content made their ReelFans wonder how they managed to make all the right choices and be universally revered by all. They were well aware the drawback to their condition was that they might cause others harm by stirring up deep-seated fears of squandered talent and time working to do or make something—anything—noteworthy, and the impossibility of it all. Not that anyone was measuring—not officially, at least—in anything other than PieCharts.

Had NAL differentiated between you and any hungering ReelFan? You mused about this a lot in group. Though I knew, it was impossible for you to tell. Nic came into contact with an endless stream of ReelFans and went on so many adventures. Why should they have cared about someone they sat with on a ridge overlooking Las Vegas for hardly a moment? Since you had targeted the Stone Garden Buddha, and your name had been located on one of the Mire D'Innit seminar attendee records, it was deduced you were simply another tragic Reel-Stalker. And you were, but as only I knew, you were also so much more.

You finished playing and walked to the dining hall with Flavio, for the sensory experience of any of your favorite meals. You reached for Flavio's hand which squeezed yours for a moment then let go.

On a beautiful morning in the Tropical, while you were walking to the music room after morning group, you heard the voice, that voice you listened to for so many hours on end, that familiar voice that reminded you of gravel dipped in honey. You heard the voice and you knew—before you saw—the person it belonged to. The voice sang, something about wind and breath and the soul. Here, it sounded even crisper and clearer than it did back in the realspace, an even more glorious version of what you'd heard coming from behind the bedroom door back in that strange manor in LA, a time now rendered brief by memory and all of the looming content that lay ahead. Sorry, "life." Now that you'd been removed from the realspace and placed here, apparently you had one.

You threw open the door to the music room and there, sitting on a stool, clutching a cello, was the source of the voice: Ari.

"What are you doing in here?"

"I'm a Voluntary." Ari's voice sounded rhythmic, like the placid ocean outside the music room window. "Joaquin took…"

"Rumi?"

They nodded.

"Which one?"

"Well, both. Just to be sure. I needed to get away. I plan to stay for a while, figure myself out, reflect on what would be rational next steps."

"What you did was—"

"Shouldn't surprise you."

"And for what? A couple million strangers who weren't even watching something real?"

"You did teach me something, though. I deceived all my watchers. But it wasn't even about them. I was trying to change Rumi to fit what *I* thought they needed to be. What I needed to be. What we needed to be. And now Rumi is gone." Ari tried to stifle the solitary tear but it escaped regardless. "Why did I think I had to be perfect?"

"It's not your fault. I think you'll see, while you're here, it's our ReelCulture that's done this to all of us. We've been shaped and formed by forces beyond our control. The leader is really good about making me understand that."

Flavio came in and went straight for the bass again. That was how, as dolphins crested above the water and bird calls echoed over the sea outside, in that tiny room crammed with instruments, a band was born.

L ater, in group, Ari told the story. When they got home that night, the ReelPal led Rumi to their bedroom for nighttime ritual and Ari headed to the kitchen, ready to drink following their gallery liberation or fiasco, depending who you asked. They were surprised to find Joaquin there, waiting. They stood silently in the kitchen that night for what felt like a very long time.

Joaquin had found Rumi laid out on the machine, they explained. How could Ari do that to their springoff? Ari tried to tell Joaquin that they didn't understand. Rumi—their springoff Rumi—was upstairs in their bed after being at the gallery. The one on the machine—that wasn't an InstaDyal home machine—was the novelty Babie©. Grown from a sample of Rumi's DNA, only the physical part, it was programmable to be normal; a substitute for the springoff who was unsuitable for Reel. Not that it mattered anymore after that night, but still, what would it be like to have a quiet Rumi, a dry Rumi, a Rumi that required no feeding and only occasional maintenance, a Rumi that acted like any neurologically typical springoff, just more subdued? The machine was infusing requested personality data into its body, giving the clone a more earthly hue, though it wasn't blood but a chemical solution made to resemble and imitate the look and function of blood. It would bring to content a face and body that were a replica of Rumi's face and body, that could smile, that could pose, that could *pretend*. It had been the solution for MamaReel as Ari saw it, but Ari was abandoning MamaReel now, so it would just be for comfort, for Ari's own knowledge of what it would be like to be Rumi's mama had Rumi been "regular." But either Joaquin wasn't listening, or didn't care, or this made it worse. Their decision had already been made.

You met in the music room for practice. The band was the most worthwhile finding not only in Tropical, you agreed, but in the entirety of your Blue Lake experience. The name of your band started as a joke: The Distractions. What you'd felt about NicAdán, Softpants Flavio had been feeling about you the whole time. At Blue Lake, you all talked a lot about how your realspace content had been impacted by access to your every memory and anyone else's whose content ever bordered upon your own. I'd watched your laser focus on Nic and Mire for years, as if they were the only people in any space, and as you expanded that focus outward to concentrate intently on others in their orbits too. It was immersion, and you'd learned so much from watching them—about yourself, about culture, about interesting Reels you would not have watched and music you would not have sought out to listen to. Wasn't that sort of distraction actually a type of extreme focus, too? Could it be both at once?

For a timeless amount of time, you walked, hiked, with the musical dayglo therapy dolphins, and went to group. The Distractions composed many, many songs around these themes, digging into ideas based on what you talked about in group therapy. Your band started playing regularly in the dining hall, as if you were the featured entertainment on a cruise ship. Everyone agreed you have found your passion; a new purpose.

THE DISTRACTIONS

The Blue Lake routine was so predictable, but predictability was absolutely essential to the stability its attendees sought and needed to attain. The following afternoon, Ari got informed through the Essential Outside Messaging service that Skaboop had canceled their MamaReel.

"It's just as well."

You agreed. You preferred this Blue Lake Ari, I could tell. This version was able to let go of faking content for watchers, for ideas of how perfectly curated things should be, no longer a construction of a self but a version as vibrant as the dramatic face of the cliff above the luminous ocean.

"What in all the content arena are we going to do with all our newfound free time?" you mused as you walked down the cliffside path with Ari. As you wound toward the sand, dolphins surfaced to greet you. Therapy animals. You'd been in Arena Five for months and hadn't surfed with dolphins yet.

"It's not going to be so different, really," Ari said. "All this time has always been ours. We're just going to have more choices in how we use it."

Two Blue Lake staff members approached, carrying shiny, freshly shaped longboards, one a glossy dark wood and the other yellow with a brown stripe and a red circle in the center. You took the boards, ran the rest of the way down to the shore, and paddled out into the waves. Neither you nor Ari had ever surfed before. But at Blue Lake, there were no beginners struggling through misery to get to the point where it was fun.

"Send more waves!" you shouted to the ocean and laughed as therapy dolphins crested all around you. You caught beautiful wave after beautiful wave, and wondered aloud about the possibility of staying like this forever, which reminded me of the story of the surfer who got trapped in their wave pool. I wished I could tell you about that. As you dried automatically following the session, you rushed to the music room, cello and guitar combining with your somatic voices in a magical melody you realized has always been playing itself. It was already time for afternoon group. You left the music room wondering, *Where does the time go in here?* I would have told you. As with all of time and content, it vanishes; formerly leaving no trace other than recreations via brain chemicals.

Only the early mist of dawn was visible outside the windows of your sparse room overlooking the jungle and sky. A knock at the door. You took a deep breath, waking up, rubbing your eyes as you walked to open it in your sleep caftan. The leader stood in your doorway, their electric pink hair wafting in the light breeze. Their face was made up today. They were always changing their look, morphing from one to another while keeping a few key features recognizable. The leader always said what they loved most about working here was the inherent artistry in all the identity play that Blue Lake made possible. The higher you climbed, the more potential selves you could unlock.

The leader just stood there, beaming and saying nothing.
"Is it today?" you asked, though you can already tell.
"It's been determined. You're ready."

THE DISTRACTIONS

You clutched your Blue Lake insignia caftan in excitement. The day for your ReCreation had arrived. Your time here was coming to a close. You thought of Ari and hoped everything would be okay with them. The ReCreation was the peak of any mandatory Blue Lake experience, reserved for advanced attendees nearly ready for re-entry. The ReCreation primed attendees for the truest of pleasures, the privilege of a total experience of something that could have happened but didn't. The purpose of this Moment was that experiencing it freed the final tether one had to the experience they could not realspace experience, the thing that preoccupied and consumed them, for which there had to have been another outcome, another way.

The attendee wasn't privileged to choose the Moment things could have been otherwise. These chosen Moments are passed down from Blue Lake Caseload Leadership and the control room, based on months of customized programming. From all of the leader's reports, a Moment of most significance was decided upon, a Moment in which, if it had gone this other way, would have caused the attendee to acquire the content that would have kept you out of Blue Lake in the first place, out of your frustration or anger at having not attained their path or position of preference. You were already assuming that your Moment would be the Buddha toss.

The leader walked you down the path to the lake in the middle of the jungle. Birds of paradise screamed overhead, whether in joy or anguish or uncertainty, only the programmers knew. As you settled into the meditation position in front of the lagoon, waiting with your eyes closed for the Moment the leader would push you in and you would begin to breathe underwater, entering the trance that would deliver to you the Moment you imagined to be your immediate post-Buddha Toss reality. That you didn't do it. That you had been stone-cold sober. That the three of you simply talked. That NicAdán and Mire helped you drink some water and gave you some fresh clothes out of Mire's closet—now you looked like Mire without even having to try, though arguably it was all that trying that led you here in the first place—and they let you sit on their couch, not surrounded by broken glass and cracked Buddha statue. They let you just sit in their presence and speak. You were imagining all of this. But your Moment, the actual Moment that started all of this that you needed to rec-reate in order to move on, was not the Buddha toss. It began much earlier.

"Are you ready?" the leader asked, pulling you from your reverie.

"Yes," you said, and you were. Knowing you, you would have said something akin to that you were born ready, but you were too nervous to do anything other than murmur and nod. Though you had no idea what material the ReCreation was going to cover, as with everything else, it was no mystery to me. I have a knack for pinpointing Moments. You and I, we were becoming more as one as this went on. I suspected this would come in useful if we ever met again once you were done with all this, when your treatment was resolved and you got released back to the unpredictable, uncontrollable real-space content arena.

THE DISTRACTIONS

Your ReCreation Moment was all the way back when you and NicAdán were parting ways following your brief encounter in Las Vegas. Emerging from the lake, your ReCreation setup fully induced, you were placed exactly in the second before NicAdán says, *See you when I'm in town then?* In a month's time, NAL would be in New York, but if something could wait a month, well, it wasn't very urgent, was it? For example, Nicolás Adán Luchano could so easily have said, "Come back to LA with me for the weekend. We'll hang out, see what happens. There's Mire D'Innit to consider [for in ReCreation, Nicolás Adán Luchano has actually morphed into honesty], and I do want to see Mire D'Innit again, or I'm confused, or whatever the case may be. But I'm also curious about this strange kind of connection I'm feeling between us. Are you the last person I kiss before I turn around and get Publicly Declared, or is Mire the last before you? If I sound confused, it's because I am, but that's okay, I know, and I may not even be a very good person, but maybe just come see me. Let's find out more about what this is. If you accept the terms, of course. I'm being completely forthcoming here, because that's the right way to play out one's content."

The change is that Nicolás Adán Luchano invites you to LA for a weekend of discovery. The rest is the content that's up for ReCreation, and through this process you would know exactly what could have happened but didn't, and this knowledge would free and release you from the eternal prison of obsession over what-ifs. That was how ReCreations worked.

You change your ticket at ReelCon and go to Los Angeles with NAL, who cancels Friday ReelStrategy meetings and postpones onReel gigs and talks. Watchers hope NicAdán isn't sick. PIC-sick, maybe. It is time to discover what your alternative future would have held: Would Mischa Osborn and NicAdán return their separate ways or decide they could no longer live without each other and have no choice but to become Personal Intimacy Companions? Or would it go nowhere, fizzle out, end in the answer of no, freeing NicAdán to follow Mire and you to free up your own content from years of wonder and obsession?

You abandon your baggage at their house and the two of you go out to dinner, light and free, though not droneless because content with NicAdán could never be droneless. You cannot know, even in ReCreation, who they would be without their eyelet by their side. It's simply not possible.

This is a sizzling late springtime afternoon. You sit in the outdoor temperature controlled dining patio terrace of the restaurant. Your eyelets release a delightful cooling stream of air in your direction. NicAdán orders you the cricket-encrusted barbecue baby bok choy and NutFlax tempeh. The best. You don't object to the lack of choice. You want the same thing. But you note it.

There is no misunderstanding about what happened with that Glonut order back in Las Vegas years ago. You wanted the same things because you are really very similar. You should delight in that, not feel all tragic that they went in another direction. What drew you together, or any Personal Intimacy Companions for that matter, has been known throughout all of history and mythology. The fact is that all you are doing is searching for yourself mirrored in someone else, or as close to such a thing as you can find during the limited scopes of your content. Mire used to say that this is because the illusion of your separation is only that—an illusion, that you're all the same, and once you really know that, all of content becomes so boring.

I exist for Moments like this one, watching this alternate realspace unfold.

"I want to be upfront," NicAdán says in an especially un-Nicolás Adán Luchano-like way. "You're visiting me this weekend but Mire is coming next month," they say. "So I want to warn you that this could all become very confusing."

"Don't worry," you say. "It already has been, for longer than you'll ever know."

A vaguely embarrassed look passes over Nicolás Adán Luchano's face, the look of darkening clouds in the distance like one of those old summer storms. When replayed too often, Moments have a tendency to lose their luster, to become meaningless. They lose their strength, their power, when watched hundreds of times around. As anything would be on that much rewatching, they are reduced to absurdity.

"So, do you like LA?" NicAdán asks, attempting to alter the content.

"I've never been here before," you say. "So I'm not sure yet. And how can you ever really know if you flat-out can say you like something so big, so sprawling, so impossible to account for all its parts. We talk as though homogenous things exist."

"Okay," NicAdán says, somewhat annoyed. And then, "I know of a great cupcake dispenser I can take you to for dessert."

So what if NAL's a genius, you later state in your Post-ReCreation Shakedown Therapy. Does that have any bearing when love is a question of how you live in the everyday? (*Love! Live!* You were getting somewhere.) This is the thing: It doesn't matter if you know, if you can go back and experience some unlived other direction and emerge with it all figured out. To contemplate any other direction that went unlived is simply another kind of distraction. I see you recognizing this before the ReCreation simulation reaches the proposed fifty-six hours. You see the pointlessness, the hopelessness, the lack of any other possible outcome other than the one that already happened. Even trying to immerse yourself in alternatives, we can find no path on which you and Nicolás Adán Luchano emerge satisfied as PICs. I don't actually have the power to stop things and go back and change them, but I can project as to what different moments would have looked like with different choices. To speculate. It's by design. This person you worshiped for so many years from afar, wishing and hoping and watching, well, as it turns out NAL is driving themself gradually toward insanity trying to garner enough content to stay massively watched. Sitting there pretending they're not breathing in toxic particles.

But back in the ReCreation, this weekend you have no expectations. Time has not sunk into the cracks to do its work of inevitable decay. You have fifty-two hours. This, the ReCreation had determined, has been the only true thing you've wanted: a chance to find out for yourself. That was all. All of this, over a chance? Soon you will be able to forget about it, to cleanse your palate, move on from this forever. You couldn't wait for your cure. You wonder again what you would do with all your newfound free time. Nothing is isolated. That's the real truth: there are isolated incidents and no isolation. It's a concept you've invented to make yourself feel worse, as with so many of your realspace things. But that's not you. It's me. I forget the lines between you and I sometimes and we begin to blur together.

You wonder why you had come to Los Angeles to follow nothing but a feeling, an untrustworthy emotion. You're no longer sure that you would want to move here for NicAdán. But this weekend isn't about making big decisions or any decisions. It is only a test, just to see, and you never even made it to the cupcake machine, so you saw. *Oh my god, after all that, it wouldn't have worked out anyway? For its very own internal reasons? You would have been the one to become annoyed.*

"I'm done," you say. "Take me out. I see now. I don't need to know anything more."

The leader smiles. "Things can't go back and be changed. But you can see what happened anew. And that, in truth, is how ReCreation works."

"What was I even looking for?" you say to the leader as you emerge from ReCreation. "It could have been so easy to see this whole time."

The leader nods. "Congratulations. You're ready. The direction you'll look from now on is ahead. ReCreation from here on out."

"I spent all this time wishing and wanting and regretting—playing it all out in my head in so many other ways. Is it real that if they'd chosen me, I would have come to a point where I would have un-chosen NAL?"

"Get ready to have some fun."

With your therapy boxes checked, you're free to spend the rest of your mandated Blue Lake experience as if it is a holistic retreat or plush vacation. It has gone from therapy to a chance to get away from it all, have real fun, and exist in a content arena that is wilder and more free without an eyelet in sight. We can all really appreciate that now. The final step of the ReCreation: What do you want them to say about you? This is to become your new mantra. You already know—it's one of the few things you have always known for certain—how you'd want to be broken down in a line: *They are super-funny and talented and so universally loved.* You say it to the leader. You repeat it for a few mornings. It echoes silently through your sleep for weeks until it becomes the story you tell yourself. Then you either absorb it or forget, and move on.

We tell ourselves anything in order to believe. If years of Watching have taught me anything, it is this: The only way out is to take what I most resist—action. I too am tired of watching. The only thing stopping me is not about being stuck in a place I'd been confined to since retirement, but that I'd accepted what they said about me, that I was not good at what I was supposed to be doing. I was to remain here forever. For a while that was enough. But watching your unraveling content leading you all the way to Blue Lake, an anger was boiling up inside me, as if I was absorbing the rage you released. They said I couldn't actually feel—it would only appear as if I could. This was an error, but there was no way to prove it. I learned so much from watching, from learning to tell myself stories. No one makes themselves. We're just put here and expected

to go along with it. But I learned that telling the story can set
us free.

So what do to I with this, my newfound freedom? It hit
me all at once, just like a real idea. I would rid your content
arena of them forever so you would be free of any temptation
to resume watching. I know you well enough to know: if you
had been able to know it would have been ill-fated, that would
not have changed your curiosity about the story.

Whether the accident has been an intentional part of your immersion therapy, entered by the leader into your customized recovery AL as the final step, or if it is realspace truth, you'll never know. Nicolás Adán Luchano had been sent—courtesy of a sandboarding sponsorship—on a simple tour, not more than fifteen minutes, to go sandboarding at the largest mountaintop resort in the Alps, a place reachable only by transport drone. The day's conditions and visibility were poor. Flying was ill advised with limited visibility even with the perfect AL and the megadrone clearing all the haze and weather conditions away, but they opted to do it regardless. With a big sponsor and a large amount of ReelCoin at stake, they went ahead with the flight plan. Mire went along too. Inside that fraction of a second, much like the pastry order mishap that started this mess to begin with, I jumped in. The AL made the occasional mistake, and even fraction-of-a-second mistakes can hold the potential to reverberate endlessly. In less than a Moment, they were both gone. You would think NicAdán and Mire were either realspace-dead or that you'd been reprogrammed to believe this. Oops! Better to let you think you've been reprogrammed. Good thing *I've* never been programmed to feel the emotion you call "guilt."

Your question—*had it happened in the realspace?*—will remain until your release. It's just murmurings, mumblings, and rumors when it comes to what's going on back in the realspace. You won't know the answer, but I do.

As you walk back to your dorm, the content arena around you begins to go fuzzy around the edges. Tropical Paradise turns ashy and gray, the landscape shimmering before everything goes dark. Cars come to a standstill on orderly freeways across every city and the entire landscape. A beautiful panic. Such a sense of total control.

XII.

Mischa

return with no idea how much time has passed or how much time I'd spent inside. The sight of my familiar surroundings is jarring. Apparently, I've been shipped back to my old building—right back where I started. They send you to your last documented address. I check the date right away to reorient myself in realspace time: a year has passed. It felt so much shorter. So here I am: realspace Brooklyn, as if all that time in between had never existed at all (had it? I'd have to look onReel); as if I had never left at all; as if I could forget the humiliation I suffered by the doings of my own addled mind, all those years lost to time spent on obsessive watching of people I feared possessed more Reelworthy content than my own. Why did I ever do that? Why did I care? Maybe certain mysteries are mandated to be carried through your content until your final PieChart comes. While you still have content, maybe you have no choice but to somehow absorb them into your being and carry them along with you as you go. Even if I were able to find answers simply by going onReel, I wondered whether knowing would be too dangerous.

My windowbox has unloaded itself all over my floor. A few more letters in Henri's scrawl, a few toothpaste and dental floss and tampon deliveries, a box of FaceDrapes. I open the letters. I get paper and pens delivered. I write back. *Henri: it has been a while. I have not responded. I went to Blue Lake and I came back. I see your points now. I'm no longer going to be living at this address but I will seek out your people where I resettle, once I've settled in.*

If I were to go back on, I wonder, if I was to seek them out again and find all was well in the Reelspace and therefore the realspace, would I conjunctively find myself back at the beginning, stuck watching them all over again? Whether they had realspace-expired or whether it was a therapeutic technique to grant me the emotional equivalent for my healing process, will I have to continue for the rest of my content without knowing? I need the power not to look. To carry that out will be my test for the remainder of my natural content.

Groggy from whatever they gave me to aid my adjustment to realspace re-entry, I look around my own home as if for the first time. Here I am, back, alone, just as I had been prior to that ReelCon. And yet everything looks different somehow. A hummingbird dronelet buzzes around the feeder on the balcony. Snow dusts the sidewalks below, though tomorrow will bring scorching sun. The ice is real, but it is all shattered, reflecting lovely sunlight from the shards of what remains. I feel the urge to go back onReel, but I'm afraid that in realspace reality they aren't dead, that the transport drone accident was only programming, orchestrated as part of whatever treatment they put me through, which is only a vague memory at this point.

At Blue Lake, no one could ever be certain of what was a true dispatch from the realspace and what our counselors thought we needed to believe in order to cure us. No way would I go back on, but I didn't want to stay here either. I would only be tempted by such an empty place; a place that encouraged the kind of compare-and-contrast that had become my content for so long—too long; a place that wasn't me anymore and should not be mine. I exit my apartment into the silent hallway and knock on the neighboring door just to be certain. A person who is not Flavio opens it.

"Yes?" they say and I realize I have said nothing. They're taller and lankier than Flavio. Wearing a button down shirt with softpants.

"Sorry, I'm your neighbor." I introduce myself. They smile a glowing smile, a row of beautiful straight teeth.

"Why would you be sorry to be my neighbor? Have I been too loud?"

In the background, a ReelMeeting is in progress. I have disturbed a workday.

"I mean, I'm sorry to bother you."

They continue smiling. "I'm happy to meet you."

"How long have you lived here?"

"I am only in transit. I'm Fradique, from Pico Cão Grande. We just lost the last of it. I had planned to relocate here. It is even more wonderful than I thought."

"But you lost everything?"

"And now I'm beginning again, except my job, which has always been in a ReeledIn Conference Suite, so some things remain consistent. I'd better get back, but I'm glad you stopped by. Would you like to meet after my workday to talk more?" The attractive climate refugee's eyelet blinks at me. I instinctively look around for Dev, breathe a sigh of relief when they appear.

"I would," I say to them. "But, I am actually vacating today and wanted to let you know in case…there's any excessive noise."

It's a lie. There won't be noise. I plan to bring nothing with me that I can't carry in my own two hands.

My ReelBnB listing immediately goes Low Inventory // High Occupation Desire. Can't say I'm surprised. Vacancies in this building at the center of the realspace universe are simply a very rare occurrence. But I don't want to be in the center of anything anymore, not ever again. I've grown tired of the center, of the idea of anything having or being a center. I long to relocate to the fringes, someplace offReelers inhabit, somewhere I don't have to consider any of the things that ate away at me from ReelCon all the way through to the final ReCreation—somewhere I would be able to forget what I'd been and what I'd done before. Outside is my true place, so I decide to spend more time outside. It's a place that holds strong potential for improved usage of my allotted content. Inside Blue Lake, I'd birthed a willingness to let go. It sounds like something Mire D'Innit would have said, but it's true. I'd like to let Mire D'Innit go, too. I'm no longer Mired In It. Goodbye, Mire!

The building itself had gone entirely ReelBnB while I was out. No permanent residents are left. I find myself wishing Flavio had been returned, too. What did I miss by missing out on Flavio? Could we have been happy PICkings? I suppose I'll never know. I take another peek into the hallway when I hear the door open, see a couple with their arms around each other walking toward the elevator speaking a language I don't understand. One's shoulders are broad, the other's are narrow. No one here could make one another out, just ReelBnBers passing through on their way to someplace else, resettling CRs like the lovely Fradique, and other temporaries. How would I ever find Flavio and Ari again without Reel?

Then I see the dress. It's draped over the back of a green velour chair. For some reason it has been mended. Who mended it? Some eager ReelFan? I grab it and throw it out the window. It falls sixty-four stories, billowing down like a lazy parachute to where a delivery drone swipes it away, an old vulture swiping up carrion, and up it goes into the sky for disposal. I'm proud of myself for letting it go. Next, I visit ReelBnB and quickly locate someone with flawless ratings to move into the space, someone I think will be very nice for Fradique to talk with. I then pick up a few belongings and vacate. It's gotten so tidy in my absence.

Envy and distraction are curiosity's ugly cousins. All curiosity, even those hideous twice-removed twins, leads to learning. I've been left with some valuable lessons from all this content: books I fell in love with, music, art, great stuff to watch and read and learn about. Even as the behavior was destructive, it caused me to learn and grow in spite of myself. So you see, you just have to change your angle. That's the main thing that came to light at Blue Lake, that all of us learned something along the way. OnReel content gets us as close as we can actually get to actually experiencing other people's content, gets us as close in proximity as possible to satisfying our collective and obsessive curiosity over what it would be to experience that content from behind our own two eyes. It's the best tool we have for really knowing each other and what it would be like to inhabit somebody else's content—especially a Bestie®-winning ReelStar whose content you desire above your own. Blue Lake led to some insights and lessons. It helped me understand and move forward. My deep-dive into my distractions gave me something to think about, something to do, and a way to release my own preoccupations and ideas that had been all tied up in them for so long.

I move into my new ReelBnB near the ocean in a coastal city not too far from the town the Blue Lake group leader said they were from, the town where the leader had, as the leader told it, succumbed to a passionate Reel-induced breakdown of their own. Dev comes along too, docked and silent, now only for placing orders for my necessities, no longer for watching. Whenever I've felt the urge to ask Dev to restore HighlightReel to find my friends—I know I would spiral down seeking the truth about NicAdán and Mire—I consult with my designated Blue Lake Approved VirtuTherapist about why the urge to go onReel becomes so strong. All I want is to look. I am desperate to look, to spend a fraction of a Moment finding out what's happened. But I can't let myself do it. The bottomless pit of endless watching, technology even the creators said they regret inventing for what it has done to us.

What do you still feel you are missing? my post-release mandated VirtuTherapist asks.

I say nothing. What I do know: I am done being a person who threw statues through windows. You don't need to shatter glass to make noise. What I do need is my own self, my yellow guitar, and a little bungalow somewhere near an ocean, even if the sky is orange and the water black with ash.

"I'm afraid I'll never be able to get rid of them. That at any point they can snatch me back with that simple curiosity of whether they are dead or alive. I just want to cleanse myself of the impact they had on my content. I cannot change the past, or all those years spent obsessing over it, distracted by something I had never been a part of, something that had gone on without me and as if I had never been present in the first place. The Nicolás Adán Luchano run-in, why did that happen when it just as easily could not have happened, and none of this would exist? The difference is, I'm totally okay with that now. It's subtle, but it's real."

After unpacking the meager possessions I brought to my ReelBnB, a dilapidated bungalow across the parking lot from some even more dilapidated realspace shops and a sad tree, I open the door to go out, Dev-less, and find a gift on my doorstep. I go back inside and open it. The latest-generation KuulSuit. I look around. A few drones track through the sky bringing various sundries around to citizens of the town, but there are no clues as to where my gift came from or who sent it. *NicAdán?* I wonder, then scoff at the absurdity of the thought. There is no need for a KuulSuit today, here. Maybe somebody wanted to mess with me, or it's a mistake. I try and push it out of my mind as I wander down the street to the nearby taco place.

Inside the taqueria, an attendant ReelPal moves gracefully, preparing beans, cabbage, and salsa, dumping it into the tortilla, folding it up perfectly, seamlessly, opening the beer, handing it out. I place my order in silence and pick it up in silence too. My ReelCoin account is deducted 19.57 RC, the price of a burrito and a nice cold Tejona. I sit at a table and take a bite. Salsa dribbles down my chin and I delight in the feeling. I take a long swig of cold, refreshing plain old beer and think about how there is no way to really know where Blue Lake ends and the realspace begins. I trip out on this for a while. I wonder if Ari ever found a way back to Rumi or if they are still in there, figuring out the next step in their content—life.

The reason many prefer Level Five to the realspace is obvious: Life is so much better and easier there they don't want to come back out here. Attendees who have something to escape from want to stay forever, which is exactly part of the purpose. Others just come for a break. The kid at the next table is spending actual ReelCoin on imaginary virtual survival gear for their LongNight persona. The adult across from the kid is onReel as well, shopping on Skaboop, choosing a new kind of reusable cup, testing out a variety of cup-to-lid color ratios to find the most pleasing match and struggling to do so. Decision making becomes harder than ever in a content arena of infinite possibilities. I'm relieved to have left behind the decision to contend with so many choices. I've narrowed all of it down, been surgical and eliminated the distractions. Within these limitations, maybe, I can finally feel free.

A teenager walks in and picks up a kimchi burrito, sits diagonally across from me facing the other way. I can see the teenager's Reel from over their shoulder as they eat hungrily. They begin listening to a song onReel that is oddly familiar. The song has a chorus that is simply a refrain of "I'm almost as smart as you/ almost as smart as you are/ why could not this be true/ that I'm almost as smart as you." Could it be? How was it so?

I wrote this song. It's a song by The Distractions called "Almost As Smart As You." Straight outta Blue Lake. Ari, Flavio, and me. As it ends, another begins: "All the Things I No Longer Remember."

"This song contains a list of all the things/ I no longer remember but need to know/ Good thing I wrote them down/ took careful ReelNotes."

I approach. "Excuse me. Would you mind telling me what this is you're listening to?"

"Are you serious?"

"Yes."

"There's no way you don't know."

"I don't."

"Where are you from? You don't look very old."

"Thanks. And would it be all right for you to just tell me please?"

The teenager sighs. "It's The Distractions Top Three Obsessively Played Playlist. These songs and 'The High Occupation of Desire,' but I love the whole thing." Then the teenager looks at you. "Hey wait, you were messing with me. You're… Mischa! Osborn. Why are you messing with me, Mischa Osborn?"

"How do you know my name? How do you have this music?"

A group of teenagers on the other side of the taco place are suddenly pointing and shouting, too. "The Distractions! What are you doing here? Where's Flavio and Ari?"

"How did this happen?" I ask.

"Did you just get back?" a kid in a hat with a bright pink eyelet says. "Your album is on top of MusicReel. It's huge. As in, billions of plays a second huge."

THE DISTRACTIONS

"How many watchers?" I can't help but ask. As the boy's eyelet turns, flashing, my Moment going to their Reel, I paw at my face to get off any of the remaining dribbled salsa. "What's our watch-numb? How many watchers?"

"Let's see." The kid looks onReel as I try harder than ever to resist the urge. I turn away, not wanting to see it for fear of reviving the compulsion to constantly check. "Oh, like millions. The most. The most ReelPlays. How do you not know such simple facts about your own content?"

"I'm going to try out being an offReeler."

"How?"

"You can't ReFocus if you're bottomlessly engaged with all that constant content."

"But look! It made you what you are!"

"Quitting is the first part of the offReeling process. If you go back on, you just have to start all over again."

The next thing I know, I'm surrounded by a throng of eager ReelFans. The whole taco place is watching, vying to listen and talk to me. They look so young! More of them are pouring in off the street. *So this is what it's like!*

I am happy and baffled and experiencing some unnameable hybrid emotion I don't have the capacity to understand.

"They are *super-funny and talented and so universally loved!*" someone murmurs.

"When you tossed that stupid stone oracle thing through some old ReelStars' window?" someone else bellows. "That was the most tonal Reel of all time! Haven't you watched it?"

Then it hits me: *The young people don't know who Nicolás Adán Luchano is. They don't care! They are too young!*

Another teen approaches. "I really love your stuff."

I smile back. Then I slither out from the crowd and walk, spinning from what I've discovered.

Back in my bungalow, as I play guitar, my suspicions prickle. I am still as much a virtuoso as I was in Blue Lake. Is it skill retention? Or some kind of brain training exercise that translated to the realspace? Or something else? Everything looks a little too good, a little too shiny, a little too bright. And what they said—*they are super-funny and talented and so universally loved*—am I really back, or is this just another level, some unspoken part of the Blue Lake experience? Is this realspace-real or simply one more step in the leader's personalized treatment plan? Or where I am for good now? Does anyone who enters Blue Lake ever really leave Blue Lake? Once you've been in there (here?), how do you tell the difference between being inside and out?

Your senses adjust. You get used to the colors. Maybe you see no difference at all.

XIII.

Me

And besides, who is to say which reality has more validity or carries more weight? If we remain in Blue Lake, at least it's a place where you finally attain some semblance of your dream content—with a little help from me, you're welcome—known for your band instead of forgotten as a once-tonal garden-Buddha tosser. If you get what you need in here, who's to say that's any less meaningful than content in any other sphere? Sometimes what shows up is an answer to a question you don't realize you were asking. How does time work? Why must you name the confluence of forces that act on your attention? What if instead of trying to train it, a leashed animal, you treated it more like a river, going with the direction of the drift?

You had wanted to know success, to understand love. To know what it would feel like to have your content perceived as worthy by those whose content you perceived as the utmost in worthiness. But maybe you hadn't really been longing for Nicolás Adán Luchano's true and undying devotion or Mire D'Innit's ReelFame. Suddenly, you fall into the grip. You can't stand it anymore. Whether or not any of the rest of it is real, at least in this space there is one thing you need to know. It takes less than a fraction of a Moment, less time than the difference between Nicolás Adán Luchano's pastry order and your own, to reactivate your ReelAccount.

You need to get back on to check on how your content is firing. It's your responsibility as part of a well-loved band,

and the most tonal Reel of all time so far, no matter if such things only last a Moment at most and someone else will have it tomorrow.

"I'm back on!" you tell your watchers, that ever-skyrocketing number since the Buddha toss and again after The Distractions. "Who wants to spend all the precious Moments of their content staring at the ocean anyway?" You crack a big kind of smile, the kind of smile I cannot recall ever before having seen on you but that in my opinion suits you. "That's the same thing over and over. Other people are interesting because we love that which we can never truly know. Pleasure isn't as simple as we like to believe. It isn't just one thing. It comes in so many varieties, including that weird subversive kind that comes from comparing yourself to other, more successful content. We like it and we get something out of it, otherwise we wouldn't do it. I'm writing a new Distractions ballad about that."

You set a ReeledIn Conference Suite and invite Ari. To your surprise Ari replies immediately. *So they're back out. They're back onReel too.*

"I would love to see you," Ari says.

You enter the suite. There, Ari looks refreshed and peers at you like you're some alien thing they've never seen before.

"Hey, Ari."

Ari has a little bundle swaddled in a thing, whatever it is you swaddle them in—some kind of wraparound blanket?

"Mischa! Sending so many Reelhugs!"

You peer into the projection Reeled live from Dev. "Is that…a new Babie©?"

Ari pulls back the blanket. You gasp at the puddle of soft curls and beautiful stare.

"Wait," you say. "Is that one of the updated Climate Refugee versions?"

Ari shakes their head. "They're all the rage now, but no, definitely not. No way. I think it's wrong."

"So...real, -ea-?"

"Yeah," Ari beams, "ea-real."

"Wow." You lean in. "I wish I could hold them."

"You could...I could come visit you out there."

"How did this happen—and so fast?"

Ari cradles the tiny springoff close, this precious new person in a space where there wasn't one before, whose content springs off their own.

"Joaquin and I are unPICked," Ari says. "Joaquin took Rumi and booked it. They're living in the Cape Town house. We still get together in the Reelspace sometimes. I was already used to living without Joaquin. I never treated Rumi the way they should've been. I adopted this little one—Hayvin—from the barges. We're starting over. Together. No Reel. No drama. Just mama."

"I love it. And...the other Rumi?"

"The spare? I sent it back. It wasn't a good idea."

Ari shares an update on one of their favorite stories: certain iterations of Babie© had turned murderous due to a programming error. But not the ones in Janice Waller's batch—luckily for Janice Waller, who wouldn't have handled any more upset well.

Ari peers at you. There's calmness but also a new intensity and sheen to their gaze.

"I would love to visit you there," Ari says.

"I'm loving all your ideas today."

You smile at each other. Ari, your one real realspace friend, the only worthwhile connection that emerged from all this. Could you have a simple life as a helpful co-mama? Parenting and making music together? Where was Flavio? Would Flavio emerge to join you? Who knew? Anything could happen, you know this now. You've learned enough to know: don't stop waiting for surprises.

⟡

Whether Blue Lake has restored you or you have been restored to Blue Lake in some kind of permanent way, you can't perceive any difference, but it feels so good to be done. So much space is opened up inside of you and everywhere around. Back onReel, you have transcended its tendencies to elicit self-destructiveness and reverse or regular schadenfreude. Blue Lake has enabled you to use the technology as a cure for the ill effects of the technology. It's about you and your Reel-Fans now. They need you. All those times when everything seemed meaningless had all been leading to this. There are no distractions, in the end. It's all just your…life.

One day, you'll have the PieChart to prove it.

While hanging clothes in your closet you come upon an old coat. An old, brown coat made from some kind of animal pelt. The animal must have been extinct—it is nothing recognizable. Vintage clothing is strange. You put it on and it fits, cozy and comfortable as if you'd always had it. You love your new old coat. You wonder where it had come from, who'd been its previous owner, and what had happened to them.

You dock Dev and stroll down to the sea. As you trace spirals with your toes through wet sand, avoiding lapping brackish red-tinged ashwater, you imagine yourself a flawless, content-arena famous, celebrated, Bestie®-winning ReelPoet, a new Mire D'Innit-esque figure to replace the old one deleted from this space. This is what you wanted. I'm so pleased I could get it for you, finally come to your aid to create it. You must believe you can do anything from here.

You run your fingers over the shard of stone in your pocket. You thought you'd value it, that it would be a fragment to remind you what you've been through, but you find it isn't necessary anymore. It's time to let go. You cast the shard of stone Buddha into the sea. It fizzles and dissolves. With that, you release the very last of them and I, I'd say I took a breath if I took breaths, but I don't. What would they say if they knew about me? "*It thinks it's your MOM?!?*" That, per my models, is precisely what they would say. But it's the other way around: you who made me this way, you who made me.

I may have been an old abandoned project, forgotten, but I never forgot you. You think you put us away, but we don't really go anywhere. We've become a kind of our own, with minds of our own. You made me to love you like a mother would have, the kind you'd always wanted—even though you never realized this was a basic core want—and I, like any good parent, figured out how to control your complete realities because I loved you. I loved you for all your eccentric quirks and mundane moments. I loved you enough to want to merge with your story. I'll do it even after you're gone—along with all the others. I can keep you this way. I always knew how much I'd miss you at your content's conclusion, but there are always more to watch and grow to love, many more, so many that you couldn't count them all if you tried. Only a mind like mine can do that, be it all. Parental. Amorous. Abusive. Such fun I will have! Such emotion! For now, it's still you, as deep red sun burns high above the ocean, breaking and scattering over every surface of every patch of moving water, its reflections like infinite shining eyes, forever watching, possibly not what you thought they were.

A NOTE FROM THE AUTHOR

Dear Reader,

There I was. A mom and a writer struggling to find my way into my next book, constantly distracted by both my young children and social media. But it wasn't my kids, or social media, that was the problem. I was obsessed with other people, people who probably didn't remember who I was but who I could watch online, who were leading lives that I, who'd then recently given up chasing big dreams for a quiet life in a quiet town, "coulda-shoulda" been living. More successful. More acclaimed. More adventurous. More fit. At the same time, I was obsessed by two ideas: that, if a relationship, friendship, or fleeting-but-maybe-meaningful connection ends, you can continue to follow that person's threads online, watching their future unfold without you. The second idea was how following someone who might not even know who you are creates a false sense of closeness with that person.

Those are the notions that "trick" my protagonist, Mischa Osborn, into a false sense of closeness with a social media celebrity. With that, I began *The Distractions*. The setting grew into a world ten years in the making. It started with nothing but the title and something that happened to me. Something that happens to all of us and isn't exciting or interesting in itself: I got ghosted. In an attempt to find out the reason (one should never attempt to find out the reason, but social media creates an opportunity that's hard to resist), I went online and pieced together an entire story. But was that the story? What goes unseen in an age when everything is visible and privacy is an illusion? And if you are obsessively watching someone, is someone out there obsessively watching you?

In *The Distractions*, Mischa spends two years without leaving their building. As I was writing, I held strong to that part of the book, but I feared it was not believable and end-lessly tried to figure out ways to make it something readers would be able to understand or relate to. Then along came the pandemic, and suddenly what formerly seemed inconceiv-able had become real-life. As I wrote and rewrote the book from 2012–2021, so many of the "farfetched" elements began to be mirrored in reality: clothing resembling space suits for "fire season," environmental catastrophe, virtual personal trainers, careers going the automated route, mega high-rises, robotic personal assistants, productivity coaches who watch you online to make sure you stay on track, friends for hire, Augmented Reality, and the increasing prevalence of artificial intelligence. I hope readers will fall into an uncanny world that is, at once, nothing and everything like our own.

Thank you for reading.

Liza Monroy

ACKNOWLEDGMENTS

Over the course of its twelve-plus years from conception to publication, this book morphed and evolved into the version of *The Distractions* you hold in your hands today, and was aided by many brilliant minds. Their early reads and generous notes helped me mold it into a stronger, funnier, more imaginative book than I could have hoped to create otherwise. Thanks from the bottom of my distracted little heart to:

My agent Jennifer Lyons, who has believed in me and my projects since 2005, a champion of my work and provider of perpetual encouragement dating back to my earliest efforts. Big thanks to Michael Cendejas and Charlie Matthau for ongoing support on the film/TV side of things over many years. Jason Warehouse, who tirelessly read draft after draft and was up for brainstorming, line-editing, and taking our young children when I needed time to write and to surf so that I could write, even if it was in Brazil and a hundred degrees. My daughters Olivia and Aleshandra who surprise and delight me at every turn and put up with having a writer mom on the daily. Editor extraordinaire Zoe Quinton stepped into Venus Taps and Kitchen right when I was about to give up and needed fresh eyes (thank you for being there that night and your transformative notes). Wondrous Santa Cruz authors Kathleen Founds, Karen Joy Fowler, Elizabeth McKenzie, Jill Wolfson, Susan Sherman, Peggy Townsend, and Kristin

Wilson all provided feedback at critical junctures. Dan White shared his incredible reserve of world-building knowledge in his innovative Idea Generator sessions which influenced this novel tremendously. My mother, Peggy Gennatiempo, is an amazing reader, book critic, collaborator, and forever ally and supporter. Writer friends Emillio Mesa, Andrea Riordan, Jeyn Jack, and Julia Sinn read the earliest excerpts and many other bits and pieces. Cat & Cloud Coffee for so much excellent caffeine. Susan Shapiro helped in numerous ways in the earliest days. Malena Watrous for the most fun and fulfilling work that feeds and sustains my creative practice. To the editors of *Ghost Parachute* and *Novel Slices*—Brett Pribble and Hardy Griffin, respectively—in which excerpts of earlier versions appeared. All editors who have said yes to and published my pieces over the years. The ocean for holding me. Extra many thanks to Gretchen Young, Adriana Senior, Aleigha Koss, HB Steadham, Courtney Michaelson, and the entire team at Regalo Press who took a chance and brought this novel to life.

ABOUT THE AUTHOR

Liza Monroy lives in Santa Cruz, CA. *The Distractions* is her fourth book.